FAMILY

AFFAIRS

The Eighteenth Hawkridge Book

The characters in this book are fictitious.
Any resemblance to any person, living or dead, is coincidental.

British Library Cataloguing In Publication Data
A Record of this Publication is available from the British Library

ISBN 1846853281
978-1-84685-328-9

First Published 2007 by
Exposure Publishing, an imprint of Diggory Press,
Three Rivers, Minions, Liskeard, Cornwall, PL14 5LE, UK
WWW.DIGGORYPRESS.COM

BY THE SAME AUTHOR

The End of an Era

In the Hawkridge Series

Murder in the Park
Murder in Providence
It couldn't happen in Dorset
The Qatar Affair
Diamonds in Dorset
Bedsits in Bath
Problems at Portland
Nuclear. No! How?
Submarines and Swindlers
Requiem for a Sapper
Politics and Property
The Body in the Churchyard
Chain of Circumstances
Murder in the Theatre
The Irish Affair
The Spetisbury Mystery
Death isn't Particular
Family Affairs
Nemesis
Satan's Disciples

ABOUT THE AUTHOR

Jack Daniel lives in Bath, England with his wife, Elizabeth and two small longhaired dachshunds. He has two sons.

He is a naval constructor, now retired.

He saw sea service with the British Navy in World War 11 and was assigned to the US Manhattan Project for the Bikini atomic tests.

He subsequently designed several classes of warships for the Royal Navy, notably frigates and nuclear attack and ballistic missile submarines, reflecting his lifetime association with submarines that began in the war.

He was Head of the Royal Corps of Naval Constructors when he resigned and joined the Board of British Shipbuilders.

His memoirs, the End of an Era, were published in 2003.

Family Affairs is the eighteenth of twenty books featuring the Hawkridge family and their friends in pursuit of the ungodly.

For Liz and the two boys
Who make everything enjoyable

Chapter One

THE Chancellor of the Exchequer looked up from the papers before him on his desk and his face creased into a wide smile as his PS opened the door and said, "Mrs Davis, Chancellor" and there she was, his lovely Peggy, looking a million dollars as usual.

He hurried round his desk, took her in his arms and kissed her.

"Put me down, William," she grinned, "you'll have people talking."

The smiling PS closed the door as she smoothed her dress and walked over to the windows saying, "Finish what you're doing, love, I'm a trifle early."

"Couldn't keep away from me," said William, his gaze already back on the documents on his desk.

"I think that this is an even nicer view than you had from the Ministry of Defence," mused Peggy, speaking her thoughts. "What a pity that there is so much traffic."

She perched on the arm of an armchair from where she could see Westminster Abbey, Saint Margaret's and the Palace of Westminster beyond the seeming unceasing stream of traffic going round Parliament Square. In her mind she could still hear her mother's voice, telling her that she mustn't sit on the arm of the settee. This reminded her that it was some time since they had been back to visit their parents in Barrow in Furness. She'd have to drag William away from those wretched red boxes one weekend soon, it wasn't as if they didn't want to go, it was simply a matter of finding the time.

She looked at the Abbey and marvelled that people had built it on what was marshy land all those centuries ago. How it must have dominated the skyline in a city in which all the other buildings were only two stories high. What faith and craftsmanship to have passed from generation to generation as the building took shape. It reminded her that their parents wouldn't always be there for them to visit. Both their fathers were now retired from the shipyard and she hoped were enjoying the small luxuries that they had been happy to provide for them.

It seemed a world away. Well it was a world away. William was the skilled fitter installing nuclear reactors in submarines and she was a shorthand typist in the accounts department, six years younger and madly in love with the handsome, athletic William. They had married and she'd made a home for him in the little house that they'd bought, with a 90% mortgage, in Dalton. Andrew, Williams's younger brother and a draughtsman in the Ship Drawing Office, had been a frequent visitor and they had tried to find him a bride but Andrew was determined upon a career in politics and had no time for girls.

Andrew had become an MP the hard way and was now the Minister of State for the Armed Forces in the MoD, a few hundred metres from the Treasury where she was sitting. William had had no wish to be an MP but was interested in trade union affairs and got on well with people. He had become a union official and by a fluke, because the man who had been nominated had been killed in a road accident a few days before the nominations were due, had been nominated to become a trade union sponsored MP in a safe Labour seat. He had entered parliament as the member for Wolverhampton North in 1992 and was now in his fourth ministerial post.

Andrew, being on the Labour party's list, had twice fought Tunbridge Wells and lost before winning Blackpool East in 2001. He was in his second ministerial post, both in the MoD. Peggy knew that he was recovering only slowly from the devastating shock of having his fiancée, Wendy, murdered in his flat.

Big Ben struck half past six and Peggy got up and wandered round behind her husband, put both arms over his shoulders and pressed her cheek against his, saying,

"Come on lover, its time that we went, the card said six-thirty."

"They won't be there yet," said William.

"No, but we're the hosts and we have to be there when they arrive."

"I still feel stupid, standing there being polite and not understanding a word that they say."

"They all speak English, well American, and anyway you'll have an interpreter."

"Yes, and did you know that both Stuart Harcourt, the PM's foreign policy adviser and Roger Stevens, the PPS, have served in Budapest and speak the language?"

"Good for them. Come on love, we won't need our coats."

He stood up and Peggy stood in front of him, straightened his tie, let her lips touch his for a moment and led him towards the door, which she opened, saying, "I can't see why it takes you so long dealing with those papers, love, all you've got to do is to say No."

"I know darling but I have at least to know what I'm saying No to."

This last was as they passed through William's Private Office and brought smiles to the staff.

"We'll be back for our coats but no ones to wait for us, just put my box in the usual place."

"Very good, Chancellor," said his PS, then, looking at Peggy, "Have a nice time and don't eat the savouries."

She grinned back, he'd heard her remarks on a previous occasion about the gastronomic danger of eating the food offered at receptions on the London diplomatic circuit.

They walked along the corridor and down the stairs to the private road that connects Downing Street with Parliament Square, crossed Downing Street and were admitted to Number 10, saying hello and goodnight to the members of staff who were going the other way. They made their way towards the back of the building, past the prime minister's study and up the main stairs to the large room where a number of guests were already assembled. Roger Stevens immediately came over and said hello, asked after Peggy's health and saw that they had a drink. He asked if she knew Sir Stuart Harcourt and took her off to meet him and then left the room. William guessed that he'd gone to bring the PM. William wasn't alone for long, most people have a bone to pick with the Chancellor of the Exchequer.

A minute or so later, the prime minister came in with his wife and William knew that the Hungarian delegation wouldn't be far behind. The prime minister's wife mouthed "Where's Peggy?" at him and William grinned and pointed towards her. The two of them were firm friends, a situation not usual in political circles, where wives most-times have axes to grind.

Not so with Peggy, with two partners she had built up a public relations company and enjoyed a life outside politics that made her an interesting and undemanding companion while William had no political ambitions, he was a member of the team and didn't want to be it's captain. He hadn't wanted to be the Chancellor.

This was his fourth, no, fifth ministerial post. Following his election, with his party in opposition, he'd been asked to shadow the

Tory employment ministers and with the landslide victory in 1997 he'd been made a junior employment minister in the new Labour government.   He had barely begun to make himself known in negotiations with management and the unions than he was moved to the Department of Trade and Industry. Following the next election he'd been promoted and moved to the Ministry of Defence as Minister of State for the Armed Forces. He understood that the high security clearance that he'd had for working on submarine nuclear reactors had served him well in smoothing his path into the secret world of defence.

Another election and another promotion, this time to Secretary of State for Productivity, Energy and Industry, the new name that one of the PM's advisers had come up with for Trade and Industry and intended to underline the importance of these functions, not least the need to decide how the nations future electrical supplies would be generated.   Peggy still giggled, in bed usually, at the reason why, within a week or so, the Department's name was changed back to Trade and Industry.

William had been disappointed to be asked to leave Trade and Industry after barely more than eighteen months, just when he felt that the department was setting out a coherent energy policy embracing wind, solar cells, a few gas fired stations, a new generation of clean coal and new pressurised water nuclear stations. The prime minister called it promotion to the second most important post in the cabinet. William called it something else – only to Peggy, of course.

There had been rumours, there always are, but these were persistent. It was hinted by those who professed to be close to the Treasury, that after many years in the job, the Chancellor was dissatisfied and felt that if he couldn't move up, he should move out. The same sort of people who claimed to be close to Number 10 said that such talk was rubbish and that the Chancellor would see this government through. Even insiders like William and Andrew found it difficult to distinguish 'spin' from the truth but it made sense. Perhaps more than the press and the general public, they could see how tired and touchy he had become.

Then one morning William's PS had poked his head in the door and said, "I've just had word from Roger Stevens, Secretary of State. The prime minister would like to see you as soon as convenient." William recognised this as the equivalent to a US president saying 'get your arse over here pronto' and thought that he preferred the British version. Peggy was always on about him getting more exercise so he had walked the short distance from Victoria Street and was ushered straight in to the prime minister's study.

"Good of you to come over William, we've got a bit of a crisis on our hands."

Williams mind went into overdrive, there weren't many things that he dealt with that could cause a crisis and in any case he would have heard about it before the PM. He hoped that it wasn't another of those Russian stations spreading deadly fission products but it couldn't be, the other members of the Cabinet Emergency Committee weren't present. He said,

"What crisis, Prime Minister?"

"Lloyd has said that he wants to leave the cabinet."

"Good Lord," said William. "I heard the rumours but didn't think that there was any truth in them. He'll be a great loss, you mustn't let him go."

"I know. The fact is that he hoped to have my job but I'm not going until we've achieved what we set out to achieve when we first came to power. I've offered him the Foreign Office and the Home Office and he's declined, so there's nowhere else for him to go but the back benches. He says that he wants to have some directorships in the City."

"He'll certainly raise the standard."

"Now, now William, you're speaking of the people who contribute to our party funds."

"There is that, of course. Who can possibly take his place?"

"You, William."

"Me?" said William, aghast. "I was never any good at arithmetic at school and the best economic principle that I know is Mr Macawber's."

"That's exactly the reason that I want you for the job. Lloyd suggested you and I agree with him, he said that you're the only member of the cabinet who will say No and keep saying No to the other members daft ideas."

"But I never went to university."

"Nor did Jim Callaghan and John Major."

"Well, with respect, Prime Minister, I wouldn't call them great Chancellors," said William.

"Nor great Prime Ministers," echoed the present one, "but you're different, you've served in three departments of state and done a good job in each. I want you for Chancellor and Roger will show you the announcement that I intend to make at noon today."

"Very well, Prime Minister, but I'll be sorry to leave DTI, we've just got things moving the way that you want."

"Ah, William, I've got the answer to that as well. In a year's time I'll give Andrew a leg up and make him Secretary of State for Trade and Industry, how's that?"

"He won't let you down," said William and added as an afterthought "nor will I, Prime Minister."

"I know that you won't, William."

So that was how Peggy Davis came to be able to sit on the arm of a chair in the Treasury, marvelling at the faith and skill of the medieval people who built Westminster Abbey with hand tools and wooden scaffolding.

The delegates from Hungary arrived and one by one were introduced to the prime minister and his wife before passing on into the room and being adroitly spread out to meet the waiting Brits. Peggy who was talking with Stuart Harcourt while keeping an eye on the door, as he was, was conscious that, momentarily, he caught his breath. She followed his gaze and saw that an attractive girl had just entered. She corrected the thought, young woman would be a better description. When she had been introduced to the Prime Minister and his wife, the young woman came across the room and spoke with Sir Stuart in Hungarian and he introduced her to Peggy, before she herself had been buttonholed by another interpreter and introduced to other Hungarian guests.

The reception progressed and the visitors and their interpreters circulated. Some time later she saw Stuart talking animatedly with the young woman and some time later again, when the PM's wife was having a quick word with her, she realised that they were no longer in the room.

The following morning Roger Stevens, the prime minister's Principal Private Secretary, rose with a smile and gestured to the chair in front of his desk. His visitor, a slender girl with deep auburn hair and green eyes, sat, crossed her shapely legs and smoothed her uniform skirt.

"Good of you to come over Jackie, this place has been somewhat disturbed this morning."

"Isn't it always?" said Captain Jackie Fraser, head of the Director of Military Security's Special Investigation Unit.

"Well, especially so today. It's not every day that you find a dead body in Number 10."

"I suppose not," said a surprised Jackie. "Who's body?"

"Sir Stuart Harcourt. It takes a bit of getting used to especially when the deceased is someone you have known for years and were talking with only yesterday."

"Of course, you probably knew him better than the others, you're from the Foreign Office and Sir Stuart was the PM's chief foreign policy adviser," said Jackie. "Did you ever serve together?"

"Yes, in Budapest, but it was some time ago, my first foreign posting, in fact, he was a second secretary and I was the dogsbody. He was a pleasant person to work for. He went back there as the ambassador, it was his last posting before coming here. I hope that I didn't drag you away from something important?"

"No, nothing that can't wait."

"Well, knowing that you've got a nose for this sort of thing, the boss thought that it might be helpful if you had a look at the scene before it's all tidied up. I'm not putting it as clearly as I should but you know what I mean and before you say it, yes, I know that your remit only covers the MoD and that you have no jurisdiction elsewhere and that it's a matter for the civil police and all that sort of stuff but we'd like you to have a look at it the day it happened, so to speak."

Jackie noted the we.

"Is there anything suspicious about his death, I mean, how did he die?"

"As far as the doctor could tell he died from natural causes," said Roger.

Jackie was about to say 'then why send for me?' but said instead,

"Who's been here from the police?"

"We've had the protection squad and our friends from over the river, and now that I come to think of it the head of the anti-terrorist lot looked in as a precautionary measure."

"Assistant Commissioner David Vowles?"

"The very same."

"But there was no sign of external injury, no smell of almonds and no empty pill boxes or phials?" said Jackie, smiling.

"No nothing. Come and see for yourself."

He stood up and led the way out of the room that he shared with the prime minister's chief of staff. Instead of turning right to pass in front of the main stairs he turned left and entered a corridor past a series of offices and entered the last one in which several sombre people were sat at desks. The PPS said, "Excuse us," in somewhat hushed tones and exited by yet another door into another passage that led to the chief foreign policy advisers room. He opened the door and he and Jackie entered a largish office by No 10 standards, with windows, including a bay window, looking out on Downing Street.

"This is it, Jackie, I understand that he was slumped over his desk."

"As if he was sitting at the desk when he died?"

"Yes."

"Who found him?"

"The security guard on his midnight rounds. He'd noticed that the light was on all the evening and seen people coming and going," said Roger. "There was nothing unusual in that, there are always people busy doing something at all hours in Number 10. But he knew that Stuart seldom stayed very late after a reception and so he poked his head in at about five past midnight and found him slumped across his desk."

"What did he do?"

"Sensible chap went and told the duty PS. We take it in turns to cover the nights."

"And the PS?" asked Jackie.

"David Graham, he's sleeping at the moment but you can talk with him later. He went and pulled Stuart upright in his seat to see if he was alive. He said that his first thought when he saw him slumped there had been that he was the worse for drink, but when he got him upright he could see that he was dead. So he sent for the doctor and rang me and then did a thing for which he deserves full marks, he went along the corridor to Number 12 and got the duty press wallah and had him take photographs of the body and everything, reasoning that the doctor and the ambulance people would probably disturb things in Stuart's room and that if there was anything odd about the death, it might well be moved or lost."

"Most people would probably have phoned for an ambulance," said Jackie.

"Not from Number 10 they wouldn't," said Roger with a wry grin, "we endeavour to keep things in house. Put another way, the only publicity that we want is that which we control. Of course, if there had been a chance that he was still alive it would have been different."

"Of course," echoed Jackie.

She studied the room, knowing now that there were photo's to give the detail. The room had two doors, both in the room's inner wall. The desk was at the end of the room remote from the bay window with two chairs in front of it and a side table which obstructed the nearer of the doors. There were two comfortable looking armchairs in the bay window with a low coffee table. Some excellent prints graced the walls and there was a small built-in cupboard for coats.

"What time did the members of his staff leave?"

"I don't know," said Roger, "let's ask them."

He led the way back to the room in which the sombre looking people were and said,

"Sorry, folks, it's dreadful, isn't it? This is Captain Jackie Fraser from Military Security who we've asked to look at things in case there was something funny about Stuart's death. She asked me what time you went home last night."

"I went first," said a young woman in the corner. "At about six."

"And I think that I was the next," said a young man with fair hair.

The other two staff members looked at each other and smiled, and the man said in a mock-cockney voice

"We're caught red handed, gov', the boss had gone upstairs so Sybil and I left together at half past six and had a drink at Charing Cross station before catching our respective trains."

"And Sir Stuart was alive and well when you left?" asked Jackie, more from want for something to say than a search for knowledge.

"Yes," said the woman. "I think that I was probably the last, he asked me what time the Hungarian party was due to arrive."

"Did he go to the party?" asked Jackie.

"Of course," said Roger, "we both did, we're the only people in the building who can understand Hungarian."

"You mean that you can both speak the language," said Jackie, smiling.

Roger smiled back

"As it is spoken in the better circles in Budapest, if you get my meaning," said Roger. "Stuart was also fluent in Serbo-Croatian. Now, that is a very diffuse country. How Tito managed to get not only the Serbs but also the Croatians and all the others singing from the same hymn sheet, I'll never know."

"Perhaps having a brutal police force and army helped?" offered Jackie.

"There is that, of course."

"Tell me about the reception," said Jackie.

"The guests were beginning to arrive as we were leaving," said the woman called Sybil. "The Chancellor and his wife were in the hall, she's ever so nice. So's he, actually, not grumpy like his predecessor."

"Clearly the influence of a good woman," said the young woman in the corner.

"I'd say that it was the influence of having a beautiful younger wife," said the fair haired young man.

"Peggy is something special, isn't she?" said Jackie.

"You know her?" asked Roger then his brain registered, "of course you do, it was you who solved the murder of brother Andrew's girl friend, wasn't it?"

"Yes, I'll go and see her," said Jackie, "being in public relations she probably noticed more of what was going on that evening than most people."

"I wonder if she and her partners have got any Hungarian contacts?" mused Roger.

"They're bound to have but I doubt if any of them were close to the delegation, she's scrupulous in keeping clear of anything that might embarrass her husband."

Chapter Two

JACKIE phoned Peggy Davis from Number 10 and asked if she could come and see her about last night's reception.

"By all means, Jackie, but can't we do it on the phone to save you having to come to Regents Street, it was a very ordinary party, people talked to one another, with and without an interpreter, then the Hungarians left and a few minutes afterwards we followed them. What in particular do you want to ask me?"

"I can do that better face to face, Peggy. Clearly you haven't heard, Sir Stuart Harcourt was found dead in his room last night."

"Good Lord, I was talking with him. I won't ask you anything on the phone, why don't you join me for a sandwich and coffee lunch here in my room at, say, 12.30?"

When they were sitting in Peggy's office with their sandwiches and coffee, Peggy said,

"Now, Jackie, about Sir Stuart, how did he die, not by poison gas in a scent bottle, I trust?"

"As of this moment we don't know, there was no sign of injury or noxious substances, it looked like natural causes."

"Then why you?" asked Peggy.

"Because Roger Stevens said that 'we' would like me to take a look at it."

"That's because you solved Wendy's murder."

"I suppose so," said Jackie, "but it does make things awkward with the proper police."

"Never mind, what time did he die? He was alright when he talked with me."

"We don't know and we probably never will. He was found slumped over his desk by the security man making his rounds at midnight. He thought that it was unusual for Sir Stuart to be there so late so he looked into the room and found him."

"I see, so it might have been any time after the end of the reception," said Peggy.

"You're an observant person, Peggy, try to run through the reception as you saw it."

"William and I arrived in Number 10 just after six-thirty. Members of the staff were leaving and we said hello and goodnight – have you

17

noticed how silly it sounds to be saying goodnight when the sun is still high in the sky? Where was I?"

"You had just entered the Hall at Number 10," said Jackie.

"We'd left our coats in William's office so we went straight upstairs into the reception room. Roger Stevens steered some drinks our way and the PUS from the DTI came and spoke with William. They got on well together."

"What did you do?" asked Jackie.

"Sir Stuart came over and drew me away, asking if we were bothered by the tennis crowds."

"And are you?" said Jackie, momentarily side-tracked.

"Not at home, our house isn't near the All England Club, but the traffic coming into and leaving Wimbledon is a nuisance."

"Sorry," said Jackie. "What then?"

"The prime minister and his wife came in and Stuart said, "Our guests must have arrived," and sure enough the Hungarians came through the door and were welcomed by his nibs and his wife."

"What then?"

"Stuart said that he should really be at the PM's elbow but Roger was there doing his stuff and he personally preferred talking with me. He asked if I ever went to the theatre and said that if I was ever at a loss he'd be pleased to escort me. .We were standing sort of side by side watching the Hungarians pass the PM and suddenly I heard him give a sharp intake of breath as if he was startled. I looked up and saw that a very attractive dark haired woman had just shaken the PM's hand."

"Did you ask him who she was?"

"Yes and he said that he thought that she was an actress who moved in influential circles. I remember those words clearly, I wondered at the time what an actress did when moving in Budapest influential circles."

"Probably the same thing as they do everywhere else," grinned Jackie.

"The woman spotted Stuart and came straight over, said something in Hungarian and then said in American accented English 'I knew that you would be here Ambassador Stuart, and I guessed that you would be talking to a pretty girl as usual.' He said 'Hello Sonia' and she said something to him in Hungarian. She then turned to me, told me that her name was Vera Veronsomething and laughed as she said something about him being well known at all the night spots in Hungary."

"What did he do or say?" asked Jackie.

"He looked a bit sheepish. To cover the moment I complimented her on her English and she said that she had spent four years at the United Nations headquarters and what she hadn't learnt in New York she had learnt in Budapest. She added, with a careless sort of laugh that he taught all the girls the naughty bits and they told her. No, that's not right," said Peggy. "She said 'and years later they told me'. Does that help?"

"Very much," said Jackie.

"She then said that she had arrived in London only the previous day to be the new cultural attaché in their embassy. She then turned to him and said something about renewing old links."

"She seems to have been very indiscreet."

"That's clearly what Stuart thought, he muttered 'excuse us', said something in what I suppose was Hungarian, and steered her to an empty corner of the room."

"What happened then?" prompted Jackie.

"I spoke with the prime minister and his wife and a lot of other people and grinned at William who was doing his best with an elderly man and an equally elderly female interpreter. Then the Hungarians left with a torrent of thanks and after a short interval we left as well. William could hardly contain himself, he'd been buttonholed by their finance man and questioned about the future movement of sterling, inflation, the Euro, the US dollar and what have you and goodness only knows what they made of his answers."

"They knew that they shouldn't have asked him those sort of questions at the reception so they will assume that he's a very smart operator," laughed Jackie. "Did you see Sir Stuart again?"

"Now that you jog my memory, in fact I did. It was just before I saw William with the elderly couple, I looked across and saw Stuart and the actress going out of the door."

"This was before they all left?"

"Yes, I'd say something less than a quarter of an hour before the visitors left. I didn't think much about it at the time because it's not uncommon for people to leave a reception to look at the paintings that are on show in Number 10. They're part of the national collection. William has been invited to take his pick to hang in his room at the Treasury and I'm going to see that he gets colourful and cheerful ones, by British painters."

"You really are a jewel Peggy and William's a very lucky man."

"That's what I keep telling him," laughed Peggy.

Jackie made her way back to the MoD. On her desk was a message to please ring Roger Stevens on his private number at Number 10, Downing Street.

"Roger, it's Jackie Fraser, I have a note to ring you."

"Hello Jackie, thanks for ringing. We've got a preliminary report from the doctors and they say that they still don't know how Stuart died but there is an angry looking pin-prick behind his right shoulder."

"So his death might be suspicious?"

"Yes, all the more reason for you to help us."

"Don't worry, when can I have a set of the pictures that your press man took?"

"They've just arrived I'll send a messenger over with them."

"Tell him to ring this number the moment he leaves Number 10 and I'll meet him outside the main entrance, otherwise he'll have a hard time with our security."

Jackie collected the packet and put her head in her chief's secretary's room.

"Go right in, Jackie."

She opened the door and Major General 'Tubby' Lowe looked up and beamed at her,

"Come on in, my dear, sit yourself down and have some tea."

It was always the same except that it was coffee in the mornings.

Jackie sat, crossed her legs and smoothed her skirt.

Tubby studied her, she really was lovely, came from an army family, her father was a colonel, now retired and doing something in the City and her uncle was a four star General serving on the sixth floor of the MoD. He'd known her mother and had known Jackie since she was a baby. The girl had been determined to have a civilian career and had read law at the London School of Economics at the same time as Helene Taylor, now Helene Hawkridge, and gone into chambers in Lincolns Inn.

She had found a junior barristers life uninteresting and unrewarding and had joined the Corps of Military Police where she had been snapped up by the General to head his Special Investigations Unit. The unit consisted of Jackie and two sergeants, Sandra Roberts and Kim Bourne who were stationed in the Regents Park Barracks. The DMS, General Lowe – a paratrooper with a DSO – told his friends that he sometimes thought that he worked for Jackie but the girls got results, partly because men didn't think that such attractive girls could also be clever.

"What did Number 10 want you for, Jackie?"

"The PM's chief foreign policy adviser was found dead in his room last night."

"What, Stuart Harcourt?"

"Yes, Sir."

"Always thought him a bit odd, bit of a ladies man, other people's ladies. How did he die?"

"We don't know but I've just heard that the skin is punctured and angry looking behind his right shoulder. The duty secretary at Number 10 last night had the good sense to get the press office to take pictures of the scene, reasoning that if there was anything fishy, the people who took the body away might disturb the evidence. These are the pictures."

She spread them out on the General's desk and went on,

"I've also been talking with Peggy Davis, the Chancellor's wife who was speaking with him at the reception to the Hungarians last night."

"At Number 10?"

"Yes, Sir."

"Did she notice anything unusual about the reception?"

"He was talking with her when the Hungarian party arrived and he seemed surprised at the presence of one of the female members, a raven haired beauty who came straight across to him and treated him as an old friend, well, more than a friend, I'd say."

Tubby thought about that and said,

"Wasn't he our ambassador in Budapest?"

"Yes, and he had served there before. Roger Stevens was there at the same time."

"So it would be a reasonable assumption on the part of the Hungarians that he'd be there last night?"

"Yes, Sir, we're not exactly flush with Hungarian linguists."

"About this raven haired beauty….."

"I was coming to that," said Jackie. "Peggy Davis saw Stuart Harcourt and the woman leaving the reception about a quarter of an hour before the end of the reception."

"Going to show her the paintings," said Tubby.

"Or his etchings," grinned Jackie. "That's as far as I've got."

"It sounds a great deal for the first day, my dear. What will you do next?"

"I'm going to ask the FCO to let me see everything that they've got on Sir Stuart Harcourt and the people across the river what they've got on the raven haired beauty who said that she was the cultural attaché at the Hungarian embassy."

"You don't miss much, do you Jackie. Try and keep me posted."

She went back to her room and consulted the telephone directory. Jackie believed in direct action, there was no point in messing about, she'd ask the new cultural attaché what time she had left Sir Stuart? She assumed that the police would already have done so but what the hell. A voice said, "Hungarian embassy, can I help you?"

"I'd like to speak to the Cultural Attache, please."

"Putting you through."

A voice with a more marked accent said, "Cultural Attache's office."

"This is Captain Fraser of the British Ministry of Defence, I'd like to speak with the cultural attaché, please."

"I'm sorry but she's not here."

"When will she be in?" asked Jackie.

"She has just phoned me and said that she'll be back tomorrow."

Somehow the words 'be back tomorrow' seemed to suggest to Jackie that she wasn't in London. The voice went on,

"Can I help you?"

"I don't think so," said Jackie. " I want to talk with her about the Prime Minister's reception the other night."

"She was very upset to have to miss it, she'd advanced her date of arrival in Britain to go to it and then she got the news that her mother had that accident and she rushed back to Budapest, only to find that it was all a mistake."

Bells were ringing in Jackie's head.

"So she didn't go to the reception at Number 10?"

"No, she's angry about it but, as she said on the phone, since she'd only arrived in London the day before, nobody would miss her."

"I'll have to come and see her on another day, then," said Jackie. "So that I get it right, be a dear and spell her name out slowly for me."

"Some of our names are difficult, aren't they?   The Cultural Attache is Vera Veronalika and she is a professor from Pecs University. That's the earliest University in Hungary, it was founded in 1367. It's called the Janus Pannonius University now."

Jackie thanked her informant and said that she'd call again in a few days time. She had much to think about.

The following morning Jackie called on Roger Stevens at Number 10. She told him what she had learned thus far.

"So the Vera Veronalika who came to the reception was an impostor?" said Roger.

"Could be, but she could be someone who the Embassy put in at the last moment because the Cultural Attache had been called away."

"In which case why call her Vera Veronalika?"

"Perhaps simply to save trouble because that was the name on the list that they had forwarded to the FCO some days earlier," said Jackie, "and that's what I am trying to find out. Meanwhile I'm on my way to the Foreign Office personnel branch to ask if I can see Stuart Harcourt's file. Do you think that they'll play?"

"Not a hope, old dear, only the permanent secretary gets to see those and by the way, it's not called the personnel branch any more, it's Human Resources. It's all changed, they've also got a division that will build you a garage, or at least plan and manage the construction of your garage. We diplomats have to be versatile these days."

"You're pulling my leg," said Jackie.

"No I'm not, old dear, you look them up on the web."

"Getting back to the question of access to the files, what about ministers?"

"Same rule applies, if a Foreign Office minister has need to ask for that sort of thing he's given relevant extracts, not the whole thing. After all, come the next election he might be on a picket line somewhere."

"Or in a London club lobbying for a conglomerate," said Jackie.

"Same thing, we FCO types don't want them to know what our diplomats get up to."

"Has your master ever asked for such a personal file?"

"Only indirectly when we were filling the chair at the United Nations. The Foreign Secretary proposed a name and his nibs said that before the decision was made, he wanted to see the files on the three possibles and the PUS brought over what he said were the files and answered my master's questions by referring to them."

"What did the Foreign Secretary think of that?" asked Jackie.

"He resented the whole thing and protested that it was up to him to make the selection. He was foolish enough to mention it confidentially to the BBC's chief political commentator who happened to be lurking about outside Number 10 when he came out."

"Is that why he's now the leader of the House?"

"Good Lord no, what on earth gave you that idea?" smiled Roger. "Prime Ministers don't do that sort of thing. He simply told him that he was the only man who could do the vital job of organising the day to day business of the House of Commons; much more important than being Foreign Secretary. The member got the message."

"But kept a place in the Cabinet."

"Somewhat further down the table, though."

"What shall I do then, Roger?"

"Go along the road and see the PUS, I'll have a word with him and tell him that my master would like him to give you all the help that he can. Give me half an hour to smooth the way and then arrange with his secretary a time that they can fit you in."

Jackie debated whether she should change into uniform and decided against it and later that morning was ushered into the presence of Sir Lancelot Braceford, Permanent Under Secretary and Head of the Diplomatic Service.

"Now young woman, I gather that the PM has asked you to look into the death of Stuart Harcourt," His eyes twinkled. "What does the Met think of that?"

"Actually, Sir Lancelot, I don't think that they know."

He looked at her archly. "Why have you come to me?"

"There is an indication that he didn't die from natural causes," said Jackie. "If he was murdered it's my view that the reason is probably rooted in his past. I reject the notion that it was because of anything to do with his current life in London, on the grounds of why run the risk of doing the deed in Number 10 when the murderer could have struck him down a dozen times on his way home from the office."

"I follow your argument," said Sir Lancelot, "but an avenger from the past could have done the same." He went on, "So you want to know about his service history."

"The bits that aren't in Who's Who."

"To tell you the truth, most of it is in Who's Who."

"I want to know how well he got on with people, whether there was any unpleasantness between him and the host nation in any of his postings, that sort of thing."

"We never had to recall him, if that's what you mean."

"But were there occasions in some countries, Hungary for example, when things got a trifle tense?" persisted Jackie.

"There are always times when we are trying to persuade foreign governments to see things our way," said the PUS.

"I meant personally, PUS, he was in Eastern Europe when the iron curtain was still down."

"I know that you did, young woman, actually he got on rather well with the other side and that proved most useful. There are at least three British business men who have reason to be grateful to him."

"How so?" prompted Jackie.

"He negotiated their exchange."

"I gather that it's usually a set piece exchange," said Jackie.

"What do you mean by that?" said Sir Lancelot in the manner of a bridge player who has just seen his partner trump his ace.

"Well," said Jackie, wishing that she'd kept quiet. "We capture a Russian spy so they arrest a harmless business visitor on a trumped up charge and then we rush to negotiate an exchange. I wouldn't think that great brilliance was required for that."

"Sometimes it was trickier than you might think," said Sir Lancelot.

Jackie decided to get back on track.

"Was there anything in his private life overseas that came to your attention?"

"Dangerous liaisons?" said Sir Lancelot, smiling.

"Yes, I have reason to believe that his interest extended into theatrical circles."

"Bohemian circles?" said the PUS smiling even more broadly.

"Could have been useful cover," said Jackie.

Sir Lancelot's smile disappeared.

"Whatever gave you that idea?"

"Sonia X," said Jackie, awaiting his reaction.

"Whatever has she got to do with it, that was a long time ago."

"Two nights ago to be exact," said Jackie.

Sir Lancelot shut the file that was on his desk and said,

"You must excuse me young woman but I think that's all the help that I can give you and my next appointment will be waiting."

Jackie knew when she was being shown the door and thanked him prettily for his help and left. She had a lot to think about but first she'd try MI-5.

It took intervention by the prime minister's office to get her inside the fortress across the river and she was shown into the room of Brian Roberthaugh, the man with whom she'd had to deal when on the case of the spies who were stealing secrets from the underwater research establishment at Portland.

"Hello Jackie, nice to see you, how do you think that we can help you this time?"

Jackie bit back the comment that sprang to her lips to the effect that they hadn't helped the last time, and said,

"In two ways, Brian, I'm interested in two people."

"And they are?"

"Sir Stuart Harcourt...

He cut in on her, "He who died the other night?"

"The same," said Jackie.

"Why on earth should the Director of Military Security be concerning himself with the death of an elderly diplomat?"

"That's a question that you should address to the prime minister, not me," said Jackie.

"We don't concern ourselves with Foreign Office people."

"Presumably that explains why Burgess, MacLean and the others could give the Soviets our secrets with impunity and escape to mock us from Moscow," said Jackie.

"That was a long time ago," said Brian defensively. "Who is the second person?"

"Sonia Something from Hungary."

"Who on earth is Sonia Something from Hungary?"

"Come off it Brian, I expect that you know who she is. Stuart Harcourt did."

"No we don't," lied the MI-5 man.

"Very well, there's no point in my wasting my time here. I will report to the prime minister that MI-5 and you in particular, Brian Roberthaugh, have been their usual unhelpful selves."

"There's no need to be like that, Jackie, I'm only doing my job."

"Yes Brian and I guarantee to you that the PM will decide that in the next round of cuts someone should take a good hard look at you and your job."

She made her way back across the Thames reflecting on the strange behaviour of the people who work in intelligence. She could understand fully the need to preserve at all costs the identities and whereabouts of those who served in MI-6, the secret intelligence service, and for the security service, MI-5, to be secretive about covert surveillance operations but Brian Roberthaugh was being awkward for awkwardness's sake. After her experience with him on the Portland spy case she didn't see why he should continue to get away with it so she went to Number 10 and had Roger Stevens listen to the voice actuated recorder that accompanied her everywhere.

Roger listened to the recording then picked up the phone and asked to be put through to the head of MI-5. Jackie could only hear the Number 10 end of the call.

"Roger Stevens, the PM's PPS here. We have a serious complaint. Acting on the Prime Minister's personal instruction, Captain Jackie Fraser called on Brian Roberthaugh this morning to ask for information on two people. No, I won't name them over the phone. She was given what I believe is called the bums rush. As far as the PM is concerned it could indicate one of two things, either one of your officers was being totally uncooperative to an emissary of the prime minister or that MI-5 has no knowledge of the people named, in which case I'm sure that my master would consider that a root and branch review of your organisation is long overdue." He listened. "You'll look into it and ring me back? Good."

Roger turned to Jackie and said, "She's OK and is having an uphill fight to establish herself in what has hitherto been an all male domain. This might help her. Did your machine record that?"

"I suppose so," said Jackie.

"Be a dear and sit at that monitor and type it up on Number 10 paper and I'll send it across by messenger, it might strengthen her hand to have a piece of paper to shove under Brian Roberthaugh and Co's noses."

Jackie went back to her room in the MoD thinking where do I look next? The least that she could do was to set the girls to work finding out all that they could about Sonia X. What did they know about her? She is about 30 years old, slender with dark hair. She has considerable nerve, few people would have impersonated another in Number 10. The imp in her mind suggested that men are doing it all the time, they call themselves minister of this or that and know nothing about the ministry. She brought her mind back to the problem in hand, she speaks good English with an American accent. Now there might just be the glimmer of a lead, the woman would have had no need to dissemble in front of Peggy so she was probably telling the truth about serving at the United Nations for four years. But when? On age grounds it must have been in the past ten years and probably the last six. It had sounded as if Sonia X hadn't been in Budapest when Stuart Harcourt was our ambassador. She looked him up and found that he was there between 2000 and 2003. It was a long shot but she'd send one of her girls to New York to comb the UN records for a Hungarian girl, age between 25 and 29 who had served there at that time.

She phoned the sergeants and told them that she wanted a volunteer to spend a couple of days in New York. She was surprised at their reaction, each suggested that the other should go. On the grounds that Kim had done the Bosnian trip, Sandra would go. She left the next day. Kim carried on with the press search.

Jackie also phoned her friend Helene Hawkridge and asked if she might approach Charles Smith, the Head of News and Current Affairs at Hawkridge Media Central, and ask him if there was a way in which they might tap media and other sources in Budapest for a 30 year old actress called Sonia who may have spent several years in the United States. Jackie and Helene had been contemporaries reading law at the LSE and had kept in touch ever since.

Chapter Three

ASSOCIATE Professor Jose Fernandez Smith was distressed. Trust that wretched Eynon girl to lose her pocket-book. It was bad enough to lose the thing but then to go and publicly accuse the pub landlord's daughter of stealing it was the limit. Until then everything had been going reasonably well.

It had started some months earlier in New Haven. He had been speaking with a friend of his and had mentioned that he wanted to organise a field-trip to England for some of his students in the summer to study some aspects of the entomology in a chalk stream or river. The friend, Associate Professor Stephen Hamsworth had suggested going to the place in Dorset from where his wife's ancestors had emigrated at the end of the seventeenth century and where their descendants still lived in a manor house through who's park a chalk river lazily flowed. Kathryn and he had spent part of their honeymoon in the village pub and had been back since and he could recommend it.

So it was that he had organised the trip for a small group of seven entomology students to study the flying insects associated with a chalk stream. He would have liked to do it at the end of May – beginning of June - when the mayflies would be most active but that hadn't fitted in with the academic semesters and it had to be in August, when there wouldn't be any mayflies to see but lots of midges and flies. He had played on his friendship with Stephen Hamsworth in making the booking and gathered that they had been extremely lucky to secure two weeks accommodation in the village inn for all of the group except two, and those two would sleep in an apartment a few yards along the road and take their meals at the inn.

They had flown from JFK to Heathrow, arriving on Sunday morning and collected a mini-bus for the duration of the visit, driving on the motorways as far as the New Forest and then on roads that seemed to get narrower and narrower until they reached the village of Tolbrite and the Tolbrite Arms where they would stay. They had parked their vehicle at the back of the pub quite close to the gently flowing River Winterborne, a tributary of the River Stour, and humped their belongings to their rooms. Jose found that as befitted his status, he'd been allocated the biggest room at the back, overlooking the garden and the river, a room that, he gathered, was the room that Kathryn and Stephen always had. The students picked theirs.

There was some debate about who would occupy the two rooms in the house just along the road. There were volunteers, notably a boy and a girl student who, Jose had noticed, had sat side-by-side holding hands in the aircraft and in the mini-bus. He'd put two young men in the house and allocated the hand-holding couple rooms in the pub; if they wanted to creep about in the night that was no more than they could have done in a five-star hotel in the States; this way their parents couldn't claim that he'd condoned co-habitation.

The house where the two students would sleep was occupied by the maintenance manager of the Manor House estate, young Will Conway and his wife, Gloria who was the daughter of the landlord of the pub. The house was known to everybody as the antique dealer's house, a fact that annoyed Gloria, and consisted of a ground floor, the front of which had once been a shop and an upper floor where Will and Gloria lived. Each floor now consisted of two bedrooms, a living room, kitchen and bathroom and each floor had its own entrance. This meant that downstairs, one entered directly into the living room through what had once been the shop door.

The first night they all had dinner at the pub and chatted with Gloria and Will in the bar. They learnt that the antique dealer had been the leader of a gang that had been smuggling stolen antique furniture into England using a charter yacht based at the local port of Poole and making copies for sale in Britain and the USA. He and his associates had been caught, thanks to the efforts of a group of friends who met at the pub most Saturday nights and he was now languishing in a French jail. The leaders of the group of unofficial upholders of the law were the son of the squire of Tolbrite and his wife, Timmy and Helene Hawkridge. Timmy owned a lot of radio stations, including ten or so in the US Mid-west and made albums and TV documentaries and Helene and her mother Claire-Marie, owned a lot of vineyards in France.

This prompted Gloria to remark that if they were in on Saturday night they would meet them, adding that she and Will had uncovered the vital clue that had solved a murder at a place near to Bristol and they had also been with Timmy and Helene in France when they had helped the American G-man capture the people who were flooding the continent with counterfeit twenty dollar bills. This led to the story that Will had been shot in the shoulder rescuing Timmy and Helene's baby daughter from a kidnapper.

"And Tim then shot and killed the kidnapper," put in Will.

"And we always imagined that England was a peaceful place," said one of the students.

"It is most of the time," said Mrs Trowbridge, the landlord's wife and Gloria's mother who came into the bar, "it's simply that they can't help chasing crooks."

All had been well until the first Wednesday. The sun had shone and Jose and the young people had wandered along the river bank in small groups studying the little things that flew. They knew that there are more than 85,000 species of diptera – true flies identified by having two wings. These include midges, sometimes called gnats, some of which bite humans and some of which don't. The small midges, less than a millimetre long are the smallest bloodsucking insects. They also knew that in some countries there are robber flies that can have a body length of 8 centimetres, eighty times longer than a midge.

They also knew that there are over 2,000 species of ephemeroptera, with two sets of two wings, the species to which the mayfly belongs and had studied the four stages of their life cycle which culminates in a few hours – perhaps a day - of flight in all their glory, the swarming dance low over the stream from which they have just emerged, mating, and dying. In the case of a female dying as soon as she has dropped or placed her eggs on the water where they will sink to the bottom, hatch into a nymph in, perhaps, two weeks and then exist for a year or more before the metamorphosis to a winged insect occurs. A truly ephemeral existence.

The students had another research objective, they were testing some barrier creams that they had prepared under the professor's guidance, for their ability to deter winged insects from settling on the exposed parts of their bodies. The young people had reacted as he had expected; this made the trip worthwhile. After all, they could read all about flying insects and study their anatomy in books and videos without having to wander about in damp places getting stung, but experimenting with deterrent formulae was different.

All except for Miss Elfrida Eynon. She said that the creams and sprays smelt and might give her a rash and so she took no part in the trials, preferring the benefits of soap and water. Thereafter she complained continually that she had been stung.

The students separated naturally into three pairs, the two boys who slept at the antique dealer's house, the two who held hands and two girls who were room-mates at Yale. That left Elfrida who attached herself to Professor Jose or to one of the other pairs as the mood suited her.

The first day had been spent exploring the banks of the river and the adjacent meadows. Will said that they had the squire's permission to explore along the river where it passed through the park and they used the hay-cart bridge close to the manor house to cross to and fro to the other bank.

Their movements did not go unnoticed. Each morning the squire, General Sir David Hawkridge, sat in his study over the front entrance of the Manor House, read the Times, surveyed his park and snoozed. He would be visited by his wife Margaret and by the butler, Hodges, his former batman/driver known to one and all as the Sergeant. Mrs Hodges was the cook/housekeeper. Sometimes the fifth member of the household, Ah Ming, would bring the General's coffee. On the Tuesday morning, when Margaret looked into his study, he said,

"I say, Margaret, who are those people messing about on the river bank?"

"They're the Americans Will told us about, they're from Yale looking for flies and things."

"Yale, eh, is it that fellow who married Kathryn, the one who played their football? What was his name, Stephen?"

"Yes, dear, Stephen and no dear, it's not him, he's a professor of English."

"And this one's into bugs, is he?"

"I understand that he's a very nice man called Jose Smith and he's an entomologist who's interested in deterrent creams and sprays."

"I suppose somebody has to be," said the General. "Pity we didn't have his stuff in Malaya and Borneo."

"They say that malaria's on the increase," said Margaret.

"Terrible thing that, kills millions every year. If your American friend can come up with something to keep the mosquitoes away, they ought to give him a Nobel Prize."

"They probably will, dear. Has anyone you know died?"

This latter was because it was a family joke that the General always read the obituaries first. It was also true that the names of an increasing number of his contemporaries seemed to have been appearing in the columns of late.

The undergraduate pairs went out on Wednesday, equipped to do tests. There were several formulations to be tested and to start with they would all test the same thing on a given day. This involved putting the cream or spray on the exposed arm and leg on one side of the body and nothing on the other side to act as a control. Elfrida Eynon added herself to the professor and complained about the smell when he put the cream on his bare arm. Nevertheless she followed him as he walked along the river bank, making notes and endeavouring to photograph the insects with his digital camera. In places they had to force their way through thickets growing close to and in some cases, overhanging the bank. Professor Jose was conscious of a steady monotone of complaints from behind him. 'Did we have to come this way?' 'That branch nearly hit me.' 'My shoes and slacks are getting dirty' 'How much further are we going?' 'Oh I nearly fell over' and so on. In the end he switched off, if the wretched girl fell into the river he wouldn't bother to pull her out.

By the end of the afternoon he had decided that the first cream wasn't effective, the winged insects that he had encountered seemed to select either arm at random and to be quite undeterred by the cream. The other three teams reported the same before hurrying upstairs or along the road to have a shower and change. They had decided to take the mini-bus and go into Bournemouth for the evening. They had the advice of Stephen Hamsworth via Jose Smith as to the best night spots to visit.

The professor had barely reached his room when he heard shouting. He recognised the voice and went downstairs again. Mrs Trowbridge was behind the long bar and Elfrida Eynon was standing in front of it, shouting,

"Somebody has stolen my pocket-book."

"Where did you take it?" asked the landlady.

"I didn't take it anywhere; it was in my room. Somebody has taken it."

"They couldn't have, you are the only people occupying rooms, Gloria and I tidied your rooms and made the beds this morning, otherwise no one has been near your room. You must have mislaid it."

"Then one of you must have taken it, mustn't you, if you're the only people who have been upstairs today?" said Elfrida.

As three more of the students clad in their dressing gowns came down, the professor stepped into the bar and said,

"Please ignore what she's just said, she's upset and doesn't mean what she's saying."

"Yes I do," screamed Elfrida. "I know good what I'm saying, one of those two has stolen my pocket-book, I expect that it was her daughter or they're all in it together." She turned on the professor, "It's all your fault, we should have stayed at a proper hotel with a safe for guests valuables."

The two girl students went into the bar and attempted to take her arms, saying, "Come and sit over here and tell us all about it."

Elfrida shook them off and shouted,

"There's nothing to tell you. I left my pocket-book in my room and now it's gone."

"Where did you leave it?"

"I said, in my room."

"Yes, but where in your room? In a drawer, in the wardrobe or where?" persisted the girls.

"I don't know. All I know is that I had it in my room this morning and now it isn't there."

"You're sure that you didn't take it with you?"

"Don't be silly, why would I take all my money and my cards to look for a lot of flies?"

"What was in it?" asked the second girl.

"All of my cards, about two thousand dollars in travellers cheques and about eight hundred pounds in English money." She started to cry.

"You must cancel the cards right away," said the professor.

"I can't," wailed Elfrida, "I haven't got the cost of the phone."

"Don't be silly, I'll let you have some money," said the professor, thinking inwardly 'what, on a Yale associate professor's salary!'

"I don't know the numbers," wailed the girl who then turned on the landlady and spat at her. "See all the trouble your daughter's thieving has caused."

"She doesn't mean it," said the professor helplessly.

"Oh yes I do, they're all in it, I didn't want to come anyway but daddy made me, I'd rather be on our yacht in Newport."

And we all wish fervently that you were, thought Jose.

Eventually Elfrida was given forty pounds by the professor and persuaded to go to her room, have a shower and change and then make the necessary calls about her lost credit cards and money.

Since Elfrida had earlier announced that she had no intention of joining the party that was going to Bournemouth, the other six went as planned and the professor had the burden of her company at dinner in the pub's dining room, the other side of the entrance hall from the bar.

On Thursday morning Sergeant Kim Bourne set about the task of finding all that was published about the late Sir Stuart Harcourt and the raven haired Hungarian girl who had said that she was the cultural attaché.   Jackie was aware that the police would learn of their activities for the simple reason that Kim was engaged to, and lived with, Detective Inspector Tom Burton who filled a similar role for the head of the anti-terrorist branch as she filled for DMS. Thanks to Tom Burton's good sense, to date it hadn't hindered any of their investigations, quite the reverse in fact.

Jackie made her way to the Hawkridge Media headquarters at Canary Wharf to speak with Helene and Charles Smith.   She explained, not for publication, that there was reason to suppose that the death of the prime minister's chief adviser on foreign affairs was not due to natural causes and that one of the last people to have been seen with him was the Hungarian girl. She described Peggy Davis's account of the meeting with the girl who had said that she was Vera Veronalika and Stuart Harcourt's reference to Sonia and the woman's reference to re-establishing the old links. For a starter she would like to know if those old links were amorous or professional.

Helene suggested with a grin that in some circles those two functions were not necessarily exclusive.

Jackie described her reception at the FCO and at MI-5 and explained, hopefully, that she had no way of looking for possible references to Sonia in the Hungarian media.

"And you hope that we may have?" smiled Helene.

"Or Clare-Marie's friends might," said Jackie tentatively.

"That's fishing in dangerous waters and I suggest that we keep it to the Brits for the present," said the half French Helene.

"Yes," said Jackie. "That was stupid of me, what I really meant was the French press."

They discussed the matter for a while and Charles Smith promised to see what he could do.

Jackie declined Helene's offer that she should share her and Timmy's coffee and sandwiches lunch and made her way back to the MoD where a message awaited her to ring Roger Stevens' number. He was at a meeting but his secretary told her that he had wanted to tell her that the post mortem had finally confirmed that Sir Stuart Harcourt had been killed by an injection of a poison. They were still trying to find out which.

That same morning in Grosvenor Square, Charles Howard was summoned by the ambassador. The post of ambassador in London had been unfilled for nearly a year while the President sought a suitable and rich enough person to fill it. To Charles, scion of one of the old Virginia families, this had been an insult to an old and constant ally. But then, he thought that these days the leaders on both sides of the Atlantic were upstarts.

Charles was the senior US Treasury agent in Europe. He had been stationed in Paris until Jacque Chirac had been so deliberately awkward about Iraq, whereupon he had transferred to London He was a friend of the Hawkridge family and Timmy and Helene and their friends had been drawn into several encounters with the ungodly that involved Charles on the side of the angels.

Charles was reticent about his precise role in the embassy. Pressed he would talk about the T-men who had arrested Al Capone. Timmy thought that he was really CIA but suave, sophisticated Charles only admitted to having friends out at Langley – after all, he was a Virginian.

He was in his late thirties and enjoyed the company of younger women. Some years ago he had pursued Elizabeth, Timmy's sister, but at the time she was intent on her medical career and not interested. More recently he had lost no opportunity in trying to get past first base with the shapely Jackie Fraser.

He passed the US Marine Corps sentries and was waved into the holy of holies by the ambassador's secretary.

"Good morning, Mr Ambassador."

"Good morning Charles, are you well?"

"Fighting fit, Sir."

"And nothing to worry me with from the, er, shop?"

"No Sir, apart from the search for potential terrorists and persuading the British to extradite those we want to the States, everything's under control."

"Good, that's what I like to hear."

Charles wondered when he'd get to the point.

"I expect that you're wondering why I sent for you?"

"Well, er, yes Sir," said Charles.

"I had a call from Marvin Eynon this morning."

"Assistant Secretary of State Marvin Eynon?"

"Yes, it appears that someone has stolen his daughters pocket-book."

Charles bit his tongue. It was none of his business if both the US ambassador at the Court of St James and the person the US President had appointed to be Assistant Secretary of State in the State Department were having a funny five minutes. Lost her pocket-book, indeed. He said,

"How unfortunate for her."

"It was stolen by an inn keeper here in England."

"Oh I see," said Charles, "Where?"

"In a village called Tolbrite in Dorset."

"There's only one inn in Tolbrite. I know it well and I'd trust the owner's family with my life," said Charles.

He thought that this was a rather clever remark, although the ambassador wouldn't appreciate it. The actual owner of the Tolbrite Arms was the squire who owned the estate that consisted of the Manor House and park, six farms, and the village of Tolbrite including the school and church and the pub.

"That's as may be but they stole his daughter's pocket-book."

"Frankly, Mr Ambassador, I very much doubt that."

"Well, somebody has and Assistant Secretary Eynon wants us to find out who did?"

"That's a matter for the British police," said Charles.

"Don't be difficult, you're supposed to... well, it's the sort of thing that I'd expect you to do, so get on with it."

Charles wondered what his chiefs back home in Washington would have made of that, but never mind, he liked the pub at Tolbrite.

"OK Mr Ambassador, We'll look into it and since its for Assistant Secretary Eynon, I'll give it my personal attention."

"Good man, that's what I like to hear."

Charles left the room and grinned at the ambassador's secretary on the way out. She was an old State Department hand, she had doubtless listened to the call from Washington and his conversation with the ambassador and shared his views on Assistant Secretary Marvin Eynon and his daughter. She said,

"Looking on the bright side, it's another day out in the country, isn't it, Charles?"

and he replied,

"Yes, it's all part of the heavy cross we have to carry."

Chapter Four

HE ARRIVED at the Tolbrite Arms that afternoon and was greeted by Gloria who was helping her mother clear up following the lunchtime trade.

"Hello Charles, how nice to see you, I hope that you didn't plan on stopping the night but we're full up with a party of students from Yale."

"No, this is just a flying visit and I will have to be back in London tonight. I gather one of the students has lost her pocket-book."

"Yes and it's cast a shadow over the whole party, she's accused us of stealing it."

"Silly girl. Where are they now?"

"They're somewhere along the river bank looking for flies. The professor gives them fancy names but that's what they're doing, looking for flies with two wings and flies with four wings."

"And how did she come to lose her pocket-book?"

"Goodness only knows," said Gloria. "She swears that she left it in her room when she went out on Wednesday morning and that it wasn't there when she got back at tea-time. I tidied her room and made the bed and I didn't see it."

"Where in her room did she leave it?"

"She doesn't seem to know, she just keeps saying that it was in her room when she went out."

"Could anyone else have got into her room during the day?"

"It's not possible for a stranger to get upstairs during the daytime and the only guests are the students from Yale."

"If she came down first, one of the other students could have gone into her room before himself or herself coming down, couldn't they?"

"I suppose so," said Gloria, "but they'd have been taking a big risk what with the professor and the other four students milling around upstairs."

"I understand that there are eight in the party from Yale, so that would make it the professor and six, surely?"

"No Charles, two of the boys are sleeping in our downstairs flat."

"Along the road?"

"Yes."

"Do you happen to know what was in the pocket-book?"

"All of her credit cards, two thousand dollars in travellers cheques and several hundred English pounds."

"And she left all that lying around?"

"Evidently," said Gloria.

"Has the theft been reported to the police?"

"Yes, I phoned Sergeant Clare Thornton and told her and because they were all out on the river banks she said that she'd come out at six this evening and take statements."

"Good, I'd like to sit-in on that session, I don't think that I knew that Clare had been promoted, I don't see how she can object, me being here officially from the embassy."

"I'm sure that she'll welcome it," said Gloria. "She's got a special job these days, she's attached to the Head of the CID at the police headquarters at Winfrith and works in all the four police divisions."

"That must be a bit awkward at times," said Charles.

"It helps that she was once one of them, patrolling a beat in both the Bournemouth and the Poole Divisions and she's good at getting on with people." Gloria looked at him with smiling eyes and added, "and in case you've got any ideas, Charles, Clare is now going steady with Doctor Simon Watts, the pathologist."

"It's tragic isn't it?" He grinned, "All the attractive girls in England are either married or spoken for."

"Except Jackie," said Gloria, in whom the girls had confided.

"The beautiful Jackie is married to her work," said Charles. "Any chance of a spot of tea while I wait for Clare at six o'clock?"

Professor Jose Fernandez Smith and Elfrida Eynon were the first of the party from Yale to return from their afternoon labours on Thursday afternoon. To be absolutely honest they were the first back because the professor could no longer stand her constant stream of complaints. Why she had come on this expedition to England he could not imagine because she so evidently didn't seem to be enjoying it. Come to think of it he wondered why she had enrolled in the entomology course because she didn't appear to be interested in that, either. It pained him to realise that it was probably because that was the only course that would take this very pedestrian daughter of a Yale benefactor.

All day she had trailed along behind him, complaining. It had started where she had left off the night before, the pub was noisy. He had pointed out that the only guests were her classmates and she couldn't blame the Trowbridges. Then it was the breakfast, why couldn't she have waffles and maple syrup? That finished, she got on to her immediate surroundings, why had he come this way, it was damp and the grass and reeds were making her slacks uncomfortable and she'd got her hands and face wet when he'd deliberately let those willow trees swing back on her.

And so it had gone on all through the day with background comments in the vein of why he hadn't moved the party to another hotel and away from that den of thieves. He gathered that her father would be having a word about it with his superiors at Yale. As to the insects, he'd made some interesting observations but not as many as he would have done had he been alone or with a more congenial companion. He smiled inwardly, if the companion was female and really congenial he might not have made any discoveries at all. Well, not about insects.

Elfrida was first in and stamped wearily up the stairs. Jose was about to follow but saw Gloria beckoning and came into the bar whereupon she said,

"You have a visitor, Professor."

Charles stood up and stretched out his hand, saying, "Charles Howard from the embassy in London, Professor Smith, I've come down to see if there is anything I can do in the matter of the lost pocket-book."

"Good Lord," said Jose, "how did you hear about that? We haven't seen the police yet."

"Ah, there are wheels within wheels and Grosvenor Square moves in a mysterious way," said Charles.

Light was beginning to dawn with the professor.

"Her father's been pulling strings, hasn't he? And wasting peoples time because a stupid girl has mislaid her pocket book. I'll bet that you wouldn't be here if it had been one of the other students."

"Now Jose, don't read too much into my being here. This is one of my favourite English country pubs, the local gentry are friends of mine and so are Will and Gloria." He added as an afterthought, "and the landlord and Mrs Trowbridge."

"Oh, I see. That's alright then and if you have to write a report you have my permission to tell her father that we are all heartily sick of his daughter."

"Now about the police who I understand are coming here at six to hear all about it," said Charles. "The sergeant who's coming is a friend of mine and if she'll let me, I intend to sit-in."

"Good, that might shut the wretched girl up," said Jose.

"You really do sound fed-up," said Charles.

"To me this has been the worst field trip ever. Such a shame because the other six students are delightful, this pub is my idea of what an English country pub should be and the river is exactly right for our studies. The landlord and the family couldn't have made us more welcome and the weather has been fine. Because the other students won't have her near them, I've had to take her out on field trips each day and she complains the whole day long."

"Sounds like her father's daughter," said Charles. "Gloria has given me the bare bones of the story; on Wednesday you all left the pub in pairs at about nine a.m. and came back between four and five. You and the girl were the third pair to get back and go upstairs to wash and change. A few minutes after she had gone to her room the girl came down screaming that somebody had stolen her pocket book. She then accused Gloria of theft and has continued to do so."

"Yes, that's about it."

"Well, we'll leave the rest of it until the police get here. Off you go and change."

By a quarter to six the other six young members of the party from Yale were in the bar, chattering and laughing about their day and what they intended to do that evening in Bournemouth. Gloria had served their drinks and told them of the night spots that she could recommend. There was a slight pause in the chatter when a fourth girl came in and went and sat on the long bench that ran along the road side of the room. A moment later Professor Jose came in and introduced Charles to the students as the man from our embassy who had come about the lost pocket book.

"Good" said one of the boys, "perhaps that will shut Elfrida up."

"I wonder if you would have come if it had been one of us who had lost her pocket-book?" said one of the girls.

"I'd have volunteered," said Charles with a smile. "This is one of my favourite English pubs."

"I expect you to search her house," said Elfrida, from her seat, gesturing towards Gloria.

"I must warn you to be careful what you say," said Charles, "there are laws about that sort of thing in England and anyway, we're guests in their country."

"I insist that you search her house and this pub, they can't have got rid of my traveller's cheques."

"I've warned you and I suggest that you should be more careful in what you say," repeated Charles.

Just then young Will came through from the back, kissed Gloria on the cheek and exclaimed,

"Hello Charles, how are you, what brings you here in the middle of the week?"

"The lost pocket-book," said Gloria.

"And I thought that it was about time I saw you again," said Charles with a smile.

"You know these people?" shouted the girl. "You're on their side, does the ambassador know about this? You wait until Daddy hears about it, he'll have you moved."

For the benefit of the professor and the other students, Charles said,

"Just so as we get this right from the outset, miss, your father has absolutely no authority over me or my work. You remember that." He turned to Gloria and said, "I expect that the sergeant will want to question people separately, will you let her use the dining room?"

"Yes, provided that she's through by half-past."

"We had hoped to have an early dinner," said one of the students.

"If half-past six is too late you could always have it in here," said Will.

"Yes, lets do that and we'd better have something that won't spoil if we have to leave it to be questioned by the policeman."

"It's not a policeman but a very clever policewoman," said Gloria.

"And I suppose that she's also a friend of yours?" said Elfrida, scornfully.

"As a matter of fact, she is," said Will, "and here she is now," as Clare walked in followed by a constable, and said,

"Hello Gloria, hello Will." Then she spotted Charles. "Charles, what are you doing here, come to find a missing professor?"

"Not this time Clare, the embassy asked me to keep a watching brief on the missing pocket book thing. Do you mind if I sit in?"

"Not at all, pleased to have you, in fact. Now who's the injured party?"

"I am," said Elfrida. "I'm the one who had her pocket-book stolen here in this place."

"That's what I'm here to look into Miss...."

"Elfrida Eynon, daughter of Assistant Secretary of State Marvin Eynon."

Clare turned to Gloria,

"Can I use the dining room? I promise not to take longer than necessary."

"You don't need to take any time at all," said Elfrida. " All you have to do is search this pub and their house." Gesturing towards Will and Gloria behind the bar.

We've got a right one here thought Clare, saying,

"We do things differently in this country, Miss Eynon, come with me please," and she, Charles and the girl went into the dining room.

"Phew," said one of the boys, "she is the flaming limit, isn't she?"

In the dining room, Clare and her constable sat on one side of a table and Charles and Elfrida on the other.

"This interview is being recorded," said Clare. "Tell me what happened"

"There's nothing to tell you," said Elfrida. "I left my pocketbook with my cards and all that money in it in my room when I went out on Wednesday and that waitress stole it."

"I'm afraid that you'll have to be more specific than that. Where did you leave your pocket-book?"

"I remember now, I put it in the inside pocket of my anorak hanging in the cupboard in my room."

"You're sure of that?" prompted Charles.

"I'm not stupid," snapped Elfrida. "I remember thinking shall I take it with me or shall I leave it here and if I do, where shall I put it? Good hotels have safes for peoples valuables."

"So you put it in the inside pocket of your anorak?" said Clare.

"I said so, didn't I?"

"Were you the last one down that morning?"

"No, I'm always the first, Daddy says that the first hours of the day are the most valuable."

"What next?"

"I went out with the prof. Looking for flies and things."

"Did you come back to the pub for lunch?" asked Clare.

"No, that's another thing I object to, the prof makes us take a packed lunch to save time and we have to eat it by the river with flies and wasps buzzing about."

"So you came back at tea-time?" asked Clare.

"Yes, sometime between four and five. I went to my room for a shower and looked in the cupboard and my pocket book had gone. I came down and said so."

"Do you know who might have been upstairs during the day?"

"That's the point," said Elfrida, "the landlady says that only she and the waitress were upstairs, tidying our rooms and making the beds, so one of them must have taken it."

"Were you and the professor the first people back that day?" "No, two of the sets were back before us."

"So the landlady and her daughter weren't the only people who could have had access to your room," said Clare.

"Of course they were, who else is there?"

"The professor and four students in the morning and four students at tea time."

Elfrida looked shocked but not for the reason that Clare expected. She half shouted,

"Don't be stupid, woman, they're American."

"Nevertheless they had the opportunity to go into your room."

"You don't know what you're talking about," shouted Elfrida, turning to Charles. "She's just trying to put the blame on the kids because they're American."

"No she isn't, she's looking into who had the opportunity," said Charles. "She's not accusing anyone, simply exploring the facts."

"The kids wouldn't take my pocket-book, the waitress has got it, why don't you search the pub and her house like I said?"

"If we search these premises we will search all the rooms occupied by students as well," said Clare. "Tell me again what you lost."

"I lost my pocket-book containing two thousand dollars worth of American Express travellers cheques, over eight hundred English pounds in notes and all my credit cards."

"How big was the pocket-book?"

"It was like all the other pocket-books. Don't you people know anything?" said Elfrida.

"About seven inches by three and a half, I guess," said Charles, "and fairly fat by the sound of it."

"Did you tell the professor or anyone else where you'd left your pocket-book ?"

"Of course not, I'd hidden it, hadn't I?"

"Very well," said Clare. She debated whether she should question the students separately and decided that could wait, she couldn't occupy the dining room much longer. "We'll ask the others' permission to search their rooms."

She led the way back into the bar and informed the assembled company that it might clarify things a little if they would volunteer to have their rooms searched, she would do the girl's rooms and DC Hutchinson would do the male rooms.

"What about this pub and her house?" said Elfrida pointing at Gloria.

"They will be included," said Clare, at nods from Mrs Trowbridge and Gloria.

"What is this intended to prove, Sergeant?" asked one of the boys.

"Miss Eynon has accused Mrs Trowbridge and her daughter of stealing her pocket-book on the grounds that only they had the opportunity. But that isn't so. Elfrida was the first one down stairs on Wednesday morning which means that Professor Smith and four of you students had an opportunity to go into her room and four of you got back to the pub before Elfrida on Wednesday afternoon and hence had the opportunity to go into her room."

"But that's ridiculous," said the boy.

"No more ridiculous than accusing the pub staff," said Charles.

"Do you agree?" asked Clare. "You may be present during the search"

There were grudging nods and muttered comments that they would have tidied their rooms had they known.

Clare made Elfrida go through what she did on Wednesday morning and spent some time examining the anorak in the cupboard and the floor beneath it.

Charles accompanied Clare and her constable when they searched the pub and the antique dealer's house at the end of which he professed himself satisfied that Elfrida's pocket book was not in the pub or the house.

The searches produced nothing.

"That only proves that they've hidden it somewhere else," said Elfrida.

"Look, you silly girl," said Charles, "you can't go round accusing people of theft. Mrs Trowbridge would be justified in taking legal action against you and I, for one, wouldn't blame her, then you'd have to stay in England for the case to be heard."

"Daddy wouldn't let that happen."

"Daddy wouldn't be able to prevent it, child, why don't you start acting your age?"

Elfrida sat down and sulked.

"What will you do now Clare?" asked Charles.

"The credit cards have already been stopped, haven't they? I'll circulate a description of the missing articles and the serial numbers of the traveller's cheques. That would seem to be all that we can do at present."

"Gloria tells me that you work for a central unit at police headquarters."

"Yes, it's a bit complicated. My chief is Detective Superintendent Harding and my immediate governor is Detective Inspector Wyatt. They're both out at Winfrith now. Because the bulk of my work is in the two most heavily populated divisions, I have a desk in the Central Police Station in Bournemouth. It seems to work alright."

"And you don't have problems with the locals?" asked Charles.

"Oh I get a bit of it, but where possible, we let them make the arrests and don't claim all the credit."

"What about that crazy Inspector Clouseau look-alike, is he still with you?"

"He's on schools liaison duties or some such thing in the Blandford Section."

They chatted for a few minutes longer and Clare and DC Hutchinson left. Shortly afterwards Charles departed to drive back to London.

Elfrida went off to phone her father.

Will had listened to the exchanges. He decided that he'd ask the General's permission to drive into Dorchester the next day and consult the Hawkridge family solicitor, Mr Swain.

Chapter Five

NO SOONER had Charles Howard reached his office the following morning than the ambassador sent for him. Charles had half expected this. He passed the marine sentry, grinned at the ambassador's secretary and entered the presence to be greeted with,

"What did you think you were doing yesterday?"

"Why, Mr Ambassador," said Charles, feigning surprise, "I was carrying out your orders and looking for the lost pocket-book."

"No you weren't you were bullying that poor child who had lost it."

"With respect, Sir, were you there?"

"Was I where?"

"In the pub at Tolbrite."

"Of course I wasn't, I was here."

"Then how do you know what I did?"

"Marvin Eynon called me late last night."

"I didn't see him in Tolbrite."

"Don't be an idiot man, he is in DC."

"Then I say again, how do you or he know what I did?" said Charles.

"His daughter phoned him. She also told him that both you and the police were on the side of the crooks who stole her pocket book. He's demanding action."

"Look, Mr Ambassador, I advise you to distance yourself from this. Do you really believe that the British police aren't doing their best or that I would cover up a theft because I happen to know the people who own the place where the pocket-book was lost?"

"Marvin Eynon evidently thinks so."

"He's reacting to phone calls from his daughter," said Charles. "She's a spoilt, stupid girl who no one likes. She's the despair of the professor who's leading the group because she complains from morning to night and he, poor chap, is stuck with her because none of the other six students will work with her. God knows where her pocket book is but as to opportunity for theft, the professor and four of the American students as well as the landlady and her daughter, had an opportunity to steal the pocket book. The police and I searched every room in the pub and the annex and found nothing. And it wasn't in anyone's satchel or pocket either. Yet at the end of all this activity, the stupid girl still accused the landlady or her daughter of theft in a bar in which other customers of the pub were present."

"She's very upset."

"You're still not understanding how serious this is, Sir. She has repeatedly made accusations in public against the people who run the pub. They would be justified in bringing a charge of slander against the girl and claiming substantial damages, not only for the harm done to their reputation but also for loss of trade."

"Surely they wouldn't do that? They should make allowances because the girl's upset." said the ambassador.

"Look, Mr Ambassador, I went to Tolbrite yesterday as a favour to you. I will write up what I've reported to you this morning, including what a poisonous girl Miss Elfrida Eynon is and the fact that the people who she has accused in public would be justified in suing for slander, and submit it to you. You may wish to forward it to her father, indeed I think that you should, it's no skin off my nose, Assistant Secretary of State Marvin Eynon isn't my boss and I don't give a damn whether he's happy or mad."

Upon which Charles turned on his heel and walked out. He knew what his chiefs in Washington (or is it Langley Va?) would think of an ambassador who ordered their top man in Europe to go looking for a student's pocket-book.

Will took Gloria with him to Dorchester and she came into the solicitor's office as well. She'd had a soft spot for Mr Swain ever since the day when, at Timmy's request, he'd dropped everything to get Will out of jail where that idiot Inspector Stevens, known to one and all as Inspector Clouseau, had mistakenly put him.

For his part, Mr Swain liked Will and Gloria, and, of course they came with the blessing of the Hawkridges. Actually, Margaret Hawkridge had phoned him that very morning and told them that they were coming and asked him to try and fit them in.

"Now Mr and Mrs Conway, what brings you here, nothing serious I hope?"

"You might not think that it's serious but we're fed up with an American girl who's staying at the pub calling Gloria a thief," said Will.

"She says that I stole her pocket-book on Wednesday," said Gloria. "The police and Charles – he's from the American embassy in London – have searched everywhere and found nothing and she still insists that I stole it."

"How much was in the pocket book?" asked the solicitor.

"Oh, she says an awful lot, thousands of dollars in traveller's cheques, over eight hundred pounds and all her credit cards," said Gloria.

"I see," said Mr Swain, "well worth stealing. Why does she say that you stole it?"

"Because she said that only mum and I were there, making the beds and tidying up."

"But the police proved that the American professor and four other students also had an opportunity to go into her room," said Will, "so they searched everywhere and found nothing."

"And you say that she has accused you of the theft. Did other people hear her say that?"

"Oh yes, all the customers in the bar on Wednesday and yesterday," said Gloria.

"You possibly have grounds for slander," said the solicitor "would you like me to write to her threatening her with a claim for substantial damages because of her alleged slander?"

"Oh, yes please but you'll have to be quick, they go back to America next week."

"Now give me her name and all the details and I'll see that she has a letter before the end of the day."

"I could come and collect it," offered Will.

"That would spoil the effect. I'll arrange for my man to personally hand it to her."

They drove back to Tolbrite relieved to have done something.

In London Sergeant Kim Bourne wasn't having much luck searching the press for references to Stuart Harcourt and even less for a Hungarian actress called Sonia . The only recent reference to Hungary being one paragraph dealing with the return to Budapest of the previous cultural attaché and the expected arrival of her replacement.

The British Council knew the address at which the previous cultural attaché had lived and Kim investigated and found that her immediate neighbour had found her to be an exceedingly nice person who spoke excellent English. They said that they hadn't seen her since last weekend and here it was, Friday. My how time flies. On that, at least, Kim agreed with her.

Professor Jose Smith was having a better afternoon, for one thing Elfrida had decided to remain at the spot where they had eaten their packed lunch where, she said, there were less flies than elsewhere. So he was spared the sound of her incessant complaining. The other students were no longer taking part in the tests of the mixtures Jose had prepared as insect repellents. One of them had caused a reddening of the skin of the arm of one of the girls whereupon they had all politely declined to experiment with other formulations. The professor had persisted and this afternoon his arm with the cream had been fly-less. His satisfaction was tempered somewhat by the realisation that due to a stupid mistake, the preparation that he had on his arm had become contaminated ever so slightly by another cream and he didn't know the exact proportions. But it couldn't be by more than five percent, he reckoned.

At four o'clock he retraced his steps to where Elfrida was sat listening to her iPod. She was unaware of his approach until he stood before her. He thought how vulnerable she was. She gave him a scowl and said,

"About time, I would have gone back to my room except that I don't trust that blonde waitress."

Jose didn't bother to ask what she feared that Gloria might do. He rather thought that she wasn't at the pub in the afternoons.

They crossed the river by the Manor House bridge and made their way along the river bank. They could see two of their sets ahead of them, Jose noted that the arrangement had changed from a two girl, two boy, boy and girl, arrangement to three sets of boy and girl. Good luck to them, he thought and here was he, stuck with Elfrida.

He looked at her as she trudged ahead of him, she had a trim figure and nice legs. If she did her hair differently, put some decent make-up on and stopped scowling and finding fault with every one and everything, she might be considered to be attractive.

The sets ahead had left the park through the narrow pedestrian gate by the church rather than take the slightly longer route keeping beside the river behind the church, some houses and the pub and turning inland, as it were, through the pub car park. Naturally, Elfrida took the shortest way and reached the pub slightly ahead of the professor.

He arrived in the entrance hall in time to see a young man in a dark business suit put an envelope in Elfrida's hand and say,

"Miss Elfrida Eynon, I represent Swain's of Dorchester on who's instruction I present you with this letter."

Whereupon he bade all and sundry a cheerful "Good afternoon," and strode out of the entrance.

A startled Elfrida was still standing there holding the envelope when there came the noise of him driving off. She turned and mounted the stairs. Jose wondered who Swains of Dorchester might be and when he reached his room he looked them up in the telephone directory. They were solicitors. Why on earth would a firm of solicitors be writing to Elfrida? He hadn't long to wait. He had just undressed to take a shower when there was a knock at his door. He put on his dressing-gown and opened the door, Elfrida pushed past him and said,

"What do you make of this?" thrusting a letter under his nose.

The professor took the letter and read,

> *Miss Elfrida Eynon,*
>
> *My clients, Mrs Conway and Mrs Trowbridge, the daughter and wife respectively of the licencee of the Tolbrite Arms in the village of Tolbrite in the county of Dorset, claim that you have publicly accused them, individually and / or jointly, of the theft on Wednesday last, of a pocket-book that you claim to have secreted in the room that you currently occupy at the Tolbrite Arms.*
>
> *My clients claim that you have voiced these accusations of theft without restraint to the police and to a representative of the US Government and to members of the general public gathered for refreshment in the bar of the said Tolbrite Arms.*
>
> *Notwithstanding the continued stream of accusations of theft, my clients have made every effort to assist you in finding the missing pocket-book but to no avail.*
>
> *Accordingly I am instructed to inform you that it is intended to proceed against you in the matter of your slander of my clients.*
>
> *Yours sincerely,*
>
> *Solicitors at Law*

"Well," said Jose, "It means that your chickens have come home to roost, I warned you and that man from the embassy warned you that you simply mustn't go round accusing people of theft. But you wouldn't listen, would you? And now they are taking you to court."

"They can't do that, everything that I've said is true, that waitress stole my pocket book."

"There you go again, when will you learn to keep a civil tongue in your head?"

"But it's true. You're all against me."

"Then you must face the consequences, Elfrida, you wouldn't listen to me or to your class-mates or to the man from the embassy and thanks to your behaviour you haven't got a single friend here in Tolbrite."

"Daddy will soon sort them out."

"You don't begin to understand the mess that you've got yourself into, do you? Once that solicitor starts proceedings against you, the Queen of England herself couldn't stop it, so don't begin to imagine that anyone over here gives a hoot about your father."

"Well then he'll see that the people at Yale know how you got me into this mess by not staying at a decent hotel that has a safe for guests to put their valuables in."

"You really are an objectionable bitch, aren't you? Get out of my room and let me take my shower. I'm through with you and you should remember there are seven of us who can tell the people in New Haven how badly you have behaved."

He practically manhandled the girl out of his room while thinking what a fool he'd been to even allow such a devious and vicious creature into his room, particularly when he was clad only in a dressing gown.

When having drinks before dinner he quietly told the other students that Gloria and her mother had started legal proceedings for slander against Elfrida. Their reaction was 'Good,' 'Serves her right,' 'Does that mean that she'll have to stay here?' 'Does that mean that we'll have to stay here?' and so on. No one expressed any sympathy.

Elfrida did not come down to dinner and was busy phoning home.

The following morning the ambassador sent for Charles.

Charles walked past the marine sentry, had a word with the secretary who mouthed 'He's been on again and the boss is getting sick of him' and walked into the holy of holies.

"You wanted me, Mr Ambassador?"

"Yes, I don't know what you did down at that place in Dorset but the goddamned Brits are taking Assistant Secretary Eynon's daughter to court for slander."

"Good for them," said Charles.

"I'll pretend that I didn't hear that," said the ambassador. "The point is what do we do?"

"You shouldn't be surprised at this development, you had my report and in it I said how her professor and I had warned her repeatedly that she simply couldn't go round loudly accusing people of theft. The police had investigated, I had investigated, we had identified five other people who could have had the opportunity to steal the girl's pocket book and still she went on accusing her hosts of theft in front of a bar full of people. The girl is a thoroughly nasty person. Did you send my report to the State Department?"

"No, I couldn't let anyone see that, Secretary Eynon would have had me recalled. You didn't send anyone a copy, did you?"

Charles chose to ignore that question and said,

"The question now is what do we do?"

"What do you mean, Charles?" asked the ambassador sensing a glimmer of hope.

"Well, they only sent the girl the letter yesterday and today's Saturday. Their solicitor won't have instituted proceedings yet. Assistant Secretary Eynon could make a gesture."

This struck the ambassador as funny,

"He already is, he's shaking his fist and talking of sending in the marines."

"He'll be a great success on the international diplomatic scene," said Charles, "what he's got to do in the present situation is to eat humble pie and try to buy them off."

"He won't like that."

"Well, he's got the choice, hasn't he? He either does that or he and his daughter's behaviour will be plastered all over the British press."

"They wouldn't," said the ambassador.

"Believe me, Sir, they'd have a field day. Probably cost Secretary Eynon his job."

"This is very embarrassing."

"I would remind you that if this had been any other American girl student who had behaved that foolishly, this embassy wouldn't have turned a hand to help her beyond seeing that she was being treated fairly under British law."

"Yes I know Charles, as I said it's very embarrassing, couldn't you go down there and talk them out of it?"

Charles said, "I still don't think that you realise how damaging the present situation is. Those people down there are friends of mine. They uphold law and order and on at least two occasions they have helped me catch the crooks who were damaging Uncle Sam's interests. They meet most Saturday nights in the bar of the Tolbrite Arms. Are you with me so far?"

"Of course I am. What's this got to do with it, get on with it, man."

"The leaders of the people who meet there are Tim Hawkridge and his wife Helene. His number one henchman is the husband of the girl who Secretary Eynon's daughter said has stolen her pocketbook."

"What's that got to do with it?"

"Tim Hawkridge owns Hawkridge Media and has close on forty radio stations, ten of which are in the US mid-west. Are you beginning to get the picture?"

"You mean that he could blow the story in the States?"

"Yes, Mr Ambassador, I would think that tonight, when he and Helene hear about the accusations that Assistant Secretary Eynon's daughter has made, it will be touch and go whether the story breaks on his stations on Sunday morning and if I go in trying to stop it they'll know that they're on to a scoop."

Charles hoped that this sounded convincing.

"Then what do I do?"

"You send a message to Secretary Eynon advising him that the Brits have got an open and shut case against his daughter and that he must try to negotiate with them to stop the case getting to court, to buy them off, in fact. If you like I'll draft the message."

"I'd like you to do that and send it, then I can play the honest broker and back you up if he argues."

You spineless creep, thought Charles, this is the risk a president runs by making political appointments, give me a career diplomat every time.

Even the ambassador's secretary raised her eyebrows when she received a copy of the message that Charles sent to the State

Department that Saturday afternoon for the attention of Assistant Secretary Eynon. It contained the meat of the earlier report that the ambassador hadn't sent, concluded that the plaintiffs had an open and shut case and recommended that he buy them off.

Chapter Six

UNLESS there was an urgent business reason, Timmy and Helene and the children spent three weekends a month with his parents at the Manor House. On one of those weekends Helene's mother, Claire-Marie, was usually present and on the forth weekend Timmy and Co went to Burgundy to stay with Claire-Marie. In this way she got to see her grandchildren twice a month and Francoise and Peter were growing up to be fluent in both nations languages and customs.

This was a Claire-Marie weekend and they all arrived at the Manor House in the armoured stretched car that the children had named Le Tank. There was another Le Tank at the Bouchier Chateau, with its steering wheel on the other side. The family used to make the trip from Chelsea to Tolbrite in two cars but since the awful afternoon when both cars had been side-swiped off the road in the New Forest and Francoise kidnapped, they all travelled together in the limo, Timmy, Helene, Claire-Marie, the two children and Brigitte their nanny.

Their time of arrival was dictated by the need to feed and bath the children and put them to bed, which meant that Timmy brought his Friday afternoon work with him.

Weekends at the Manor House followed a regular pattern. On Saturday mornings the General sat in his study and read the Times, looked out of the window and dozed. The ladies walked across the park to the village or drove to one or other of the farms and Timmy worked at the computer in his study, by means of which he could access the records in his London office. The children played in the rumpus room or in the park, with Ah Ming, the Sergeant or Towers, the gamekeeper, in attendance.

The General watched the three ladies walk across the park. The family always went that way rather than the long way down the drive and along the Winterborne road. It was safer, too. He knew that they would go through the narrow gate by the church and then walk to the end of the village before turning back to the Cosy Tea Room for a coffee and a chat with the elderly sisters who ran it. He wondered if Mrs Ford, the vicar's wife, would 'just happen to be in her garden' when they passed.

He shrugged off the unworthy thought, Mrs Ford did a great deal of unpaid and unsung good in the village and anyway, they'd see her in church the next day. Margaret said that she sorted the problems out for her. His mind wandered; the popular image of a squire is a busybody poking his nose into everybody's business when, in fact, he and Margaret were often unaware that one of their elderly tenants was in trouble until late in the day. For years he and Margaret had depended on three main sources of information about what was going on; Mrs Ford, the Roberts sisters in the Cosy Tea Room and the public bar in the Tolbrite Arms via the Sergeant. Nowadays they had young Will, the estate maintenance manager, born and bred in the village, home after a spell as a Royal Marine Commando and married to Gloria. There was not much that went on in the village or the estate farms that escaped Will's attention and the estate had never been so well maintained and managed.

As a child Will had played in the park and had become the friend and companion of the Hawkridge children when they came home from school in the holidays. The friendship had endured and young Will was the friend and confidant of all the Hawkridge family. He was called young Will because when he came back from the marines he had worked for his father, old Will, who ran the ailing village garage. The garage was now the estate maintenance depot and old Will, the caretaker. All this had been made possible by Timmy and Helene setting up and financing the Manor House Trust.

The three ladies had turned back at the end of the village and made their way to the tearoom. A small bell tinkled as Margaret opened the door and the elder sister, Daisy, hurried forward saying,

"Good morning Lady Hawkridge and Mrs Timmy, Bon jour Madame."

"Good morning Daisy," said Margaret on behalf of the three of them.

"The usual?"

"Yes please, three black coffees, no milk or sugar."

Daisy disappeared through a bead curtain and almost instantly reappeared with a tray on which was a coffee pot and three cups and saucers. Walking behind her came her sister Mary carrying a jug of milk, her passport to join in the conversation.

Margaret addressed her.

"What's been going on this week, Mary?"

"There's a lot of Americans staying at the public house. They're looking for insects. Fancy that, you'd think that they had enough insects of their own in that great big country, wouldn't you?"

"One of them has been saying awful things about Gloria," put in her sister.

"What sort of things?"

"That Gloria stole her purse with ever such a lot of money in it."

"Have the police been told?"

"Yes, that nice young girl came out yesterday evening and searched everywhere."

"She's a sergeant now," said Mary, not to be left out.

"There was an American from London as well," said Daisy "and he proved that other people could have taken it as well as Gloria but the American girl keeps on accusing her."

"Someone should shut her up," said Claire-Marie.

"I gather that the American professor has tried but she won't be silenced, Madame."

"Silly girl, she could get into trouble."

"We think that she already has," said Mary. "Two of the American students came in for a coffee this morning and they were talking about a letter from an English lawyer."

Margaret said nothing. Well done Mr Swain.

Brigitte had Saturdays off and had gone into Bournemouth for the day. After lunch, Timmy and Helene took the children for a walk in the park. They no longer took the big pram and Helene looked forward to the time when they would be big enough to go across the river and the water meadows and into the Long Wood where they used to take Timmy's brother David's, children before she had babies of her own. For the present they stayed this side of the river and Francoise had recently taken to exploring the river bank west of the bridge.

This afternoon Claire-Marie came too and took charge of the small girl, patiently talking to her in French, as she wandered between willow trees looking for fish in the river. Timmy, Helene and baby Peter kept abreast of them.

There was a sudden cry from the little girl. They turned towards the river but Francoise wasn't to be seen. Claire-Marie was disappearing into the foliage of a willow tree that stretched down to the ground. Timmy and Helene ran towards the spot as she reappeared with Francoise who was clutching a dark coloured object.

"Look what I've got, Mummy," holding it out.

Helene took it and saw that it was a purse. Light dawned, the American girl had accused Gloria of stealing her pocket-book. She opened it and saw the name and an address in New Haven, Conn.

"This is the missing pocket-book that we were talking about at lunch, the one that Gloria is accused of stealing. I wonder how it came to be out here?"

Timmy turned to Francoise. "Show Daddy where you found it, baby."

The little girl turned and disappeared behind the willow fronds with Timmy following. She pointed to a spot in the undergrowth quite near to the edge of the bank. Despite its size it could have been difficult to see. They returned to the others.

"What shall we do with it?" asked Helene. "Take it to the pub?"

"No," said her mother, "there will be a police file on the loss and we should let them return it."

"Let's temporise," said Timmy. "We'll ring the police and tell them that we've found it and that we think that we know who it belongs to, do they want us to hand it to them or to the American girl?"

"That would take the rest of the day, I'll ring Clare," said Helene.

They returned to the Manor House where Francoise told her English grandparents about finding a great treasure on the river bank and Helene went off to their study to find Clare's home telephone number. As it happened, Clare was on duty,

"Clare, its Helene Hawkridge,"

"Hello Helene, to what do I owe this pleasure on a rotten Saturday afternoon?"

"I understand that an American girl who's staying at the Tolbrite Arms has lost her pocket book?"

"Yes, that's right and she's accusing Gloria of stealing it, Why?"

"Our little daughter was exploring the river bank and she found it. It's got the name Elfrida Eynon and an address in New Haven which is where Yale is."

"What a liar that girl is, she must have had it with her and lost it. When I looked at the anorak in her wardrobe I couldn't see how she could have put a bulky purse in the pocket that she said that she'd put it in."

"My question, Clare, is what shall we do with it?"

"I'll come out and take charge of it, Helene. I wouldn't miss this for a fortune."

Clare duly appeared, met the clever little girl who had found the purse and accepted a cup of tea while she checked the contents against the list that Elfrida had provided. It was all there.

Helene told Clare that Gloria had taken the first step towards suing Elfrida for slander.

Clare drove to the Tolbrite Arms. The other students had just returned from a sightseeing trip in their mini-bus and were sitting around prior to changing for the evening. She went up and asked the professor and Elfrida to come down into the bar. As Elfrida passed her, Clare went into her room and took the anorak out of the wardrobe.

When they were assembled, with Mr and Mrs Trowbridge behind the bar as interested spectators, Clare said,

"I want you all to witness this. This afternoon a little girl who was exploring the river bank to the west of the Manor House found this."

She dramatically produced the pocket-book and turned to Elfrida,

"And in case you are about to accuse the little girl of theft, I've checked the contents and they are exactly in accordance with the list that you gave me."

"She must have lost her nerve and thrown it there," shouted Elfrida.

"Who?" said Clare, rather startled.

"The barmaid, you fool, you're supposed to be a detective."

Elfrida went to take the pocket book but Clare moved it away and said in a quiet voice,

"And you insist that you left your pocket book in the pocket of this anorak when you went out on Wednesday morning?"

"How many more times do I have to tell you, YES."

"Very well then," said Clare. "Before I make you sign for the lost article there is one thing that I want to check. When we searched your room last evening I looked at the anorak and thought that the pocket seemed to be too small to take a reasonably sized pocket book. Now we can try it."

She passed the anorak to one of the girl students and said,

"Elfrida swore that she had put this pocket book in the inside pocket. Please do so."

The girl took the items but couldn't begin to get the bulky pocket book in the pocket. The boy beside her had a go and said,

"In no way can you get her pocket book in any pocket of this anorak."

Clare turned to Elfrida and said,

"Your entire story has been a tissue of lies, you took your pocket-book with you on Wednesday and lost it. If you had admitted the loss I'm sure that the professor and your fellow students and, I expect, half the village, would have joined you in searching everywhere that you had been that day. But no, instead of admitting that you had taken it with you and lost it, you invented the robbery story and falsely accused Gloria of the theft."

Elfrida kept her eyes down. Clare went on,

"In English law deliberately wasting police time is an offence and I shall have to discuss with my superiors whether you will be charged. In so doing they will be aware that you not only caused a lot of people a great deal of bother but also accused an innocent person of theft, knowing the accusation to be false."

"I didn't want my father know that I'd lost it," said Elfrida, starting to cry. "Now he'll tell everybody that I'm stupid."

"Well, you are," said one of the boys.

Oh God, thought Clare, she did it because she's frightened of her father.

"There was that man from the embassy," said the professor "will you tell him?"

"Of course," said Clare, turning to the girl. "Now if you'd check the contents and sign to say that everything's there, you can have your pocket book."

"And I can have the money that I've loaned you," said the professor who was by now thoroughly sick of the girl.

Clare drove back to the police station and sent an e-mail to the US embassy for the attention of Charles Howard.

Francoise Hawkridge found Elfrida Eynon's pocket book by the river in the Manor House park on Saturday afternoon and her parents surrendered it to the police. Subsequently it has been established that

63

Elfrida knew that she had lost her pocket-book outside the hotel and invented the theft story to avoid her father knowing of her carelessness. We are considering whether to press charges for public mischief and wasting police time.
  Clare Thornton [Detective Sgt]

That evening, as was usual on Saturday evenings, Timmy and Helene walked across the park to the Tolbrite Arms. Clare-Marie came with them, which was also as usual. They entered the bar to a chorus of hello's. Will and Gloria were behind the bar talking with the other three members of the Hawkridge Irregulars, Fred Smart and his wife, Angela, and Paula. Fred and Paula had worked for a firm of accountant-detectives that undertook confidential enquiries for clients in the City of London. Fred had fallen in love with Angela, the assistant to the Poole harbour master and had resigned to set up his own detective agency in Bournemouth with backing from Timmy and black-belt Paula had joined him some time afterwards. Their office was in the complex of shops, restaurants and offices that surrounded the Hawkridge Bournemouth radio station.

Claire-Marie perched on a bar stool and showed a great deal of her legs. Timmy thought that it was difficult to believe that she was Helene's mother and not her sister. The landlord, Mr Trowbridge, always came into the bar when Claire-Marie was there. They talked about vintages and grape varieties and good and bad years while she also took part in the other conversations going on around her. Helene was the same and both mother and daughter could do it in both languages at the same time. At parties at the chateau they would be speaking to one guest in French and at the same time speaking to Timmy or to another guest in English, all without a pause for thought.

Timmy looked at Helene and smiled, he knew what she was thinking. Sometimes he saw a small tear in her eye as she thought of her father, and the RAF fighter squadrons that he had served in or commanded. The Home Counties were peppered with pubs adjacent to airfields from which he had flown, pubs adopted by the squadron and in which Claire-Marie had perched on bar stools, showed the young men her legs, and adored her husband. These were among her most treasured memories. They had eventually retired to the Bouchier family estates in Burgundy where he had died a year or so before Helene met Timmy. The Tolbrite Arms now stocked Bouchier wines.

Gloria was full of anger at Elfrida Eynon's behaviour but grinned to say that her mother was relieved that now there should be no problem with the girl's bill when the party from Yale left in a week's time.

Professor Jose Smith came in after dining across the hall and Gloria hastened to introduce him. They had something in common, their dislike of Elfrida Eynon.

"She shouldn't have been allowed to come on this visit," said Gloria.

"Unfortunately we can't deny people coming on field trips if they want to," said Jose, remembering what a struggle it had been to get the seven students necessary to make the trip worthwhile.

"What do you think will happen now, Tim?" said Will.

"Because Elfrida is leaving the country in a weeks time I wouldn't think that the police will press charges."

"What about our action?"

"That's up to you," said Timmy. "The girl's lies make your case for deformation much more telling, she not only lied about her loss but then deliberately attempted to implicate Gloria. I'm not sure that isn't a criminal act in itself."

"How does it stand at present?" asked the professor.

"As I understand it, our solicitor has told Elfrida that we intend to take action against her. Now it's up to her side to respond, if their response is not satisfactory the Swains will set the wheels in motion."

"What would you consider to be satisfactory, Tim?" asked Will.

"A proposal that the matter be settled out of court."

"How?"

"Well, Swains will leave that to you but I expect that they would suggest that you ask for a public apology and a substantial cash settlement," said Timmy.

"But she'll be back at Yale by then," said Gloria, who had been listening intently.

"That isn't an insuperable problem," said Timmy. "In this case it depends on how much her father values his reputation."

"He's an Assistant Secretary of State," said the professor.

"That's the whole point," smiled Timmy. "Will he want my radio stations in the mid-west telling the US public how his daughter screwed up in England because she is scared of him?"

"But if he settles out of court and makes a public apology the public will know anyway," said the professor.

"His solicitors will suggest that since the slander was local, the apology should be local, such as a brief announcement in the Bournemouth paper," said Helene.

"He doesn't know that we've got Timmy on our side," said Will.

"The power of the press in modern form," smiled the professor "Have you really got radio stations in the States?"

"Yes, ten so far."

"Radio has taken the place of books for a lot of young people."

"My stations transmit more educational material than most," said Timmy.

He turned to Fred, "Any interesting new cases?"

"Yes, in addition to the usual cases of suspected infidelity and drugs we've had two sets of worried parents who've found replica guns in their sons possession."

"Have you questioned the boys?"

"Paula did. One attempted to laugh the whole thing off and the other said that it was because of the bullying at school. She gathered that youngsters carrying weapons is more common than adults think. Like our sample of two shows, half carry them because it makes them feel important and the other half carry them because they're scared."

"And we've also had a woman who says that the Bournemouth Council planning department is dishonest," said Paula.

"Someone who's had a planning application turned down, I suppose," said Gloria, "There was a case like that in Bath and it turned out to be more serious than they thought."

"Was someone accepting money?" asked Angela.

"I don't know but one of the planning officials was found to be bending the evidence in case after case to secure rejections of proposals."

"Perhaps the applicants wouldn't pay a bribe," said Helene, turning to Paula. "What about the woman in Bournemouth?"

"She only came in a few days ago and we haven't done anything yet."

"Surely her best course would be to go to the police?"

"She doesn't want to do that until she has more positive evidence."

"I would think that would be very difficult to get," said Timmy.

The conversation continued until, at about half-past nine, Angela sat at the piano and played. This, too, had become a Saturday night routine. It had been on the afternoon that the irregulars had rescued the infant daughter of Tanya, one of Hawkridge Media's top recording stars, that they had heard her play and realised that she had a rare talent. She had played in her school orchestra and after rehearsals would play popular tunes and jazz for her classmates. The music teacher had heard her and given her a spot in the school concert and there it had ended. Timmy and Tanya had insisted that she make a trial recording and after putting two tracks on the disk that Tanya was recording at the time, she had since made four albums on her own. She had steadfastly refused to go on tour or make public appearances and playing for the patrons of the Tolbrite Arms most Saturdays was the only way that she broke this rule.

Sergeant Sandra Roberts arrived back at Heathrow early on Sunday morning. Dusty was there to meet her, not in his cab but in the family car that his mother used. He told her that he loved her and took her to her flat. Before she would let him show her how much, she phoned Jackie.

"I think that I found her, Cap, name of Sonia Berolinka, 30, black haired and worked as a cultural assistant in the Hungarian delegation for just under four years. She went back to Hungary in November 2004. I got a copy of the photo that was on her UN pass."

"Well done, are you home?"

"Yes Cap."

"See you in the morning then."

Chapter Seven

ON MONDAY morning Jackie checked that Peggy was in her office and took a cab to Regent Street. She showed her the photo of Sonia Berolinka and Peggy confirmed that this was the girl with whom she and Stuart Harcourt had talked at the prime minister's reception.

On that same morning the US ambassador's secretary rang Charles to say that her chief had received another call from you-know-who and would like to see him, now.

"That's convenient," said Charles, "because I want to see him."

He walked past the marine sentry, grinned and blew a kiss at the ambassador's secretary and was waved in.

"Good morning, Mr Ambassador."

"There's nothing good about it," snapped the ambassador, "I've had a call from Marvin Eynon. He's hopping mad at the report that you sent and is going to talk with your superiors. I warned you. Of immediate concern he's asking what we're doing about this English lawyer Swain."

"What does he expect us to do about him?"

"He thought that you might go and lean on him a little."

"I can't believe what I'm hearing," said Charles. "What does he think England is, a central American banana republic?"

"I think that he means you to go and reason with the man."

"The only thing the English lawyer wants is a reasonable response to his letter."

"Such as?"

"Well if it was me, I'd offer an apology and a cash settlement."

"He won't do that, they stole his daughter's pocket-book"

"But we now have proof positive that they didn't," said Charles. "I was on my way to see you when you sent for me. I thought that you should see this and with reference to Secretary Eynon's remark about speaking to my superiors, I have this morning sent copies of this British police message to my chiefs and to Secretary Eynon."

He put a copy of Clare Thornton's e-mail on the ambassador's desk. The ambassador read it and asked,

"When did you get this?"

68

"I saw it when I looked in yesterday morning."

"Why didn't you phone me?"

"Do you really consider the antics of a girl who has been caught lying through her back teeth important enough to spoil your weekend, Sir?"

"Well, no, not if you put it that way." Then he added, "but he is an Assistant Secretary of State."

"His daughter isn't," said Charles, "and it looks as if she's broken the law in a foreign country."

"You know that policewoman," he consulted the e-mail, "Clare Thornton. Have a word with her and see if you can persuade them not to bring charges. If you can he ought to be grateful for that."

"With respect, Mr Ambassador, the most urgent thing required is for Secretary Eynon to react to the solicitor's letter, otherwise the story might well break in the mid-West."

"On that Englishman's radio stations?"

"Yes, most of his radio stations are in Illinois, Wisconsin and Michigan, his headquarters are in Milwalkee and Secretary Eynon is a former senator from Wisconsin."

"He'd better be careful, Secretary Eynon has probably got friends who could cancel his license."

"After the story breaks I'd be surprised if his friends would dare do anything," said Charles.

The ambassador looked at his wall clock and said with a smile "I expect that he'll be on the phone before one o'clock. What shall I say?"

"You tell him that his daughter and, by implication himself, is in big trouble and that he must respond positively to the British solicitor's letter. You then tell him that he's extremely fortunate to have someone dealing with it who actually knows the people at Tolbrite and who might be able to prevent a dozen radio stations in the mid-West breaking the story. You must make him realise that politically, he's in big trouble."

"That message from the policewoman does rather change things, doesn't it Charles?"

Charles noted the altered tone and still thought that the ambassador was a creep.

On his way out he gave a copy of Clare Thornton's e-mail to the ambassador's secretary. Quite early in his career he'd learnt to cover all the bases.

Kim had drawn a blank as regards gathering information about Stuart Harcourt and a Hungarian called Sonia. For the former they had what he had written about himself for Who's Who and for the latter they had only the one mention in an arty periodical that a Hungarian girl called Sonia Berolinka had performed well in Vienna.

When they were in bed together, Kim asked Tom Burton how the anti-terrorist branch would go about getting information about someone from another country, a country that was once part of the communist bloc.

"You mean Hungary?" said Inspector Tom.

"How did you know?" asked his lover.

"You've been mooning about looking up references to Sir Stuart Harcourt and that Hungarian woman ever since the PM called Jackie in to look into his death."

"We didn't think that you knew," said Kim.

"Of course the boss knew, Tubby Lowe told him."

"Well I'm blowed, our own General shopped us."

"If you think about it, darling, he had to if our organisations are to continue to work together."

"I suppose so. Jackie was embarrassed but Number 10 asked her not to tell anyone what she was doing."

"Well, she didn't, Tubby did," said Tom.

"That brings us back to Oscar Wilde," said Kim.

"You mean the one about him having no difficulty keeping secrets?" said Tom who had heard Kim on the subject before.

"Yes," said Kim, determined to complete the quotation. "Yes, it was the people that he told them to who couldn't keep a secret."

Tom idly caressed her breast. "You know, you are too nice to be a soldier."

"Being a soldier doesn't mean that a girl can't be attractive," pouted Kim.

He kissed her and showed her how attractive he thought that she was. Afterwards he said,

"Didn't you ask me a question?"

"Did I?" said Kim dreamily.

"Something about a Hungarian girl," said Tom.

Kim came alert,

"Yes, that was it, how would you go about finding out about her?"

"I'd do what we always do, go and talk to the Free Hungarians or whatever they call themselves these days."

"Who on earth are the Free Hungarians?" asked Kim.

"They're the émigrés who escaped from Hungary at great personal risk when their country was part of the Soviet bloc. In those days they were welcomed as hero's and heroines and interrogated in the West. Many of the stories that they told have since been proved to have been invented or embellished to ensure good treatment in the West."

"Haven't they all gone back now that it's a part of the EU?"

"No, it's like the Iraqi's who arrived here pleading that they would be tortured by Saddam Hussain if they went back. Saddam's gone but they haven't gone back, because no-where else would they get the free handouts they get in Britain. In the case of the Hungarians, they encounter a degree of resentment if they go back for a visit, so they stay here."

"It's a long time since the Soviet troops pulled out of Hungary," said Kim, "and the woman who we're interested in would have been a child, well, a teenager when they left, so she can't have been a spy."

"You mean that it's unlikely that anyone who escaped from Soviet occupied territory would have known her," said Tom.

"But it could be the only lead that we're likely to get, so where do I find them?"

"I'll have to look them up. I'll ring you tomorrow."

Inspector Tom was true to his word and later in the morning Kim made an expedition to sight the shop in Islington that was owned by one of the leading lights of the Hungarian émigré movement. It was a modest, single-fronted shop, painted a decorous dark green, that proclaimed its purpose as D. Dalponov, Clockmaker, in gold leaf on the glass door.

Sandra and Kim visited the shop that afternoon and asked to speak with Mr Dalponov. A courteous young man behind the counter asked,

"Which Mr Dalponov would that be?"

"Are there more than one?" asked Kim mischievously.

"There are three generations," said the young man seriously.

"All clockmakers."

"No, some of us make watches and I'm studying to be an accountant. What can we do for you?"

"We want to talk about Hungary, well a Hungarian girl," said Sandra.

"Why come to us?" asked the young man.

"We were told that you have roots that go back a long way in Hungary."

"That's true, but if you have somebody in mind, why don't you ask at the embassy?"

"We did and they said that there must be dozens of girls with the same name," said Kim.

"Oh, I see," said the young man who didn't see at all. All he could see was two very attractive girls who were the only customers he'd had since lunchtime and they didn't seem to be proper customers.

"The information that we want is background information about her parents and other family back in Hungary," said Sandra.

"How old would this mysterious girl be?"

"We think something like thirty."

"So she'd have been born in about 1975?" said the young man.

"Yes, while Hungary was under Soviet domination," said Sandra.

"And a member of the Warsaw pact," said Kim for good measure.

"I see," said the young man. "You could go to Budapest and make enquiries, it's a country that now belongs to the European Community."

"We were told that your family had escaped from Hungary and had kept in touch with people and events there and might know something of the background to those events."

"My grandfather and grandmother escaped to the West after the 1956 revolution and arrived in London two years later and my father was born two years after that."

"So he's forty-five," said the literally minded Kim.

"And I'm twenty-one," said the young man.

"Can we talk with your grandfather?" asked Sandra.

"He's a trifle frail these days."

"But I expect that he would enjoy talking about the old days."

"He doesn't see anyone other than family since granny died. Tell me, are you from the police?"

"Yes, sort of, we're army police."

"Redcaps?"

"Yes," said Sandra. "Would you please ask your grandfather if we can see him?"

"Why grandfather?"

"We were told that he knows all the important émigrés from Hungary."

"That's true but these days they are just relics of the past."

"It's the past that we want to talk about," said Sandra, becoming tired of this verbal fencing, "and if that's not possible we'll ask someone else, the Dalpronov's aren't the only Hungarian émigré family in Britain."

"Not so fast," said the young man. "I'll ask my father."

He disappeared through a door in the back. The girls stood and surveyed the shop. It didn't look all that prosperous but they were intelligent enough to appreciate that their standards were being set by shiny TV advertisements and real life wasn't always like that.

The young man reappeared, followed by an older man with a watchmakers eyepiece firmly clamped to his left eye. Without preamble he said,

"I understand that you're from the army's police and that you'd like to ask my father some questions. Could I ask why?"

"A young woman from Hungary is part of a current investigation and we would like to be able to eliminate her from our enquiries."

"Diplomatically put, young lady. Is it a serious investigation?"

"She was among the last people, perhaps the last person, to speak with a diplomat before he was found dead."

"And you think that the solution to the diplomat's death might lie in communist Hungary?"

"It's a possibility that we cannot ignore," said Sandra.

"And you won't tell us her name?"

"We'll tell your father," grinned Kim.

"He's not here, he's at his house."

"And where is that?" asked Sandra.

"Round the corner," said the younger man.

"Look," said Sandra. "Let's stop fooling around. We're from the army's special investigations unit and we've come here because we were told that your family are among the better informed people on life and personalities in communist Hungary. If you don't want to talk with us we'll find somebody else."

"Don't be so hasty, young woman," said the man who, in her mind Sandra had designated Dalponov 2. "You come here, out of the blue as it were and ask to speak to my father. In the old days we had to be careful, people came from the East who wanted to silence him and old habits die hard. Let me see some proof of your identity and I'll see if he will speak with you tomorrow."

They showed him their identification, gave him their cards and left.

"Phew," said Kim as they walked away. "You'd have thought that they were guarding the crown jewels. Hungary has been a free country since they held their first post-communist elections, fifteen years ago and it was the most liberal of the iron-curtain countries for many years before that."

"I think that the Dalponov's are simply clinging on to the last vestiges of their importance. Twenty-five years ago they would have been consulted by western diplomats and intelligence agencies about the significance of events in Hungary and today they aren't."

"Then you would have thought that they would have welcomed us with open arms," said Kim.

"I suppose that it's like he said, old habits die hard," said Sandra, "and playing hard-to-get comes naturally to some people."

They received the call the next morning, Grandfather Dalponov would see them. If they would present themselves at the shop at eleven o'clock, the grandson (Dalponov 3 thought Sandra) would take them to the old man. They debated whether to go in uniform and decided against it, on the one hand it might impress the old man with the seriousness of their enquiry but on the other, it would draw other people's attention to the authorities interest in the Dalponov's. It probably wouldn't matter but they decided to play safe.

The grandson took them to an imposing house literally just round the corner and they were ushered into a bright sitting room where a grey haired man rose to greet them. A younger woman who was with him offered them coffee and wouldn't accept no for an answer because father was just going to have his. The coffee served, the old man said,

"I understand that you wish to ask me about a young Hungarian woman?"

"Yes Mr Dalponov," said Sandra. "It happens that the young woman was among the last, if not the last, persons to speak with a diplomat who was later found dead."

"What makes you think that being Hungarian had anything to do with it?"

"The diplomat had served in Budapest."

"Your talking about Sir Stuart Harcourt, aren't you? The man who was found dead in the prime minister's offices."

"Yes," said Sandra.

"And who was this young woman? My grandson says that you have already spoken to our London embassy."

The girls noted the reference to 'our embassy'. The old man might have a British passport but in his heart he'd always be a Magyar.

"Sonia Berolinka," said Kim.

"Ah, I heard that she had been here but I have never met her. She wasn't born when we came over."

He fell silent and looked into the distance. Then he said, "It was a very unfortunate business."

There was another period of silence. Then he seemed to make up his mind and said, "I'm sorry but I can't help you. I know nothing. Now please leave me."

The grandson was clearly as surprised as the girls at their sudden dismissal but the old man was adamant, he had nothing to say about Sonia Berolinka.

They went back to their office at the Regents Park Barracks and phoned Jackie.

"You had told him that you wanted to know about her in connection with the death of Stuart Harcourt?" asked Jackie.

"Not exactly, Cap," said Sandra. "We said 'the death of a diplomat' and he leapt to the correct answer."

"And when he knew the names of the girl and the diplomat, he clammed-up?"

"Yes, he said 'it was a very unfortunate business' and asked us to leave".

"That tells us a lot, really," said Jackie.

"Like what, Cap?" prompted Kim who was on the extention.

"That there is a connection between Stuart Harcourt and the girl and something happened that was very unfortunate."

"Like she had a baby," said Kim, "and she came over here and killed him because he wouldn't acknowledge it."

"Shut up Kim," said Sandra, "this is serious."

"So's having a baby without a father," said Kim.

"I'd have thought that would be physically impossible," said Jackie, smiling down the phone, Kim's flights of fancy had suggested valuable avenues of enquiry in the past. She went on,

"Let's look at the facts, Stuart Harcourt was our ambassador to Hungary until a year ago. He could have had an affair with Sonia during the preceding three years."

"It would have had to be a very fleeting affair if she was in New York most of the time and he was in Budapest," said Sandra.

"But time to have a baby or two," said Kim.

"What's up with you, getting broody?" said Sandra and was surprised that Kim blushed.

Jackie ploughed on,

"That's one thing to check, did they have an off and on romance in Budapest during those four years. And did anything take place that might cause her to seek revenge?"

"Like her thinking that he was serious," said Kim.

"That might be the easiest of our two enquiries," said Jackie. "The second is did he do anything that would concern her when he was there as a newly promoted second secretary?"

"When was that?" asked Sandra.

"I'll ask Roger, he was there at the same time. It was before they got their freedom."

"How do we follow that up, Cap?"

"Frankly, girls, that was why you went and saw old Mr Dalponov and learned that something unfortunate occurred. Now we'll have to see, won't we?"

Chapter Eight

THE phone rang at half past twelve, not the ambassador's phone but Charles's.

"Assistant Secretary Eynon here, is that Howard?"

"Yes Mr Assistant Secretary, Charles Howard here," said Charles, switching on his phone recording machine.

"What do you mean by sending me that ridiculous message, that English policewoman must be out of her mind, you'd better get down there and put things right or you'll receive new orders."

"Are you threatening me, Mr Secretary?"

"Sure as hell I am, mister, this is all your fault."

"What exactly is all my fault, Mr Secretary?

"Blowing up a simple mistake into a crime and then sending copies to all and sundry here in DC."

"What simple mistake are you referring to Mr Secretary?"

"My little girl mislaying her pocket-book, you fool."

"I see," said Charles, "and what about the false accusations of theft that she made against the owner of a British hotel and her daughter?"

"They obviously misunderstood her. She says that the other students told her to say that those people had stolen it, she didn't mean any harm."

"When exactly did your daughter tell you this?"

"Last night when she phoned me."

"I have to remind you, Mr Assistant Secretary, that your daughter is in trouble, some would say, serious trouble, and lying won't do much to improve her position."

"What do you mean, lying," shouted Eynon. "I'll have you sacked for that."

"If you don't like the word lying, I'll put it another way, Mr Assistant Secretary. She has consistently not told the truth and the reason that she gave to a room full of people was that she's frightened of you." Charles checked that his recorder was still running.

"Rubbish, they didn't hear her properly, they're making it up."

"Let me get this straight, Mr Assistant Secretary, you're saying that two English police officers, the proprietor of the hotel and her daughter, a professor from Yale University and six Yale undergraduates and I, have conspired to incriminate your daughter?"

"You can forget the professor, he'll change his tune quickly enough when I've had a word with his Dean. You give me the name of this uppity policewoman, I'll have a word with her chief and straighten her out."

"I don't think that it's the policewoman that you have to worry about, Mr Assistant Secretary, the police will probably take a lenient view of Elfrida's mischief-making because she is not a British national and will be coming back to the States at the end of this week. It's the solicitor that you must deal with."

"Why should I take any notice of that, once Elfrida is home they can go to hell for all that I care."

"They won't give up," said Charles.

"If they try to sue my girl in a US court my lawyers will take them to the cleaners."

"I wasn't thinking of them taking action in a US court, just the adverse publicity that you'll receive, Mr Secretary."

"Rubbish, man, cases involving silly girls are ten a penny and who in the States is going to read some hick English newspaper?"

"I wasn't talking of newspapers," said Charles. "The family that own the hotel at Tolbrite also own ten or a dozen radio stations in the mid-West. In fact their headquarters are in Milwaukee. Weren't you a Senator for Wisconsin before the last election?"

"Say that again," said Eynon.

"Weren't you the Senator for Wisconsin …."

"No, not that, you fool, the bit about the radio stations."

"I said that the people who own the pub have radio stations in the mid-West."

"You said something about Milwaukee."

"Yes, their US headquarters are there."

Mr Assistant Secretary Eynon digested that, then said,

"Why should that worry me, they wouldn't dare criticise my daughter in my home state. It would be my word against theirs and I'll sue the pants off them if they do."

"That's fine then, Mr Assistant Secretary."

It had been on the tip of Charles's tongue to say that the people in the pub recorded everything and he shouldn't be surprised to hear his daughter's confession going out over the mid-Western air. And then he thought, 'Why should I?'

"I want you to go down and tell them."

"Tell them what, Mr Assistant Secretary?" said Charles, genuinely puzzled.

"My God, are you all stupid over there, the ambassador's thick as two planks and you don't appear to understand simple English. Go down to this place Tolbrite or whatever it's called and tell them to leave my girl alone."

"And you had better understand three things, Mr Secretary, the ambassador and staff of this embassy aren't stupid, I have no intention of going down there and all your daughter's troubles are self inflicted."

Charles held the receiver away from his ear as Eynon shouted,

"I'll have your guts for garters, mister, you see if I don't and you had better not make any long-term plans over there in England, I'll see that you're reassigned, you see if I don't."

"A trick that I've learnt from my British associates is to record everything that people say and you do appreciate, Mr Assistant Secretary, that this conversation has been recorded, don't you?"

With which Charles replaced his receiver.

Fifteen minutes later his secretary told him that the ambassador wanted to see him, pronto.

Charles walked past the marine sentry, blew the smiling secretary a kiss and went in.

"You wanted me, Mr ambassador?"

"Yes Charles, what did you say to Assistant Secretary Eynon, he's going beserk, he wants you sent back to DC on the first plane."

"I don't underestimate his capacity for doing harm so I recorded his phone call."

Charles put his recorder on the desk and switched it on. Secretary Eynon's voice came loud and clear,

'What do you mean by sending me that ridiculous message....'

The ambassador's lips tightened when he heard that he was considered to be as thick as two planks. When it was finished he said,

"This can't be allowed to go on, I think that I'd better have a word with the Secretary of State and warn her that Eynon is a loose cannon. Thick as two planks, indeed, I wonder where he picked up that expression."

"It's an expression used in the British Navy," said Charles.

"I know that he doesn't deserve it, Charles, but is there anything that we can usefully do?"

"As I said to the Assistant Secretary, I'm fairly sure that the police will not be pressing charges for public mischief or whatever they choose to call it and it's the solicitor's letter that he should worry about. Why can't he bring himself to have his daughter say that she was sorry? They're decent people and would probably let the matter drop."

"What about the man who owns the radio stations?"

"Tim Hawkridge? His father owns the village, including the pub and I expect that if they said sorry, that would be the end of it. Knowing Tim I expect that he would also pay the legal costs that his friends have already incurred."

"Sounds a bit feudal," said the ambassador.

"It is, in a way, except that the good works and money go from the squire to his villagers, not the other way round."

"OK Charles," said the ambassador, "I'd appreciate a copy of that recording, I'll play it to the Secretary of State. Don't you worry, I'll sort Assistant Secretary Eynon out, thick as two planks indeed, I'll show him."

In mid-afternoon the ambassador received an urgent diplomatic message to the effect that Assistant Secretary Eynon would be arriving at Heathrow the following morning for discussions with the embassy staff. The visit would be for two days.

An embassy car met him at Heathrow and conveyed him to the ambassador's residence. After a shower and breakfast he demanded an embassy car to take him to the Bournemouth police and to Tolbrite 'to sort those Britishers out.'

This was duly provided upon the Assistant Secretary of State's statement that he was engaged in urgent government business. He declined vehemently the ambassadors suggestion that Charles Howard should accompany him.

The ambassador's secretary kept Charles informed and he debated ringing Clare Thornton and those at the Tolbrite Arms and warning them what was about to descend on them. He decided to do nothing and prayed that they would have their recorders switched on.

Jackie phoned Roger Steven's private number at Number 10 and asked when it would be convenient to call on him. She went across the next morning.

"Made any progress, old girl?" was Roger's greeting.

"Quite a lot," said Jackie, "although we're no closer to proving the actual murder. That's why I want to talk with you, we've identified the girl who came to the reception and left with Stuart Harcourt. She made use of the fact that the new cultural attaché had only just arrived and wasn't known to the other members of the embassy staff, lured her away and took her place. Her name is Sonia Berolinka and I'm convinced that the reason for his murder is in the past and you were briefly part of that past."

"When was that?" asked Roger.

"Come on Roger, you can do better than that," smiled Jackie. "Where's all the brilliance that has you tipped for a PUS's job in the not-so-distant future?"

"Flattery will get you no-where old dear," said Roger, then he grinned and said, "Well, not very far."

"I've been puzzled why they chose Number 10 and my conclusion is that it's meant to show us something."

"Who is this mysterious they?"

"The Hungarians," said Jackie.

"I thought that you said that this girl gate-crashed the reception?"

"I did but someone in their embassy was helping her."

"How do you get that?"

"Well, she didn't arrive at the Whitehall gates on foot and tell the police that she was a member of the Hungarian delegation who had missed the bus. I've questioned all the men who were on duty that night and the Hungarians all arrived and left together and you can bet that they didn't stop and pick up a stranger on the way."

"OK, so someone in the embassy was helping her. What makes you think that they were sending us a message?" asked Roger.

"Their choice of Number 10 to do the deed. It couldn't be a casual murder, it has to be something to do with Hungary, so come on Roger you were part of his past in Hungary."

"I suppose that I was."

"Good," said Jackie, "then tell me all about Budapest in the mid-1980's"

"When I was the dogsbody?"

"Particularly when you were an eager beaver and Stuart Harcourt was a newly promoted second secretary."

"Why Budapest in particular?"

"Be your age, Roger, who was the last person seen with him?"

"That Hungarian woman, I suppose."

"Well, there you are then," said Jackie.

"Didn't you have any luck with the FCO's personnel section, sorry, the Human Resources Branch and our friends across the river?"

"Not a sausage, I should have asked the CIA or the KGB."

"They're not called that now," said Roger.

"You know who I mean. Tell me what sort of person he was."

"As a bachelor he was in a very favourable position, he could meet people and have friendships that a married officer couldn't have."

"You weren't married," said Jackie, knowing that he had married in the last few years.

"Yes but I was keen and ambitious and until one's well up the scale, a wife and children can be a bit of a nuisance in a diplomats life."

"About Stuart Harcourt?" prompted Jackie.

."This was 1984, Hungary was the most western-orientated of the Warsaw Pact countries and so we foreign diplomats could move around the country fairly freely. There were places where the Soviets had troops and military installations and that sort of thing and we kept well clear of those, but life wasn't bad. As I said, Stuart was a bachelor, and not only was he able to move about fairly freely but it didn't raise many eyebrows when he spent evenings in seedy night clubs."

"Ever since he died in mysterious circumstances I've suspected that he had duties that went beyond the normal run-of-the-mill diplomatic round, you're hinting that he was the resident spook."

"Tut tut, old dear," said Roger smiling. "I'm saying nothing. All we diplomats are spies, keeping our eyes and ears open and reporting little tit-bits to mother."

"But some do it differently than the others," said Jackie. "I suppose that it wasn't broadcast within the embassy, how long did it take you to find out?"

"Not long, actually and it could be that I was being sounded out."

"How was that?"

"Well, soon after I joined, Stuart made a lot of jocular remarks about my monk-like existence and that I should get out more and meet more Hungarians. He enlarged upon the lovely girls who were there for the asking, you know the sort of thing. In the end I was practically ordered by the ambassador to go with him. It was the usual thing, the bar-girls knew him, we danced and dined and at one in the morning he put me in a taxi and sent me back to my digs."

"Sounds fairly innocent," said Jackie.

"Oh, but it was. When I thought about it afterwards I realised that I was there to provide verisimilitude and also that he couldn't do what he was doing, three or four times a week, on a second secretary's salary, which meant that someone, somewhere in Whitehall, approved of what he was doing."

"He could have had a rich and indulgent mother."

"I checked-up on that, he didn't," said Roger.

" How did you know that it wasn't someone in the Kremlin?"

"That didn't cross my mind until a lot later so I did a bit of investigating and satisfied myself that he wasn't a double agent. I kept a rigorous check on everything that he saw and who he spoke with in the embassy and on the phone and frankly he saw nothing that would be of value to the other side."

"That wouldn't stop him being a sleeper for that period," said Jackie.

"There was always that possibility, I suppose," said Roger.

"Did he spend much time out of Budapest?"

"More than most of us. Again, with hindsight, he was better able to afford it."

"What reason did he give for these field trips?"

"He usually had a female companion," said Roger.

"He must have been a double agent, Roger."

"How do you work that out?"

"Think about it. He arrives in Budapest, settles in and starts nightclubbing. In common with all foreign diplomats he's watched by the Hungarian intelligence service and their Soviet masters. So what would they do? Why, they'd ensure that he met the most beautiful and seductive of their agents and they'd investigate every other person with whom he spoke. They'd also work out that he couldn't afford his life-style on his salary and allowances."

"That doesn't prove that he was a double agent," said Roger, "Only that he was a poor diplomat."

"I'll grant you that, so far, I've only made him look like a rather inept British diplomat," said Jackie. "But surely the fact that the Soviets let him complete his full tour of duty in Hungary without provoking an incident, must mean something?"

"There is that, I grant you," said Roger. "I happen to know that he was quite extensively investigated some years ago. They didn't want another 'is he, isn't he?' saga like they had with Roger Hollis."

"Think back, was there anything about his travels that was different from the usual pattern?"

"Not really, except that he made trips into the industrial regions, like the north-east whereas we others went south to Lake Balaton and Pecs and the spas and vineyards where the Hungarians went on their days off. His trips were justified by the fact that it was his job to foster trade. He was the Commercial Attaché."

"Did he go alone?" asked Jackie.

"I know for a fact that on at least two occasions he didn't but they might well have been isolated incidents. He explained it away by saying that the girl had discovered that he was going through the town where she came from and he had given her a lift and picked her up on the way back. Anyway, Jackie, what possible connection can this have with the Hungarian girl, she must have been a baby in 1984?"

"She would have been nearly ten years old. Perhaps she has an older sister," said Jackie as she rose to leave.

She thanked him and asked him to contact her if he remembered anything else.

When she got back to the MoD she found a message asking her to ring Peggy Davis at her office. When she was connected a voice said,

"Mrs Davis's PA, can I help you?"

"This is Jackie Fraser returning her call."

"Oh yes Captain Fraser, I'm putting you through."

"Hello Jackie, thanks for returning my call. It's not important but what was the name of that pub you spoke so highly of in Dorset?"

"The Tolbrite Arms. It's in the village of that name that Helene's in-laws own."

"Sounds a bit feudal, is it alright?"

"Yes, Timmy and Helene have spent a fortune on the village, it's probably the best preserved estate and village in Dorset. Are you thinking of going there?"

"William doesn't know it but I thought that we might slip away for a fortnight as soon as the House rises."

"That's next week, isn't it?"

"Yes, I've left it a bit late haven't I? Do you think that they'll have a room, I suppose that it'll have to be two rooms, we'll have to bring William's tame policeman."

"You can only but ask. I happen to know that they are full up with a party from Yale University this week, they leave on Saturday."

"Then I'd better be quick, hadn't I?"

"You'll probably see Helene, she and Timmy meet their friends there on most Saturday evenings."

"That would be nice as long as they forget that William is the Chancellor" said Peggy. "You don't know how off-putting it is to have everyone telling you how to cure this nation's financial ills."

"I'm sure that they won't embarrass you, I go there myself on some Saturdays and drive back to London afterwards."

"OK, I'll phone them."

"I've got the number, hold on a minute."

Jackie scrambled in her address book and gave Peggy the number.

Chapter Nine

IT WAS at about this time that an erect figure with grey hair and a florid face marched into the central police station at Bournemouth and impatiently banged the bell on the reception counter.

A police constable emerged from the office behind the counter and said,

"Yes?"

Assistant Secretary Marvin Eynon though that this was more than a little casual but decided to overlook it on this occasion.

"I want to see the boss man."

"What about?" asked the constable.

"That's my business," snapped Eynon.

"I'll get the sergeant," said the constable, disappearing. After some minutes he returned with a grey haired sergeant who said,

"I understand that you wish to see my superiors, Sir."

"That's what I already said," snapped Eynon.

"What about, Sir?" asked the sergeant.

"That's for your superiors ears."

"You want to register a complaint?"

"I most certainly do," said Eynon.

The sergeant produced a foolscap sized book from under the counter, opened it, turned over the pages and found the page where the past entries finished. He picked up a pen and said,

"If you'll just give me the details, Sir, this is the 'Complaints Book.' You can see that we get a lot of complaints."

"I don't wonder at it," said Eynon. "Stop fooling about and take me to the man in charge."

Sergeant Prior was beginning to enjoy himself. Before joining the police he'd spent twelve years as a regular soldier. As a private he'd practiced dumb-insolence and as an army sergeant he'd had to try and deal with it. Down through the ages and across the world's armies, dumb-insolence has been the peasant's most successful weapon against those in authority. Not rudeness or belligerence, simply feigned lack of comprehension.

"And who would you be, Sir?"

"Assistant Secretary Eynon from the State Department."

The sergeant laboriously wrote this down.

"And you want to make a complaint?"

"How many more times do I have to tell you, I want to see the head man to make my complaint."

"Oh but they won't let me do that, Sir, it's the system you see, it has to be written down, it's evidence in case it ever comes to court."

From beneath his brows Sergeant Prior could see this visitor getting redder and redder."

"Look, you fool, I want to complain about the way one of your sergeants has been harassing my daughter."

"There's no call to use that sort of language, Sir, we're only doing our job and we take charges of sexual assault or interference by police officers very seriously in Bournemouth. You wouldn't happen to know the sergeants name?"

"What are you blathering about man. Of course I would, you fool, how else could I complain and the sergeant's a woman." He fished out his copy of the message that Charles Howard had forwarded to Washington, DC and read,

"Detective Sergeant Clare Thornton."

"One of our very best young sergeants, Sir, I'd find it difficult to believe that she would sexually harass your daughter."

"I'm not interested in what you believe you idiot and she hasn't sexually harassed my daughter. It's what I believe that matters, don't you know who I am, I'm Assistant Secretary Eynon."

The sergeant leant over the counter and said in a man-to-man tone,

"What would you be the assistant secretary of, Sir, a golf club?"

Eynon was getting more angry but before he could explode a harassed driver came in and said,

"I'm sorry, Secretary Eynon but the police say that I'm blocking their cars from coming in and out and that I've got to leave. Here's the car-phone number, call me when your through here." With which the man turned on his heel and departed to move the car. Eynon turned back to the sergeant,

"Are you going to take me to the boss man or do I have to make a complaint about your stupidity?"

The sergeant picked up his pen and said, conversationally to the constable,

"The gentleman wants to register a complaint about our stupidity." He turned back to Eynon, pen poised and said,

"Now Sir, what precisely is your complaint, your new complaint?"

"Look you idiot, I've told you who I want to complain about and what I want to complain about and you've written it down in your stupid book. Now please go and find a senior officer who will listen to me."

That's better, thought the sergeant and turned to the constable and said,

"See if Detective Inspector Wyatt will see the gentleman."

"Is he the boss man?" demanded Eynon.

"No but he's Clare Thornton's boss and you'll have to start with him," said the sergeant and turned away from the counter.

He was taken through. John Wyatt stood up and shook his hand and invited him to sit down and describe the nature of his complaint about Sergeant Thornton's behaviour.

"First I want you people to understand who I am, I'm an Assistant Secretary of State."

"Very good, Sir," said Wyatt, "that would be in America."

"Yes, I advise the Secretary of State."

"Does she know that you're over here complaining about one of my officers?"

"What's that got to do with it?" demanded Eynon.

"Well, we have to know whether you're here in an official capacity or not, don't we, Sir?"

"What difference does that make?"

"It makes a great deal of difference, Sir. If you're here representing Uncle Sam I have to inform the Foreign Office and use diplomatic language but if you're here as plain Mr Eynon, I can use quite different language. Are you here officially?"

"I don't see that it makes any difference, I'm an Assistant Secretary."

"Very well I shall regard you as Mr Eynon, a private US citizen. Now what precisely is your complaint? By the way, this conversation is being recorded."

Eynon placed on the desk a copy of the e-mail that Clare had sent to Charles Howard reporting the finding of the pocket book and Elfrida's admission that she knew that she had lost it by the river and that she had lied because she didn't want her father to know of her carelessness.

Wyatt read it. He had his own copy on file.

"What's wrong with that?" asked Wyatt. "Your daughter made that admission in front of a room full of people. We're considering whether to bring charges for wasting police time and public mischief. I understand that the people who she falsely accused of stealing her pocket book have already started legal action."

"I'm going to sort them out after I've dealt with you," said Eynon.

"In what way are you dealing with us, Mr Eynon?"

"What do you mean?" said Eynon.

"You said that you will sort them out after you've dealt with us. How will you deal with us?"

"Well, I demand that you drop those ridiculous charges for one thing."

"And the other?" prompted Wyatt.

"I want you to get on to this small town solicitor, Swain, and tell him to withdraw his letter because my daughter didn't accuse anyone of stealing her pocket book, it was the other students who suggested it."

"You are claiming that your daughter didn't say that the hotel staff had stolen her pocket-book and that it was the other students."

"Yes," said Eynon, "they suggested it."

"Perhaps you don't know that the bar staff at the Tolbrite Arms have voice actuated recorders and that in consequence, we have a complete record of your daughter accusing the landlady and her daughter of theft over a period of days as well as her confession that it was all a pack of lies."

"Recordings can be faked," said Eynon.

"She said it in front of her professor and six other undergraduates from Yale."

"If they know what's good for them they'll forget everything that they heard or face the consequences," said Eynon. "That professor shouldn't have let her lose her pocket book and she wouldn't have lost it if he'd booked them in at a decent hotel."

"And now you're going to sort the others out," said Wyatt.

"When you've given me your assurance that you'll make no charges against my daughter."

"I can give you no such undertaking, Mr Eynon and I must insist that you leave this police station."

Inspector Wyatt pressed a bell-push under his desk and switched off the recording machine saying,

"You are a thoroughly dishonest and nasty person Mr Assistant Secretary Eynon and I can quite understand why your unfortunate daughter is a nervous wreck. Constable, see that this man leaves the building, if he creates a disturbance, arrest him."

A slightly shocked Assistant Secretary Eynon found himself on the pavement outside the police station, phoning for his car and thinking that they did things better in Milwaukee.

Detective Inspector Wyatt sent for Clare Thornton.

"I've just had that girl Eynon's father in here."

"Yes, Gov, word gets around, I gather that Sergeant Prior had given him the dumb-policeman treatment before he got to you."

Wyatt grinned at her, then became serious.

"He really is a most unpleasant creature and how the President came to accept him in a diplomatic post, I'll never understand."

"Charles Howard says that it was a consolation prize for losing his seat in the Senate."

"Well, I can't see him lasting long in the job. He's now on his way to see the solicitor and the folk at the Tolbrite Arms to get them to drop the action for slander. Frankly I fear that he'll cause a disturbance, he's certainly going to annoy people and I don't want anyone to get into trouble for assaulting a US diplomat."

"I could phone them and warn them that he's on his way and perhaps I should look in at the pub later."

"Good, you do that, your brief is to see that he comes to no harm."

Clare went back to her desk and phoned the law firm of Swain and Son and spoke with Mr Swain, Senior's, secretary. That done, she rang Gloria's mobile number.

"Gloria, it's Clare Thornton."

"Hello Clare, how's things?"

"Fine. Look Gloria, the father of that girl who said that you stole her pocket book is over here and is on his way to speak with Mr Swain and then he's coming to the pub."

"The girl hasn't said anything about him coming and he can't stay here."

"I don't think that he intends to stay, judged by his behaviour at the station he's coming to bully you into withdrawing your action for slander."

"Bullying won't get him far with us Dorset folk."

"I know. Why I'm phoning is to warn you to be careful, especially Will. On no account touch him. I'll drop in later, you must warn your parents and Will to do nothing physical, he's a thoroughly rotten person..."

"Like his daughter," put in Gloria.

"...and he'd be only too happy to put you in the wrong, him having diplomatic immunity."

After Clare had rung off Gloria thought about what Clare had said. She was worried about ex-commando Will. What a pity that it wasn't Monday when they would have the night off from helping her parents at the pub and would be in Bournemouth for Will to host his weekly chat show on Radio Bournemouth. She wouldn't tell him in advance and with luck the man might have been and gone before Will came home.

She knew that this wasn't possible, the students wouldn't be back from their field trips until, say, four-thirty and that, presumably would be when things would start to happen. Will got in at about five. Usually they had their evening meal, changed and went along to the pub sometime before seven. Today she'd make jolly certain that she'd be there when the American was there so as to protect her parents. That would complicate things with Will. Oh dear, why couldn't the wretched girl's father stay in America?

But it was her and her mother who the girl had accused of stealing her pocket-book and who's names were mentioned in Mr Swains letter and presumably it was them that this man would want to persuade to drop the case. This raised her spirits, perhaps they could deal with him and he'd go before Will came home. She knew that was a non-runner as well. In any case if she was along at the pub agreeing to drop the case, who would be back at their house – the antique dealers house – cooking Will's dinner? It was all so complicated; she wished that Will was there.

She'd have a word with Paula.

She phoned Southern Enquiries and Paula answered the phone. Gloria explained the situation and Paula wondered why she was phoning her. She agreed that it was wrong for men to come over here to bully people and that it was a good thing that Clare would be dropping by. She then got the message. Gloria said,

"Do you think that Jill would like to send out a reporter, there might be a story in it, him being a man from the American government?"

"I don't know, Gloria," said Paula, smiling at the phone, "would you like me to ask her?"

"Oh, yes please, Paula, would you?"

"Yes, of course I will, for you, and you can guess who it will probably be, can't you?"

"Yes, the students get back between four and five. You are a dear."

That was how a Hawkridge Radio Bournemouth car came to be parked in the Tolbrite Arms' car park late that afternoon. When they eventually got there, Mr Assistant Secretary Eynon didn't see it, he was dropped at the pub's entrance.

He sat in the back of the car and fumed, which should he sort out first, the small town solicitor or the staff at the pub? That stupid policeman hadn't got the message; you don't fool with ex-Senator Eynon. It had been a shock being defeated by that Democrat, he should have spent more time in the state but how could he find time to be pumping peoples hands in Milwaukee while he was busy in Washington DC, seeing that Wisconsin got more than its fair share of the federal pork barrel. He'd been given a consolation prize, Assistant Secretary of State but considered that he and not that woman, should have been given the top job.

He told the driver to take him to Dorchester and find the offices of a lawyer called Swain, reasoning that the fellow should be there in business hours and the pub would be open all the evening.

He was lucky, a pre-warned Mr Swain was in and would see him.

Mr Swain was surprised that his visitor had come without prior notice and assumed that the American had come to discuss terms of settlement. He would insist that a verbal apology wouldn't be enough.

Eynon was ushered into the presence, his hand shaken and invited to occupy the chair opposite the desk.

"Now Mr Eynon, to what do I owe this surprise visit?"

"My name is Assistant Secretary Eynon and I demand that you stop this nonsense about my daughter."

"I should tell you that all conversations in this office are recorded, it saves so much argument later. Now, what nonsense is that, Mr Eynon?"

"Saying that she accused the people at that hick hotel of theft, she did no such thing."

"Who told you that, Mr Eynon?"

"My daughter of course."

"Then I'm afraid that she has misled you," said the solicitor, "we have tapes that we will use in evidence, that clearly record your daughter's voice repeatedly accusing the hotel staff of stealing her pocket-book."

"Tapes can be faked," said Eynon dismissively.

"But you can't fake the evidence of nearly a dozen witnesses."

"They'll change their tune after I've finished with them, that professor is as good as out of a job."

"There were other people there as well, quite well known people."

"All liars."

"Is that all that you have come all this way to say to me. Mr Eynon?"

"Yes, in plain American, back off if you know what's good for you."

"Very well, if you'll let us know the name and address of your lawyer, I'll send them a transcription of today's conversation."

"You can go to hell."

"Otherwise I shall be forced to send it to Washington for the attention of your Secretary of State."

"It'll never get to her."

"It's a chance you'll have to take, isn't it Mr Eynon? You would be well advised to settle the matter here and now."

Eynon did a quick appraisal and decided that he'd concentrate on making those people in that hick hotel withdraw their case instead of wasting his time with this small town lawyer. He said,

"If you know what's good for you you'll learn not to tangle with Marvin Eynon.

"I think that it would be wise if you left now, Mr Eynon" said Swain.

He was shown out and told his waiting driver to take him to the hotel in a village called Tolbrite.

He arrived at the pub after four o'clock and made his way into the bar. There were only two other people there, two rather attractive girls a blonde and a brunette, who were sitting at one of the row of tables under the windows, sipping tea. He stamped up to the bar, whereupon the blonde girl came over and asked,

"Can I help you?"

"You might," he said curtly, "I'm Assistant Secretary Eynon."

"I see," said Gloria. "We have a young woman of that name staying here. From Yale University."

"I know, that's what I've come about. I'm her father."

"I expect that she'll be pleased to see you," said Gloria, thinking, I bet she won't.

"Where is she? I want to see her."

"I'm afraid that they're all out on what they call field work, they'll be coming in soon, can I get you something?"

"No," snapped Eynon. Gloria turned on her heel and resumed her seat with Paula who's recorder was already switched on.

Paula stood up, hoisted her Hawkridge Radio recording set over her shoulder and walked up to Eynon. She said,

"Excuse me, did you say that you are Assistant Secretary Marvin Eynon of the US State Department?"

"Yes," said Eynon, momentarily taken aback.

"I'm from Radio Bournemouth," thrusting her hand held microphone between them. "It's not often that we have an Assistant Secretary of State visiting us, could I ask what important matter of state brings you to Tolbrite?"

"It's not for publication," said Eynon, thinking fast.

"Let me put it another way," said Paula. "Which government department's officials have you come to see?"

"I'm not here to see your government's people," said Eynon. "I've got nothing to say to the press."

"Oh, that's a shame," said Paula. "It's surprising how many US visitors come to Tolbrite. We get lots of professors and students because the district is rich in history. Are you interested in history?"

Paula was running out of things to say.

"Can't say that I am," mumbled Eynon, wishing that the girl and her microphone would sink into the ground.

"The founder of one of your most prominent Boston families came from the Tolbrite Manor House, the same family still live there, the Hawkridge's. There's a plaque in the church at Spetisbury, that's a village just across the river, commemorating their marriage in 1692.

Their descendant is a professor at Harvard and she's married a professor at Yale."

"Not the idiot who got my daughter into trouble, I hope?"

"Oh, I didn't realise that. Are you here because she's pregnant?" asked Paula, innocently.

"What are you talking about?"

"Your daughter being pregnant."

"She didn't tell me. Now I will kill that professor."

Paula decided that this had gone far enough.

"No one here said that your daughter is pregnant, the subject came up because you said that the professor had got her in trouble and in England that's one way of saying that an unmarried girl is pregnant."

"Leave me alone, my business is private," said Eynon.

"Your daughter has caused a great deal of unnecessary fuss, Mr Eynon. She said that the people in this hotel had stolen her pocket book when she knew all along that she had taken it with her and lost it. Have you got anything to say?"

"It's all a pack of lies, she told me that the other students put her up to it."

"Put her up to what, Mr Eynon, losing her pocket book or saying that the people in the hotel had stolen it?"

"All of it," blustered Eynon.

"And is that why you've come to England?" asked Paula.

"Of course it is, the police are going to put my little girl in prison."

"Surely not, they are considering whether to take any action on charges of public mischief and wasting police time. I would expect them to let her off because she's going back home at the end of the week."

"That's not what that policeman said."

"Perhaps you didn't ask him properly," said Paula.

"You mean that I should have paid him off?"

"Good Lord no, if you'd tried that they would have put you in jail and never let you out. I mean that you should be polite."

"I am polite, I was a US Senator, for Wisconsin, that's the other side of Lake Michigan."

"Oh, we know where it is alright," said Paula.

Just then the first pair of students, a boy and a girl, arrived back, looking tired but bronzed and cheerful. Two more pairs arrived in short order and the boys waved at Gloria, turned and walked along the road to their flat in Gloria's house. A few minutes later Professor Smith walked in, waved wearily to Gloria and trudged up the stairs. He was followed by Elfrida Eynon who looked mournfully into the bar before starting to climb the stairs.

She stopped, looked again, then bounded down and flung herself in her fathers arms, saying,

"Oh, Daddy, Oh I'm so glad to see you, I've been so unhappy, everybody here has been beastly to me."

"In what way, baby?"

"They stole my pocket book and when I made a fuss they threw it away along the river, knowing that kid would find it. They're all in it together."

Paula motioned to Gloria to keep quiet and made a small gesture to show that she was recording all that was said.

"Tell me all about it, honey."

"Not in front of this lot, come up to my room."

She led her father out of the bar and up the stairs.

Half an hour later the students began drifting down. News that Elfrida's father was among them was greeted with grimaces of distaste.

Some time afterwards Clare drifted in and sat with Paula and when the professor came down Clare introduced him to Paula.

Looking around, Clare got the impression of a group of people sitting on a time bomb.

Chapter Ten

JACKIE walked the few steps along the corridor and asked General 'Tubby' Lowe's secretary if he was busy. She was waved in.

"Come on in, my dear and sit yourself down and have a cup of tea."

She sat in the chair indicated. Crossed her legs and smoothed her skirt.

"To what do I owe this pleasure?"

Jackie grinned at him. Behind that benign face was one of the keenest minds in the building.

"It's the death of Stuart Harcourt, General. We've got so far and now I believe that the answer's in Hungary."

"What have you done so far? No, I put that badly, what has been done so far?"

"It has been established that he died from some sort of nerve agent administered in the back of his right shoulder sometime between eight and ten on the night of the party at Number 10. The last person to be seen with him was a girl impersonating the new Hungarian cultural attaché which must mean that at least one person in the Hungarian embassy knew that the substitution had taken place and, presumably, why. We are sure that the girl is an actress called Sonia Berolinka and that Stuart Harcourt knew her."

"What does she have to say about it?"

"That's one of the problems, she went back to Hungary the next day."

"That was rather thoughtless of her," grinned the General.

"It doesn't help. I'll come back to that, Sir."

"I rather thought that you might."

"As far as the girls and I have been able to establish, he hasn't been dating anyone in London."

"I shouldn't think so, at his age," said the General.

"The older they are the worse they get," said Jackie.

"I'm sorry, my dear, I can see that you speak with knowledge."

"If anyone bore him a grudge for what, for want of better words, I'll call a serious non-service transgression, they could have done it with far less risk to themselves at somewhere other than in Number 10 Downing Street."

"Amen," said the General. Jackie ploughed on.

"I reasoned that his murder must have a service connection, is symbolic and, ergo, it must be rooted in the past."

"Enter the beautiful female spy."

"Exactly," said Jackie, "except that she's too young."

"I wouldn't say that thirty-ish was too young, I'm told by my Sunday paper that girls as young as fourteen…."

"What I mean, Sir," said Jackie. "is that she would have been too young to have interested him when he was thcrc in the mid-eighties."

"I see," said the General. "Why are you discounting the more recent time when he was our ambassador there?"

"I checked up on that. All the while he was our ambassador in Budapest, Sonia Berolinka was in the Hungarian delegation at the United nations in New York."

"My, you have been busy," said the General.

"Nevertheless," said Jackie, determined not to be side tracked, "according to Peggy Davis, when she came into the reception she made joking remarks about him teaching the night club girls naughty English words and the girls teaching her years later. There was one other thing that Peggy said that she had said and that was that Stuart Harcourt knew all the best night spots in Hungary."

"Perhaps I'm getting old, my dear, but what's special about that?"

"Usually people say the best night spots in New York or Paris or London, not the USA, France or England."

"I see what you mean but don't read too much into it, it might be that in the mid-nineteen eighties the only night spots in Hungary were in Budapest and in that respect the names were interchangeable. Is the Peggy Davis you mentioned the Chancellor's rather attractive wife?"

"Yes," said Jackie, "she's nice and she's clever and for your private ear, Sir, she's hoping to take her husband to stay at my favourite pub next week. He doesn't know it yet."

"It's difficult, isn't it, they probably want to be left alone and people won't let them. Like most of the ills in this island nation of ours, it all comes from too much television. I thought that I might write a book on it one day after I retire."

Jackie grinned at him, if it was as good as the book that he had already written about his paratroopers experiences in the Falklands it would be a best seller.

"I went to the FCO and MI-5 and asked to see what they had on Stuart Harcourt and they told me to push-off. It seems that the PM's name cuts no ice with them."

"Right and proper too," said the General. "Mere politicians must be kept in their place. They have no right to tamper with the organs of state security."

"Except to cut off the money," said Jackie.

"There is that, of course," grinned Tubby. "It was so much easier when we all went to the same schools and understood these things."

Jackie could envisage another chapter of his book. She said,

"Now I'll go back to Sonia Berolinka. The girls went to the high priests of the Hungarian émigrés, a family called Dalponov who run a clock and watch repair business in Islington. After a lot of polite argument with the grandson and the son, they were taken to see the old man who escaped from Hungary after the 1956 revolution. He listened to the girl's story and when he learned that the person in whom they were interested was Sonia Berolinka, he said 'that was a most unfortunate business' and said that he couldn't help them. He meant that he wouldn't help them."

"He wouldn't put the finger on Sonia," said Tubby who liked gangster movies. He grinned at her and said, "So where does that leave us? As if I didn't know."

"Yes General, if the prime minister wishes us to continue with this investigation, somebody should tackle it from the other end."

"You mean that you should go to Hungary?"

"Yes but I must have the backing of the embassy, they will have to provide me with a linguist who knows colloquial Hungarian."

"I would think that might be arranged. Have you mentioned this to anyone else?"

"You mean our friends across the river? No."

"Then let them find out the hard way."

"It would be a bit of a nuisance if the translator assigned to me is the embassy spook, wouldn't it, Sir?"

"Leave it with me, Jackie, I'll ask my contacts how good the assistant Defence Attaché is and if he's any good he shall be your man. Come to think of it, you can make an army visit and sort of extend your terms of reference when you get there. All of us soldiers like helping pretty girls. When did you plan to go?"

"The day after tomorrow would do," said Jackie.

The following day she received a file containing orders from the Director of Military Security, General Lowe, to conduct a security audit of the Defence Attache's organisation in Hungary. The fact that it consisted of two rooms in the embassy wasn't mentioned. She expected that she could stretch it to cover the houses or flats in which the military personnel lived and the communications although she was conscious that the FCO had a specialist organisation for this.

She told the sergeants that she'd tried to take one of them on the trip but the boss had told her not to push her luck. She told them to try to find some other émigré Hungarians and ask them what was distressing about the Berolinka family.

Remembering their earlier conversation, she phoned Helene Hawkridge and asked her if Hawkridge Media had any contacts out there that she might use. Helene consulted Charles Smith and he phoned Jackie; from public records they had found that the birth of a female child named Sonia Berolinka had been registered in 1974 in Kisvarda, a town in Szabolcs-Szatmar-Bereg, the North Eastern-most county of Hungary and that in 1980 a family of that name with two girl children was registered in Miskolc in the adjacent county of Borsod-Abauj-Zemplenand which bordered Slovakia. Charles gave her two telephone numbers of media people who might be useful.

Jackie looked the places up. Kisvarda was close to the Ukranian border in a region devoted mainly to fruit growing although there was some light industry. Miskolc was more interesting, 90 miles north east of the capital and comprising the second largest industrial grouping in Hungary in the Borsod industrial region extending up the Sajo River valley. The original industries of Miskolc were textiles, wine and food processing, together with glass making to which the production of heavy machinery, iron and steel and chemicals had been added or enlarged in the post-war period. But the countryside with its fruit and vineyards was never far away. There was also a new university.

Looking at what she had assembled and assuming that the Berolinka's who had moved to Miskolc in 1979-80 were the same family as had registered the birth of their daughter in Kisvarda in 1974, it looked as if they may have moved to improve their employment prospects.

Jackie grinned at the sheet of paper, perhaps the name Berolinka is as common in Hungary as Smith is in England.

She flew to Budapest the following morning.

At the Tolbrite Arms there was the noise of heavy footsteps coming down the stairs and Assistant Secretary Marvin Eynon stamped in and stood in the doorway.

"Which one of you is Professor Smith?"

"I am," said Jose from a seat under the window.

Eynon advanced a step towards him and said in a loud voice,

"I'll see that you lose your cushy job at Yale. You should be ashamed of yourself bringing my daughter to this place and then letting her be robbed."

"I did no such thing as the rest of the Yale team will tell you," said the professor.

There were murmurs of assent from the other six students, one of whom had his video camera primed on the table.

"And why didn't you see that these hotel people," he managed to make it sound as if they were the lowest of the low, "were prosecuted for stealing my little girl's pocket book?"

"For the simple reason that they didn't steal it," said Jose.

"Of course they did," shouted Eynon, "they stole it and when Elfreda accused them they hid it on the river bank in that park. They knew that no one is allowed in there."

He turned on Gloria and Mr and Mrs Trowbridge, who were behind the bar wondering how they could get rid of this awful man. Gloria was praying that he'd go before Will appeared.

"Yes, it's you I'm talking about, you stole Elfrida's pocket-book."

"I'm afraid that I must ask you to leave these premises," said Mr Trowbridge.

"You're thieves. Do the rest of your customers know that?"

"Your daughter has fed you a lot of hogwash, Mr Assistant Secretary," said one of the girl students. "Why don't you behave like the statesman you're supposed to be and go away and take your wretch of a daughter with you?"

"There, you see, daddy, they're all against me," chipped in Elfrida.

"We sure are," said one of the boys.

Will appeared behind the bar and said in a stage whisper to Gloria, "What's going on, love?"

"Her father's come to tell us that she still says that we stole her purse."

"Then they're both mad," said Will.

"I must ask you to leave, you are causing a disturbance on licensed premises, " said Mr Trowbridge.

"Not until you've admitted that you stole my daughter's pocketbook and agree to tell your lawyer to take his letter back," shouted Eynon.

Will lifted the bar-flap and came into the bar. Clare could see what was about to happen and she stood up, advanced one step and said loudly to Will.

"Don't touch him, Will, that's what he wants you to do."

Will stopped, until that moment he hadn't realised that Clare was there.

Eynon turned and glared at Clare and said,

"And who are you, Miss?"

"I'm a police officer, Detective Sergeant Clare Thornton. Now Sir, the licensee has asked you to leave…"

Eynon interrupted her.

"You're the bitch who sent that note to the embassy, aren't you?"

"If you're referring to your daughter's confession, yes."

"You're a liar like the rest of these people and you ought to be horsewhipped."

He took a step forward and struck Clare twice across the face, once with the palm and then with the back of his hand.

There was a startled silence as Clare reeled with the force of the blows and fell backwards on to the upholstered bench seat that ran along the window wall of the room.

Ex-Commando Will started forward but Mr Trowbridge had come through the flap and grabbed him as Eynon said,

"That'll teach you not to tell lies."

There was a deathly silence, perhaps Eynon realised that he had gone too far. Clare rose to her feet and walked past him and out of the room to her car. A minute later she returned, walked up to the Assistant Secretary, spun him round and put a handcuff on his right wrist, the hand that had struck her. Eynon struggled but was no match for the athletic sergeant, his arms were pulled roughly across his body and the cuffs clicked on his left wrist. There was a minor cheer from the students.

"Mr Eynon, I arrest you for the offence of refusing to leave licensed premises when requested to do so and for striking a police officer. Anything that you say may be taken down and used in your trial."

"You can't do this, you fool. I'm the Assistant Secretary of State."

"That will be noted as evidence," said Clare.

"But I'm an American diplomat."

"You haven't behaved like one," said Clare.

"But I claim diplomatic immunity."

"You can tell that to the magistrate in the morning, meanwhile you'll spend the night in the cells," said Clare.

"I'll see that you're sacked over this, Miss."

"Look, you stupid old man," said Paula, coming forward, "can't you get it into your fat head that everything that you have said has been recorded and filmed." She looked at the young man and he nodded "and may be used in evidence in court. Your behaviour has been disgraceful."

"You won't be so cocky when our ambassador hears of this, I demand the right to make a phone call."

"Not on our phone, you don't," said Will.

Eynon turned on his daughter and said,

"Don't worry baby, Uncle Sam will soon sort these people out and as for you, Miss," turning to Clare, "It'll take you the rest of your life paying off the suite that I'll bring for false arrest."

The undergraduate who had spoken up earlier stood up and said,

"Why don't you shut up, you make all of us ashamed to be Americans and you can be sure that the folk back home will hear of this."

"See it too," said the boy with the camera.

Clare left Eynon standing there while she brought her car to the front entrance. She came back into the bar and frog-marched the protesting prisoner out and into the back seat of the car with Elfrida walking wailing behind. She backed out of the car and slammed the door and stood beside it while she phoned the station that she was bringing in an American prisoner who had assaulted her. She asked the desk sergeant to tell Inspector Wyatt.

Paula said goodbye and followed Clare back to Bournemouth. On reaching her office at the radio station she told the station manager, Jill Jones, that they had a scoop. Together they edited it to make it coherent to someone who hadn't been present and put it on the line to the news-room at Hawkridge Central.

The duty editor recognised it for what it was and put it on the line to the Hawkridge Radio news-room in Milwaukee and that's how the story of Assistant Secretary Marvin Eynon making an idiot of himself, the State Department and the President who had chosen him, broke simultaneously on both sides of the Atlantic.

Two hours after the arrest, the driver of the embassy car, who had parked at the river-end of the pub car park, looked in at the Tolbrite Arms to ask how long the Assistant Secretary would be. He was told that his passenger was in police custody and that he would be well advised to return to London.

Charles Howard was visiting with friends when one of them came in from another room and said,

"Do you have an Assistant Secretary of State called Eynon?"

"Yes," said Charles, "what's the fool done now?"

"He's been arrested for striking a police officer, a lady police officer. They just broadcast a recording of his behaviour in a pub down in Dorset. It sounded like a TV soap-opera."

"I can well imagine it. Did he claim diplomatic immunity?"

"Yes and the policewoman told him that he should raise that in court in the morning. Tonight he was going to jail. Do you think that you should do something?"

"Who me?" said Charles, "Good Lord no, the Brits have done Uncle Sam a good turn, he can rot in jail for ever as far as I'm concerned."

It was an hour later when his mobile phone rang. The duty hand at the embassy patched a very agitated ambassador through to Charles.

"Charles, the Secretary of State has just phoned me. She says that there's a story on the radio news that the British police have arrested Assistant Secretary Marvin Eynon."

It was on Charles's lips to say, 'Yes, good isn't?' it but prudence prevailed.

"Arrested him? Good Lord, I don't believe it."

"He was in a very awkward mood when he left here this morning."

"What is he supposed to have done?" lied Charles.

"She said that the story is that he punched a policewoman."

"They take a serious view of that sort of thing over here," said Charles. "Does diplomatic immunity cover that?"

"I don't know, the Brits could be a bit awkward about it since it was a police woman who he hit. I'll have a word with protocol."

"I hope that it wasn't the one who sent us that note."

"Look Charles, it's a bit late to try and get him released tonight but would you be a good chap and go down in the morning. If they bring him up in court you could at least confirm that he's who he is."

"Very well Mr Ambassador, consider it done but I warn you, the Brits might be awkward."

"Do your best Charles, whatever we do it's bound to be wrong."

Chapter Eleven

CHARLES HOWARD drove to Bournemouth in the morning, confident that the Court wouldn't sit before 10 a.m. He parked at the radio station and looked in on Fred and Paula and mentioned that their story had reached the highest levels of government back home and that he had been sent down to do what he could for the prisoner. Paula was also going so they shared a cab to the Magistrates Court in Stafford Road. Charles spent a good deal of his time in cars and cabs with attractive girls.

The case of Marvin Eynon was among the first to be taken. Charles had introduced himself to the court officials and was allowed to sit in the well of the court and Paula used her Radio pass to sit with the press. She noted that some of those on the press benches were Americans. They had heard the previous night's broadcast.

The usher called 'Marvin Eynon' and he was pushed, protesting, into the dock. The clerk read out the charge. Before anyone could speak, the prisoner shouted,

"I protest at my treatment. I am a representative of the US government and claim diplomatic immunity. I am the US Assistant Secretary of State."

The District Judge said in a flat voice,

"Is there anyone present to vouch for that?"

Charles rose and said,

"My name is Charles Howard, your honour, and I'm from the US embassy in London."

"And do you assure the court that the prisoner is who he says he is?"

"Yes, Sir," said Charles, not sure whether he should have said Your Honour

"Thank you," said the judge.

Charles sat down.

"I demand to be released," shouted Eynon. "Where's our ambassador? I'm a diplomat."

The judge, who had heard last night's broadcast and wondered if it might be construed to be a contempt of court, in which case he would have summoned the reporter before him and given them at the very least a severe dressing down, decided that it wasn't a contempt, this fellow deserved all he got.

"That's a trifle difficult to believe, Mr Eynon."

"What do you mean," shouted Eynon.

"You are here because you struck a lady, a police lady, in a totally unprovoked attack."

"She wrote a pack of lies about my daughter."

"Is the policewoman in court?"

"Yes Sir," said Clare standing up.

"I'll take your evidence now."

Clare entered the witness box.

The Judge addressed the prisoner,

"You have been brought before this court for the offences of disturbing the peace and striking a police officer. The first charge would normally be dealt with in this court as a Summary Offence. The more serious offence of striking a police officer could be taken to a Crown Court to be dealt with by a judge and jury because such an offence could attract a longer sentence than the six months maximum that this court can impose. For reasons that I think are obvious, I have taken the decision to deal with both offences. However, if you wish, you can insist that the case be taken to the higher court."

The young public defender who had been hastily briefed to defend Eynon, turned and spoke with him, shaking his head vigorously. He turned and said,

"The prisoner has no wish to go to a higher court, Sir."

"I said no such thing, its all a waste of time," shouted Eynon, "I'm a diplomat."

The Judge looked in Charles's direction and Charles kept his head down.

The judge got the message and nodded at Clare and said, "Please proceed."

She took the oath and the Judge asked her to describe briefly the events at the Tolbrite Arms the previous afternoon.

Clare explained that the root of the trouble went back a week and described the accusations that the prisoner's daughter had made against the staff at the Tolbrite Arms, the finding of the missing purse in the park and the daughter's admission that she had made up the theft story to avoid her father discovering that she had lost her purse.

The daughter had been phoning her father in the Unites States describing the so-called theft and he alerted the embassy in London and demanded that they clear the matter up.

"And so they should have done," said the man in the dock.

"Be quiet," said the Judge. "You'll have your turn in a minute."

"The man came from the embassy and after the daughter admitted that she had fabricated the whole theft story, I warned her that the police might prefer charges for wasting police time and public mischief. I wrote to the man from the embassy and told him. I understand that he copied my memo to the prisoner who was, of course, in the United States. That was last Saturday."

"Perhaps you'd bring us up to date?" said the Judge.

"Yesterday morning the prisoner presented himself at Bournemouth police station and demanded that the police drop any charges against his daughter because she had since denied to him that she had made the confession and furthermore he demanded that the police should lean-on the lawyer acting for the licensee of the Tolbrite Arms who had written to the daughter pointing out that her accusations were defamatory."

"I see," said the Judge.

"I understand that the prisoner then went to the solicitor and demanded that he withdraw the letter. He then went to the Tolbrite Arms, talked privately with his daughter and then came down into the bar and made a scene, shouting and accusing the hotel staff of theft. He refused to leave when the landlord requested him to and when he found out who I was, he immediately struck me twice in the face. I then arrested him."

"That was very courageous of you sergeant. How fortunate that you were present."

"I wasn't there by chance, Sir. After the prisoner's behaviour at the police station and his statements that he was going to sort people out, my superiors thought it prudent that there should be a police presence at the Tolbrite Arms to prevent the prisoner coming to harm."

"You were there to protect him?" asked a surprised Judge.

"Yes, Sir, we feared that the prisoner's wild accusations of the hotel staff might provoke a physical reaction from the male members." She was tempted to say one of whom is an former Royal Marine Commando, but didn't.

"I see," said the Judge, "very commendable. And instead of defending the prisoner, he attacked you?"

"Yes Sir, I had no alternative to taking him into custody."

"All lies," said the voice from the dock.

"There is a complete recording of what was said and one of the American undergraduates filmed it," said Clare.

"Did the prisoner know that it was being recorded?"

"Yes, Sir a reporter from the radio station had attempted to interview him and had told him that she would record what he said."

"Is that reporter present in court?"

"Yes Sir."

"Will the reporter please stand up," said the Judge.

Paula stood up.

"Please come down," said the Judge.

Paula took Clare's place in the witness box.

"Recordings appear to have played a considerable part in this affair. You are the person who recorded the tape that was broadcast yesterday evening?"

"Yes, Sir."

"And do you agree the account of yesterday' events that the sergeant has given the court."

"Yes, except for one thing," said Paula.

"And what is that?" asked the Judge.

"In her evidence she has been too kind to the prisoner. He behaved in a thoroughly obnoxious way, shouting, threatening and abusing the hotel staff, the professor and the undergraduates and then the sergeant the moment that he found out who she was. All of it was based on his daughter's persistent lying."

"The prisoner was aware that you were recording proceedings?"

"I had told him and my recording equipment was on the table in full view."

"Thank you, you may step down."

"All lies," said the prisoner, "What about my side of the story?"

"Very well Mr Eynon do you wish to enter the witness box or will you give your evidence from the dock?"

His lawyer stood up to confer and was waved away.

"All I want is for you to recognise that you're wasting your and my time," shouted Eynon. "I claim diplomatic immunity. That's why he's here," pointing at Charles.

The Judge looked at Charles and Charles kept his eyes down. The Judge was no fool.

"This is a serious case. It would appear that you weren't here on government business."

"What difference would that make, you should be glad that I only slapped that policewoman, I felt like killing her and if I had you still couldn't touch me because I'm a diplomat."

The Judge was torn between an enjoyment of hearing this objectionable prisoner dig his own grave and concern that, in the absence of measured legal advice, he would go too far. He said,

"I do earnestly counsel you to be careful in what you say. I really think that the best thing that the court can do is to remand you in custody for a further twenty-four hours in order that you may reflect on the legal advice that is offered and the unseemliness of your behaviour. Meanwhile the court asks that the US authorities urgently consider whether they wish to propose that the diplomatic immunity understanding between our nations shall apply in the present case."

"I won't have that, I demand to be allowed to leave this court today. You have no jurisdiction over me; I'm a US citizen and a diplomat. You, down there," pointing at Charles, "if you want to keep your job, shift your butt and get me out of here, now."

The Judge looked at Charles and asked

"Is there anything that you wish to say?"

Charles thought this is it. He rose and said,

"I discussed this with my ambassador before coming here, your Honour. We recognise that striking a police officer is a serious crime and cannot be justified even under extreme provocation. The fact that the extreme provocation is the outcome of a web of untruths generated by the prisoner's daughter complicates the matter but doesn't excuse it. We, too, are uncertain of the line to take and are seeking other advice. In these circumstances we must accept the interim decision of the host nation."

"You accept the courts decision."

"I don't think that we have any alternative," said Charles.

"Very well then, take the prisoner down,"

Eynon was still shouting threats against Charles as he was led away.

When he got back to London, Charles found that State Department protocol, who had heard the broadcast, had replied that the London embassy should let him sweat for a day or two and then play the diplomatic immunity card. Charles also got the impression that it had been a touch and go decision and that Mr Assistant Secretary Eynon was destined to become plain Mr Eynon in the not too distant future.

That night, when it was not possible for anyone to take action that day, the US embassy in London indicated to the British Foreign and Commonwealth Office that the US government wished to invoke the diplomatic immunity agreement in the case of Mr Marvin Eynon, currently being tried in the Dorset courts.

The following morning Mr Assistant Secretary Marvin Eynon was brought up into the dock at Bournemouth Magistrates Court for the second time. Charles was in court and listened while the formalities to release the prisoner for diplomatic reasons were gone through. It was plain to Charles that the impartial Judge didn't think much of it and would rather have sent the prisoner to jail.

Marvin Eynon couldn't accept his good fortune with good grace.

"I protest at having been kept in a British jail for two nights. I told your stupid police that I had diplomatic immunity and I told you the same the next day. I'll sue you for wrongful detention, that's what I'll do."

"Be quiet, Mr Eynon," said the Judge, turning his eyes on Charles who was sitting, embarrassed in the well of the court. "Could the representative of the US government who is present in court please point out to his compatriot that the agreement not to enforce the law only applies to the offence for which it was granted and doesn't give the prisoner the blanket right to offend on other issues. If there is another outburst like that I'll commit Mr Eynon for contempt."

Charles stood up, nodded his head to the Judge and turned and addressed Eynon.

"Mr Eynon, The police and this court are decent people doing their jobs and do not deserve the abuse you have sought to put on them. You hold the office of Assistant Secretary of State in the US Administration. Because you hold that office the British legal authorities have agreed to release you, provided that you leave the country forthwith. I have a car outside to take you to the airport and to the reception that awaits you in Washington, DC. You can shout and rave as much as you like in the car, I can't stop you but until that happens, SHUT UP."

Eynon was momentarily startled and in that time the Judge uttered the formal words of discharge and told the police to take the prisoner down. Normally a discharged prisoner walks free in the court-room but the Judge wasn't going to risk that with Eynon. He could be heard, still protesting, although he was no longer visible.

Charles bowed to the Judge who smiled sympathetically, had a quick word with Clare and Paula and went and collected the ex-prisoner and practically arm-locked him into the car.

For the journey to Heathrow Charles sat in front with the driver with the glass partition up and Eynon ranted and raved in the back. Charles gathered that he wanted to go back and collect his daughter but ignored the demand.

Two US marines had brought Eynon's bags from the ambassador's residence and took over the job of seeing that he actually left on the plane.

At the State Department morning press conference, it was announced that the President had accepted Assistant Secretary of State Marvin Eynon's resignation, effective forthwith. Among the questioners was one who asked who had paid his air-fare for what was clearly a personal visit to the United Kingdom?

The Yale students held a farewell party on Friday night and left for Heathrow in their mini-bus early the following morning to get an early afternoon flight home. With one exception they voted the visit a great success, they had learnt something about diptera and ephemeroptera and a whole lot more about each other. To cap is all, it seemed as if the professor had got a winner in his fly repellent spray. Professor Jose Smith had expressed his sorrow for the bother that Elfrida Eynon had caused and his gratitude for the helpful way in which the folk at the pub had dealt with a nasty situation.

Elfrida Eynon had sulked ever since her father had been arrested and simply tailed along behind the others, a forlorn and unhappy figure.

Mr and Mrs Smith arrived in the late afternoon with Peggy giggling to Mrs Trowbridge that she'd always wondered what it would be like to go away for a dirty weekend with a man as Mr and Mrs Smith, and now was her chance to find out. William pointed out that they should have called themselves the Jones's and Peggy protested that wouldn't be the same. Thus the Chancellor of the Exchequer and his wife – and their detective – arrived at the Tolbrite Arms. They were shown into the big back bedroom and Peggy said,

"Oh how lovely. Just as I'd hoped that it would be."

They told their policeman to get lost and went for a walk through the village before dinner, along past the Cosy Tea Room then back, past the small village green with its duck pond, past the estate maintenance depot opposite to the pub, then on, past a house with a shop front that was now curtained, to the church. Beyond the church was the Manor House set in its park. Helene had told Peggy that they were welcome to go into the park, they wouldn't encounter curious citizens there, but they decided to leave that for another day. William remarked on how well kept it all was.

When they were finishing dinner, Helene and Timmy slipped in and said hello and that the rest of their friends were already in the bar. They came into the bar and were introduced to Fred, Angela, Paula, with young Will with Gloria beaming behind the bar. Peggy recited their names and said that they must call her Peggy and William; William, to distinguish him from young Will.

Helene said that they only needed Jackie and Clare to walk in and they'd have a full team, if you included Mr and Mrs Trowbridge. Peggy reminded William that Jackie was the army policewoman who had caught the murderer of his brother Andrew's fiancée, Wendy.

"Oh," said William, "the red haired girl."

"She came here while she was investigating Porton Down," said Gloria.

"And when she was catching the spies at that place at Portland," said young Will.

This led to speculation about Jackie's present task at which Peggy admitted that she and William had been present at the reception and about which she, herself, had provided a lead to a mysterious Hungarian girl who had known the murdered man in the past.

Gloria gave a graphic account of the trials and tribulations of the Yale students and themselves in the past two weeks, thanks to Elfrida Eynon and Helene mentioned the coverage that Timmy's US stations had given to the ex-Assistant Secretary of State story.

William and Peggy took it all in and drank the Bouchier red wine to which they'd already been introduced at dinner. No one talked about finance or taxes or politics and they enjoyed every minute of it.

They were surprised when Angela sat at the piano and played and they suddenly realised who she was. In all Mr and Mrs Smith had a very pleasant evening. So did their detective sitting quietly in the corner. He'd have a lot to tell his wife when he got home.

Chapter Twelve

CORPORAL Barry Preston scanned the passengers who were beginning to emerge from the Arrivals tunnel. The arrival of the flight from London had been announced twenty minutes earlier and the waiting had seemed longer that usual. He didn't have to meet visitors on a Monday very often, usually it was mid-week.

He liked driving out to the airport, either taking people to catch flights or coming from flights. Perhaps meeting flights was more interesting if he didn't know the person who was arriving. Take today, for example, he was here to meet a woman army police captain. Imagine that, a female captain red-cap. He'd bet that she'd look like a boxer. He'd never seen a woman red-cap captain before but he'd seen a lieutenant and that was bad enough, face like a cruiser-weight and fourteen stone.

He scanned the arrivals, no need to hold up the piece of cardboard on which he'd written FRAZER, he'd recognise her on shape alone. His eye lit upon a most gorgeous girl, she must be a film star or model, auburn hair and the figure of an angel. She was studying the ranks of those waiting. Barry wondered if she was looking for one of those greasy long haired characters in a black open-necked shirt with a gold chain round their neck, who seemed to be photographed with all the nicest girls these days. He switched his gaze back to the opening through which one or two latecomers were still trickling.

Five minutes later the crowd had thinned and no she-dragon had emerged. The girl with the deep auburn hair was at the exit looking along the approach road. If this was Hollywood, thought Barry, a long white stretched limo would draw up. The vision turned away from the entrance and came back into the arrivals hall.

He became aware that she had green eyes, green eyes that were fastened on the piece of cardboard that hung limply in his hand, the card that he hadn't bothered to display, the card with FRAZER on it. The vision said, in what he called a Sandhurst voice,

"Are you here to meet Captain Fraser?"

"Yes," said Barry and added "Maam."

"Then why the devil didn't you hold up the card, I've been waiting a good fifteen minutes, wondering if the embassy had fouled up. What's your name?"

"Corporal Barry Preston, Maam."

"Where's your tansport?"

"In the car park, Maam, if you'll wait here I'll fetch it."

"Is it far away?"

"About a quarter of a mile, I'd guess."

"Then I'll come with you, after the flight I can do with stretching my legs."

And very nice too, thought Barry, I wonder what she looks like in uniform?

They walked to the car park in silence with Barry carrying her case. He led the way to a black Rover 75.

He installed her in the car, she chose the front passenger seat, and paid the parking fee, speaking to the attendant in fluent Hungarian.

"Have you been out here long, Corporal?"

"Nearly six months, Maam."

"Look, Corporal, stop this Maaming, it makes me feel old. My sergeants call me Cap and if you don't like that, call me Miss."

"Very good Miss. That's why I missed you at the airport, you don't look like a Maam, begging your pardon Miss."

"A lot of people have made that mistake, Corporal, forget it. Tell me, how did you learn the language so quickly?"

"I've spoken it all my life, German too as well as English, you see my mother's Hungarian, well, she was until she married dad."

"That's remarkable, how old are you Corporal?"

"Twenty five Miss and in case your wondering, Mum was twenty two and a BAOR sergeant's wife when I was born."

"My interest is when she came over, she came to the West the hard way?"

"Yes a group of them set out to go over the mountains into Austria, only two made it, the others were caught by the Russians."

"She's sure that they were Russians?"

"Oh yes, she speaks Russian as well as German, Hungarian and English."

"You come from a very gifted family, Corporal, what brought you into the army?"

"I was born into a soldier's family, tried civilian life and thought that I wouldn't mind a three year spell in the forces."

"It was very much the same with me. How much longer have you got to do?"

"Just under eighteen months, Miss."

"I would think that there will be some good job opportunities waiting for you if you play your cards right. How do you find life in Budapest?"

"Very enjoyable Miss." He lowered his voice and said, "we're not very busy at the present time."

."So I understand, Corporal. My advice is to keep your head down; in my father's time, a man like you who can speak several languages was just the chap to be sent to fill sandbags in Iraq. Changing the subject, Corporal, when was your office last swept for security?"

"Last week, Miss. The Colonel's from REME and is an electronics whiz, so we're up to date."

"That's good," said Jackie, while a little corner of her mind thought shame.

He drove her to a modest hotel not too far from the British embassy, and said that he'd be back at two to take her to meet the Defence Attache.

The latter greeted her with the same surprise as had been evident on the corporal's face at the airport. Lieutenant Colonel Giles Cox had been in post for just over two years, he'd a reasonable understanding of Magyar and got on well with the Hungarians. He hadn't lost any classified documents, his office was swept regularly and he couldn't understand why the MoD should want to make a special check on his security.

Jackie explained that she was from the DMS's Special Investigation Unit and that her visit had nothing to do with office security, that was a cover story. She was looking for a youngish Hungarian woman called, she thought, Sonia Berolinka, who appeared to have been the last person to see the prime minister's foreign policy adviser in Number 10 before he was murdered.

"That's a bit of a tall order, there might be hundreds of them," said the colonel.

"Oh, we know a lot more about her than that, in the past five years she has served at UN headquarters in New York and we think that as a child she lived in Kisvarda and Miskolc. That's where I plan to start. Oh and she got her degree at Pecs University."

"That's unusual," said Cox ,"in Hungary people tend to go to the local university. If you find her will you be applying to extradite her?"

"No, the only evidence that we have is that under a false name she came with the Hungarian delegation to a reception that the prime minister hosted and that she was seen leaving the room with Stuart Harcourt. Later that night he was found to have been poisoned. It's a bit more complicated than that but that will do."

"How do you intend to go about it?"

"I'll go to the places I mentioned and ask questions. I'd like Corporal Preston to act as my interpreter if you can spare him for a few days. I could perhaps get by in Western Hungary where people are familiar with German but not in the east where they have Russian as their second language."

"He can drive you in our car," said Cox. "You'll find that Hungary isn't a large country, it's barely bigger than Ireland, and if you wanted to you should be able to do each of the places that you mentioned by day trips and avoid all the trouble of finding hotels. When do you plan to go?"

"First thing tomorrow and to avoid wasting too much time travelling, I'll find a hotel in one or other of the places for the night."

"You could find people a bit preoccupied at the beginning of the week."

"That's a risk that I'll have to accept, they should have got over their weekend by then," said Jackie.

The Colonel thought her mad but said, "What will you do now?"

"Go sightseeing and get some sleep ready for an early start."

"Perhaps you'd have dinner with us when you get back."

"That would be nice," said Jackie.

Budapest was all that she'd expected. She hadn't realised that Buda and Pest had stayed as two separate towns on opposite banks of the Danube until 1873 and that there was actually a third town, OBuda in the coming together. A catalyst in their amalgamation had been the completion of the Chain Bridge in 1849. She gazed up at the archangel Gabriel dominating Heroes Square and learnt that it wasn't named for the fighters of the resistance but for the conquering Magyars over a thousand years earlier. The more recent war was remembered by Liberty Square where there was a Soviet memorial to commemorate the city's liberation in April 1945. Of more lasting glory were Matyas Church in Buda in which the Hapsburg emperors had been crowned Kings of Hungary and the larger St Stephen's Basilica which dominates Pest and is of more recent origin, having been built in the second half of the nineteenth century and survived the collapse of it's dome in a storm half way through.

She learnt that two thirds of the buildings had been damaged by Nazi or Soviet bombing and thought it a remarkable demonstration of a people's sense of values that the old buildings had been so carefully and lovingly restored for future generations to enjoy.

Early the following morning she and the corporal were off on the four hour drive to Kisvarda on the border with the Ukraine. Their route took them along the northern edge of the Puszta, the vast central plain that resembles the Russian steppes to the east. They were in Kisvarda by lunchtime. En route, the Corporal had asked the captain how she intended to proceed?

"We're going to the public library to consult all of the local directories, then we'll go to the local paper and ask to go through their back numbers from 1980 onwards. I only hope that they've got them computerised with a rapid search function."

"You mean we put in a name and read the references."

"Yes, Corporal, you do. I can't speak the language."

"I wonder if there's a Russian language paper, or rather, if there was a Russian language paper in the early 1980's?" said the Corporal.

"We'll see, won't we?" said Jackie. "The important thing is that we look. I'll explain why one day."

They found the library, parked and went in. The corporal asked to see the old local directories and was told that it would take too long to bring them up from the storeroom to do it, they'd have to get a written authority from the mayor's office. Nothing daunted, Jackie had Barry ask for directions to the local newspaper offices.

Here they were more fortunate, the sub-editor on duty had worked in Birmingham and the records were computerised. They spent an hour wading through back numbers and found no reference to the name Berolinka. Jackie asked if they could see the copies from 1970 onwards and in 1973 and 1975 they found the short announcements of the birth of two girls, Nadia and Sonia to the Berolinka family. They thanked the man and left.

"Where to now, Cap?"

"Miskolc, of course," said Jackie.

Two hours later they were in Miskolc. On the way Jackie had learned from the guide book that the town was the chief town of the

Borsod industrial region extending northwards as far as Kazincbarcika and beyond and which was second only to Budapest in industrial production. She noted in passing that the town-name was the result of joining together two villages, Kazinc and Barcika. She had a mental image of two sets of village elders in solemn conclave unable to agree on a name for the new place and finally calling it both, as presumably had the citizens of Buda and Pest in 1873.

It was late afternoon and they checked into a hotel.

The following morning, Tuesday, they did the same as they had done in Kisvarda and found no reference to Berolinka.

Jackie professed herself well satisfied with the results of the visits and a puzzled Corporal Barry Preston drove them back to Budapest. She asked to be picked up early the next day to go to Pecs.

She phoned one of the numbers that Charles Smith the news-man had provided and was pleased that a woman replied. Jackie asked if she spoke English and the woman instantly switched to it. Jackie explained who she was and how she had the woman's number and the woman asked how she could be of assistance. Jackie said that she wanted to know how to get access to the records of past students at Pecs University. The woman said that she didn't know anyone there and Jackie should ask the registrar. Jackie thanked her and rang off thinking that was a wasted call. She knew that she didn't need to go there but it was part of her plan.

The first part of their journey to Pecs was on one of the busiest roads in Hungary, the road to the resort area around Lake Balaton, then swung to the south to Pecs. As they neared the city Jackie thought that the countryside took on a mediterranean look. She studied the guide book en route and learned that near to Lake Balaton and now behind them, was a thermal lake called Heviz where people came for the cure. In fact Hungary is well endowed with thermal springs and many of the hotels have thermal baths for their guests. She also read that Pecs is the second or third largest provincial city and the centre of the growing industrial and agricultural region in the south.

The journey took 3 hours and by mid-morning they were laboriously working their way through university officials, explaining that they simply wanted to know if a Sonia Berolinka had graduated from the university approximately eight or ten years ago. The officials were clearly puzzled why someone from England wanted to know, but could see no harm in admitting that Sonia Berolinka had graduated with honours in modern languages in 1997. Jackie thanked them and told the corporal to drive back to Budapest.

Corporal Barry Preston was puzzled. The initial impression of the Captain that he'd gathered was that she was clever as well as good looking but she'd spent the past three days driving across Hungary making what seemed to him to be the most basic of enquiries, things that he could have done if she'd sent a request to the Defence Attache. A letter would have been a lot cheaper than her air fare and hotels. He knew that his chief was puzzled as well.

As they reached Budapest he asked,

"What next, Miss?"

"We wait, Corporal."

"Wait for what, Miss"

"You'll see or else I've been wasting your time and mine for the last three days."

She had dinner with the Colonel and his wife that evening. She said much the same to them, that she must now wait and see.

They came for her at breakfast-time the following morning. As she finished her second cup of coffee a young man in an immaculate uniform came into the dining room and to her table. She could see two other uniformed figures in the foyer. He as good as clicked his heels and said, in English,

"Captain Fraser, I would be most honoured to escort you to see my Colonel."

Jackie smiled sweetly at him. She was registered at the hotel as Miss Fraser and her passport gave her occupation as 'Government Service' so it appeared that somebody else had been doing their homework. She said,

"I'd be most happy to, Captain."

"I have a car waiting outside, do you wish to get a coat."

"Perhaps that would be sensible," said Jackie as she stood up.

She was driven to one of the elegant buildings that surround Liberty Square with the two soldiers in front and the captain beside her in the back, pointing out sights of interest. She agreed that Budapest is a beautiful city, two beautiful cities in fact. This observation evidently pleased him and he told her the story of the Chain Bridge.

They were whisked up in a lift and she was taken to a room with breathtaking views across the square and the city. The officer sitting at a big desk got up, smiled at her, came round the desk and shook her hand, saying,

"Good morning Captain Fraser, Captain Jackie Fraser, I hope that you didn't mind me interrupting your morning, let's sit over here."

He led the way to chairs closer to the picture windows and seeing her glance said,

"It never ceases to impress me, there is always something new to notice, I could look out all day, in fact," he smiled, "my staff think that I do."

Jackie sat, crossed her legs and smoothed her skirt. He went on

"I am Colonel Franz Matyev and one of my duties is to notice people's comings and goings."

"And you have noticed mine?" smiled Jackie.

"Oh yes, Captain, in many ways you are rather special and no-one could fail to notice you." He smiled at her and added, "We saw you on the television."

She smiled back and said,

"When a girl's just been shot at and nearly stabbed beside a load of explosives, Colonel, modesty is the last of her worries."

"It was what you English call a good show my dear." Then he smiled, realising that he had made a double entendre. "Now to business, why have you been criss-crossing our country drawing attention to yourself?"

"So that you'd notice me and ask me in for a chat, Colonel."

"But why go to all that trouble, all you had to do was ask?"

"How long would it have taken to reach you if I had gone into the police headquarters or the Army headquarters and asked to see the head of Hungary's intelligence service?" asked Jackie.

"I see what you mean." He smiled at her, "Your way was quicker, now what was it that you wanted to see me about?"

"You know already, Colonel, Sonia Berolinka."

"Ah, the young woman who you were asking about in Kisvarda, Miskolc and Pesc, what's she supposed to have done?"

"I've been asked by our prime minister to investigate the death of one of his advisers which took place on the night that a delegation from your country visited Number 10 Downing Street. Sonia

Berolinka was a member of that delegation, no let me put it another way, Sonia Berolinka accompanied that delegation and was the last person to see Sir Stuart Harcourt alive."

"Except, perhaps the murderer" said the Colonel.

She smiled at him and said,

"I will be absolutely honest with you and admit that we don't have any evidence against Sonia Berolinka except the fact that she was seen to leave the reception with the man who was murdered. No jury would convict her on that alone."

"Then why the pursuit?"

"Because I'm sure that she did it. I don't want her arrested or extradited, what I want to know is why?"

"Why, what?" said the Colonel.

"Why was Stuart Harcourt executed?" said Jackie.

"That's why you came to Hungary and laid your trail to get to me?"

"Yes, Colonel, I knew that it must have been something serious."

"Oh yes it was and your people did nothing about him. It goes back a long way."

Chapter Thirteen

THE first days of their holiday had been all that Peggy could have wished; the sun shone, there was only just enough wind to blow the stuffiness away and they spent their time wandering along, or lying contentedly on, the river bank. They didn't see a soul except at meal times or in the bar in the evening.

Peggy watched William relax and the cares drop away. Already, in her eyes, he was beginning to look like the young man who she'd married. She had put her shapely foot down and absolutely refused to let his office send him red boxes. Their plea that the Chancellor would return to a mountain of paper merely elicited the response that she'd help him burn it. Let someone else deal with it for two weeks. The prime minister was in Tuscany and William was in Tolbrite.

On Thursday morning they went into the park, along the south river bank and crossed to the other side by the hay-wagon bridge, past the bathing hole with it's sand beach that a long gone Hawkridge had created for his children. This brought them close to the Manor House and it's stables but they didn't see a soul. Once across, they wandered along the far bank with the Long Wood paralleling them on the other side of the water meadow.

On the Tuesday they had continued on the southern bank of the river and found their way blocked by the massive fence extending to the river bank that, together with big gates on the two drives, Timmy had had erected after his daughter had been kidnapped. On the other side of the river there was no obstruction and they could wander further upstream. They'd come this way yesterday and Peggy knew just where she intended that they should sit and eat the packed lunch that Mrs Trowbridge had provided.

They passed the end of the fence on the other bank and William pointed out to Peggy that despite the fence and the gates on the drives, intruders could still get into the park by way of the old hay-wagon bridge or by boat. She said that they'd probably thought of that themselves. And so they proceeded, chatting about inconsequential things, simply content with each other's company.

They wandered a good way further. They only saw one person and he wasn't fishing and didn't look like a farmer. He was hurrying towards a car which he proceeded to back along a farm track. Seeing another human reminded Peggy that if they went much further they'd reach a village so she looked at her watch and found that it was some time beyond their usual lunchtime and so they turned and slowly made their way back to Peggy's chosen spot.

They had heard all about the students from Yale and their experimentation with fly repellents and William wished that they had some with them today. Peggy was of the opinion that her toilet water attracted them and longed for some good old fashioned carbolic soap to see what the midges made of that, they hadn't been bothered much by midges when they were children in Barrow in Furness. William reckoned that was because the cold wind from the Irish Sea kept them flying. And so they contentedly made their way to the bend in the river that Peggy had chosen.

They put down their rugs and spread out their belongings and enjoyed their lunch. Afterwards Peggy lay flat on her back with her eyes closed, basking in the warm sunlight with William keeping the upper part of his body raised for conversational purposes by propping up on one elbow, while idly chewing the end of a piece of rye grass, then lying down, then up again on his elbow when another thought occurred to him to share with his wife. Much later, he said,

"There's something in the river, Peg."

Peggy said dreamily, "Yes, you idiot, water."

William was struggling up, "No. I mean it, it looks like, Oh My God, its a girl."

Peggy was up beside him as they ran closer to the river and saw that it was, indeed, a girl who was caught in the roots or branches of a riverside tree. Her dress had gathered somewhere above her waist and she was wearing the briefest of undies and was undoubtedly beyond help in this world

William wasn't stupid, he'd seen pictures of people who had plunged fully clad into the ocean to rescue people and he'd always wondered how they got home in their wet and probably shrinking clothes, so he took off his shoes and socks and trousers and waded into the shallows, clad in his underpants. Peggy looked at the cows in the water meadow and remarked inconsequentially that it was a good job that he hadn't worn his red ones.

Together they laid the girl's body on the river bank and pulled her dress down. While William dried himself as best he could and dressed, Peggy took stock. The girl was about her height with an excellent figure, attractive with a mass of blonde hair. She guessed between twenty- two and twenty-seven and she wasn't wearing any jewellery.

"We'd better call the police," said William. Peggy did so.

"And we'd better warn the people in the big house, otherwise the first that they'll know of it is a stream of police cars and an ambulance coming up their drive."

"I'll walk back and tell them," said Peggy, "while you mind the body. I wonder who she is, that's an expensive dress that she's wearing and those sort of underclothes don't come cheap."

"OK lover you go and warn them but don't be long."

"I'll phone the pub as well," said Peggy walking away.

Walking as fast as the meadow would allow, it took less than ten minutes to reach the house and ring the bell. The door was opened by the Sergeant who's wife had seen Peggy hurrying across the bridge on the CCTV screen in the kitchen.

"I'm sorry to bother you," said Peggy, "but my husband and I have just found a girl's body floating in the river."

The Tolbrite grape-vine had done its stuff and the sergeant knew with whom he was speaking

"Have you told the police, Madam?"

"Yes, I phoned them," said Peggy, holding up her phone.

"It will take them half an hour to get here, would you care to come in and wait?"

"Oh, no thank you, my husband's with the body and I should go back"

"I'll ring the estate manager, I'm sure that he'll come."

"Young Will," said Peggy, "what a good idea."

She thanked the Sergeant and went back across the bridge to where William was waiting and trying not to look at the girl's body.

About ten minutes later a 4 x 4 drove up and young Will and a more than middle-aged lady got out. Will greeted them and introduced Lady Margaret Hawkridge, who said,

"What an awful thing to happen, poor girl, what on earth was she doing in the river, it's hardly deep enough to drown. You mustn't let it spoil your holiday."

"We won't," said William.

Margaret looked at the dead girl and said, "That dress probably cost as much as I'd pay for a complete wardrobe."

William said, "That's difficult to believe, there's practically nothing to it."

"That's why it costs so much, lover," said Peggy, "her undies are good, too."

"If you two would like to go on your way," said young Will, "I'll stay and mind the er, I'll stay here. I'm sure that the police would take your statements later."

William and Peggy looked at each other and both said that they'd prefer to get it over with.

Some minutes later an ambulance arrived, bumping across the meadow, closely followed by a police car. Clare Thornton got out and was introduced to William and Peggy. She took out her pocket recorder and invited them to tell how they had found the body.

William described their walk along the river bank almost to the next village and coming back to their chosen picnic spot, setting out their rugs, having lunch and so on and then spotting something caught by the branches or roots in the river. He had waded into the river and with his wife's help they had placed the girl's body where it was now. The girl had shown no sign of life.

The paramedic said that, off-hand, he'd say that the girl had been in the water for more than an hour but not as long as a day.

William wondered if he meant a day, as distinct from a night, or twenty-four hours, but kept quiet and edged into the background. The paramedic had that 'haven't I seen you somewhere before?' look on his face.

Clare said, "There's not much point in estimating how far the body has drifted because we don't know how long it was caught-up in the tree. We'll have to look higher up the river to see if there is any evidence to show where she entered it. Her shoes and bag must be somewhere. If she doesn't live there, we'll look for a car. Did you happen to see a parked car?"

"No," said William, "the only person we saw was a chap walking back to a car that he proceeded to back along a farm track. Seeing him reminded us of the time and we turned back to come here," he gestured to their rugs, "for a very late lunch."

"Could you describe the man, Sir or you, Madam?"

127

Peggy gave her a lopsided grin. "I come away with my husband and we call ourselves Mr and Mrs Smith and now I'm a Madam." Then she became serious, "we weren't closer to him than the length of a football pitch but he didn't look country, he had a dark blue suit and lighter blue shirt."

"His car was light green," said William. "Looked like a Mondeo saloon or estate from the distance."

The paramedics were allowed to take the body away and young Will and Margaret departed after inviting William and Peggy to lunch the next day. Clare thanked them for their help and followed.

The charm had gone from their chosen picnic spot so they walked back to the pub and got their car and went and parked on the heath overlooking the channel.   They spent a pleasant time in Swanage although William had a little difficulty in navigation wearing the dark glasses that Peggy bought for him.

When Clare met her fiancée, the pathologist Simon Watts, that evening, he said,

"I've got news for you, darling, the Jane Doe in the cocktail dress didn't die from drowning, there was no water in her lungs."

"That complicates things, doesn't it?" said Clare. "How did she die?"

"I don't know at this precise moment, I'll know better when I complete the examination tomorrow. Have you any idea who she is?"

"Not the faintest," said Clare. "All we have is her body, her clothes and where she was found. We'll have to publish her picture, do your best to make her face look alive in the photographs Simon dear, please."

The next day Clare collected the clothes (and a quick kiss from Simon) at the mortuary and took them to the one place which might be able to help her in Bournemouth, Jane's Boutique. Jane was now past her mid-thirties and still slender and attractive which helped in the sale of the expensive lingerie that was the boutique's speciality. Jane lived in a house further along the Winterborne road than the Manor House and had featured in the first case in which Timmy and Helene had been forced to do their own detecting. At the time she was the exotic dancer at the Half Moon Club, it's stripper, in fact, and married to an out and out rotter . The husband had been killed and some years later, Jane had given up baring her all at the club and put her savings in the boutique. Clare-Marie kept her appraised of what rich Parisians were wearing and Helene and Margaret shopped there.

Clare laid the clothes separately on the desk – the best boutiques don't have counters – and said,

"Have you any idea who these belonged to, Jane?"

Jane picked the items up and examined them and the minute label sewn into the bottom.

"I stock them," she said fingering the pants and bra. "Haven't sold more than a dozen sets this season, nice finish and an excellent design. Where did you get them from?"

"Off a dead girl's body. I'm trying to find out who she is."

"I suppose that it could be one of mine, I stock the identical style and colours but that might not be sufficient to identify your girl."

"Why not?" said Clare.

"Because there is an increasing tendency nowadays for men buy them as presents for their girl friends. Men used to be shy about buying briefs and bras but they didn't mind buying bikinis. Funny, isn't it?"

"I suppose that it's because undies are, well, intimate, whereas a bikini is for all to see," said Clare.

"Could be."

"What about the dress?" asked Clare.

"She didn't get it from me. One of the London houses, I'd say."

"OK and thanks. I'll come back when I have a picture of the girl," said Clare, pulling a face.

"Sad, isn't it when there is so much to look forward to in life."

Clare departed with the clothes in her hand. After a few paces it occurred to her that people probably thought that she'd just bought them. On a Detective Sergeant's pay? That would be the day. Then it occurred to her that if she'd seen someone come out of a place like Jane's with an article that wasn't in a fancy paper bag, she would have thought that there was an even money chance that it was stolen. So she put them in her handbag.

Colonel Franz Matyev gazed abstractedly across the roofs and repeated,

"It was a long time ago."

Jackie sat quietly and waited for him to begin.

"The people of Britain don't appreciate how lucky they have been down the centuries to be separated from the rest of Europe by the North Sea and the Channel. The last invading army to cross it were the Normans, a thousand years ago. A century before that time Hungary was over-run by my ancestors, the Magyars, who gave us our language and the beginnings of nationhood."

"I've been to Heroes Square," said Jackie, quietly.

"But unlike the English, we suffered further invasions as various tribes manoeuvred for position and power in central Europe," went on the Colonel as if she hadn't spoken. "The Mongols came in 1241 but the worst invaders were the Turks who came three centuries later and laid siege to our cities and eventually ruled us for a long time. Then there were the Hapsburgs who spread the Austro-Hungarian empire into the Balkans and were finally deposed after the first world war."

He turned to Jackie and said,

"I hope that I'm not boring you?"

"Oh no," said Jackie, sincerely, "it's fascinating."

"The years between the wars were not happy ones for we Magyars. There was the slow rebuilding of what was left of the country and when that showed some small prospect of stability there came the rise of Hitler in the West, Stalin in the East and Mussolini in the South, all bent on expanding their power, influence and territory."

"Which or who posed the greatest threat?" asked Jackie when he paused.

"In the short term, undoubtedly Adolf Hitler, although I think that Stalin was a much more evil man. In quite a short time, in historical terms, Hungary had a frontier with Germany in the West when his storm-troopers marched into Austria and then in the North when they took over Czechoslovakia and the Fuhrer was screaming about lebensraum and the German speaking minorities in Hungary and Transylvania."

He gazed out of the window and went on,

"The Germans occupied Hungary in the second war and used us as a base for operations in Southern Russia. All was fine to start with as their army rolled back the poorly equipped Soviet divisions. But the Soviets hung on, land that was conquered spawned guerrilla bands who attacked the German lines of communication and winter set in. Soon our hospitals were filled with frostbitten and wounded German soldiers who dreaded being sent back into that dangerous and inhospitable land."

Jackie was beginning to wonder when he'd reach the bit that she wanted but daren't interrupt him.

"As you know, by enduring incredible hardship and suffering, the Soviets held the line at Leningrad, Moscow and Stalingrad and forced the German armies to retreat. They retreated across Hungary putting up such resistance as they could. The Soviets declared Hungary liberated in April 1945. There had been a small resistance movement carrying out minor acts of sabotage on the Germans and this was largely communist and the Soviet occupiers saw that communists were entrusted to form the 'free' Hungarian government. Hungary became part of the Soviet sphere in 1949." He turned and looked directly at her and said,

"Which brings me to why you came here."

Jackie smiled at him and nodded.

"The Soviets dominated Hungarian politics from the end of the war until the late 1980's. No minister could survive unless he toed the Soviet line. Those who did things that the Soviets disapproved of were removed and in some cases, shot. The people rebelled in 1956 and the rebellion was put down with Soviet tanks. There were reprisals. The revolution put back most aspects of Hungary's recovery because more than 200,000 people escaped to the West and, of course, they were the thinkers, the graduates and the skilled workers. But the spirit of freedom burned on and we were the most western orientated of the Soviet satellites and, as far as we could manage it, our borders were the most porous."

He was pleased with this analogy in English and repeated it.

"The most porous and the Soviets, who had their own power struggle going on in the Kremlin weakened their control by the late 1980's. We really triggered the destruction of the Berlin Wall and the collapse of East Germany by allowing thousands of East German tourists to escape across our western border into Austria."

"About Stuart Harcourt," prompted Jackie.

"Ah, yes, Mr Sir Harcourt." He paused for thought. "I mentioned that we had people who worked against the Germans in the war, didn't

I? Well, there were people who worked against the Soviets in the post-war years, only this time they didn't blow up troop trains but supplied information to the Western powers. This meant, of course, that there were western agents to whom they gave the information. Mr Harcourt was such an agent and Peter Berolinka was one of his informants."

"He is Sonia's father?" asked Jackie.

"He was her father," corrected the Colonel. "Peter had a degree in chemistry and worked in a plant in Kisvarda. Something to do with organic chemistry. Married with two small daughters and a dislike of the Soviet system. Being born and raised practically on the border with the Ukraine, he spoke Russian fluently. We don't know how it started but he supplied tit-bits of information to the British. In 1981 he moved his family to Miskolc and went and worked at the chemical research centre at Kazincbarcika, one of a number of research establishments financed by, and working for, the Soviets. Much of the work there was concerned with organic compounds and was secret."

An aide brought in coffee. When they were once more settled, he resumed.

"Mr Harcourt relieved the controller in 1982 and left in 1985. Within weeks of his departure all the people who had provided him with information were arrested. Peter Berolinka was tortured before being shipped off to Siberia where he died two years later."

"You think that Harcourt was responsible?" prompted Jackie.

"We know for certain that he was responsible," said the Colonel. "Now I must remind you of some more recent history. Hungary provided a route to the west from 1989, the Berlin Wall came down in October 1989, we held our first free elections in 1990 and the USSR ceased to exist on 31st December 1991. The East German state disintegrated and is now part of the unified Germany. The East Germans were the Soviet's most willing collaborators and none more so than the state security and intelligence service, the Ministerium fur Staatsicherheit, known to one and all as the Stasi.. This was a truly formidable organisation, it makes mine look puny. At its peak it had 85,000 full time officers and an even greater number of informers and had files on a third of the population. After the wall came down their offices were stormed in a popular uprising by some of this 5 million and the files had to be speedily removed into western custody. But not all the files went that way."

He paused for effect and Jackie said, "What happened to the others?"

"A Stasi General arrived downstairs one day and said that he had the files relating to Stasi activities concerning Hungary. He brought samples. We negotiated with him and got the files, hundreds of them. The Stasi were no respecters of rank, there were files on our political, military and industry leaders, their family details, weaknesses, mistresses, intrigues, finances and swindles. It was all there. There were a group of files with a red band across the top with the word Geheim These were the most sensitive and I'm sure that the KGB didn't know of their existence. They contained the names of the Western agents working in Hungary that the Stasi had identified and also, believe it or not, those working for the Soviet."

"They had spotted Stuart Harcourt?" said Jackie.

"Oh yes, they had him marked down as your man in Hungary but he also appeared in the list of active Soviet agents, together with the name of his Soviet controllers in Budapest and in London."

Jackie recalled her talk with Roger Stevens a week or more ago when she had suggested that Stuart Harcourt must be a double agent. It seemed that she was right but why hadn't other people worked it out? She said,

"He might have been a deliberate plant by MI-6, giving false intelligence to the enemy."

"Come, come, Captain, you don't believe that, do you?"

"No Colonel, they'd have rumbled him in the first six months," admitted Jackie.

"That's a good word, rumbled, to find out, I must remember that."

"What did your predecessors do with the information about Harcourt?"

"They regarded it as extremely sensitive and so they wrote it up, attached extracts from the Stasi file and our man in the London embassy delivered it by hand to the head of the British counter-intelligence service."

"MI-5" said Jackie.

"Yes, that's it. He was called Roger Hollis, or a name like that. Of course I was a relatively junior officer at the time but I know that my chiefs expected an acknowledgement but nothing came. They then assumed that the British intended to deal with it in the quiet way and we were astounded when, many years later, Harcourt reappeared as your ambassador to Hungary. This was considered to be a big insult to our country."

"I'm sure that if anyone had heard what you have told me, he would have been put on trial," said Jackie.

"Then what about this Roger Hollis?" said the Colonel in rising tones, "didn't he tell anyone?"

"It appears not. He's dead now so we can't ask him, but the Americans suspected him of being a Soviet agent. Did you say anything to the CIA?"

"We may have dropped a hint that he wasn't to be trusted when your government sent him here as ambassador."

Which perhaps explains why the Americans were so keen to stir up the suspicions about the security or lack of it, in MI-5, thought Jackie. She looked the Colonel in the eye,

"Would it be possible for me to see your copy of the file that you gave to Roger Hollis, Colonel?"

He stood up and took a buff envelope from his desk, saying,

"This is a copy that you can take away, Captain. The British traitors in this unhappy affair are dead and Peter Berolinka has been avenged. Now, I expect that you have some more important things to do in our lovely city than talk to me. It has been a true pleasure to talk with you Captain and we much admire you." He gave a courtly little bow, "And your initiative in getting here."

"It is you, Colonel to whom we will be eternally grateful and as to my initiative, I did see a great deal of your lovely country."

They shook hands and an aide took her down to where a car was waiting to take her to the embassy.

She found that the Defence Attache and his staff had been concerned for her safety. When she hadn't appeared by ten o'clock Corporal Preston had gone round to the hotel to see if she was indisposed. He was told that the army had come as she was finishing her breakfast and taken her away. The receptionist had recognised one of the soldiers as belonging to the security service. He had been to the hotel checking up on an Albanian guest only last week.

Jackie explained that all that pointless dashing about the country on the first three days of the week had simply been to trigger the interest of the Hungarian security authorities. It had done so and she had spent a pleasant two hours with their chief, Colonel Franz Matyev, who had given her valuable information to take back to the Prime Minister. It would explain things that had puzzled those in authority. The principals in the story that she would pass on, were all dead.

"What about the girl Sonia Berolinka, will she be arrested and extradited?" asked Colonel Cox.

"No. I have given my word that we won't pursue a case against her and in any case we have no evidence that would stand up in court. I can't say any more except that she ensured that, at last, justice was done. I'd be grateful if you didn't mention any of this to other people in the embassy."

"That sensitive, eh" said Colonel Cox. "When it's all over, Jackie, come back and tell us all about it."

Chapter Fourteen

JACKIE returned to London that evening and next morning reported her findings to Major-General Lowe. He studied the Hungarian-Stasi file and said "Good God, the bastard, he deserved to die."

"And so did Hollis, Sir," said Jackie.

"It raises some important issues, doesn't it?" said the General "there will have to be a root and branch review of their recruitment and promotion procedures, we've relied for too long on the old-boy network and it doesn't work any more. We should move towards the American system where nominees for the highest positions are examined by a committee in public and if there is the slightest question mark over them, rejected. Have you arranged to take this to Number 10 yet?"

"No, General, I wanted to talk with you first."

"What's the problem?"

"Roger Stevens."

"How on earth can Roger be a problem?"

"He was in Budapest when Stuart Harcourt was our resident MI-6 man."

"So were a lot of other people."

"But Roger admitted to me that at the time he wondered where Harcourt got the money to support his lavish life-style in Budapest and concluded that he must be funded by MI-6. But he didn't think it through, that the Soviet's would think the same and would set out to compromise him. They didn't and that's why I told Roger ten days ago that Harcourt was a wrong 'un."

"How do you know that they didn't?"

"Well, according to Roger, he was openly wining and dining and probably bedding, every good looking girl in town and he didn't take drugs, so they wouldn't have much to go on, would they?"

"You underestimate the evil machinations of the KCB. Say that they faked photographs of him in bed with another male?" said the General.

"Nowadays nobody would take much notice, I suppose."

"But this wasn't nowadays, Jackie, it was 1984 when there were stricter codes of morality and how do you think that would have gone down in the Foreign Office?"

"He could have told them, they would know that it's a risk that all diplomats run and especially those who carry an MI-6 card," said Jackie.

"But he knew that somebody would put a question mark on his personnel file, a very small question mark but a question mark nevertheless and when an important appointment or promotion came up, it might sway the balance."

"So he betrayed his informers," said Jackie.

"We have the evidence of this Stasi file and the Hungarian Security Service that says so."

"So you agree that it's conclusive enough to give to the Prime Minister, Sir?"

"Oh yes," said the General, "but please explain why you're reluctant to give your report to Roger."

"It's just that I want to be sure that it doesn't get watered down before it reaches ministers. I know that in the end they won't make a public announcement that Hollis and Harcourt were both Soviet spies or otherwise rock the boat but I know that the PM would want to know the bare facts. For one thing I feel that I owe it to those people in Hungary."

"It's not like you to have doubts, my dear. You prepare your report quoting from the Stasi files and also attach the Stasi file, address it to the Prime Minister personally and give it to Roger. I'll think of ways of checking up and you might think of your ministerial friends."

"Security is nothing to do with them," said Jackie.

"Forget that I said it," said the General, puzzled at Jackie's indecisiveness. "On second thoughts, don't give it to Roger, give it to me. In any case I happen to know that Roger's away and the PM's away for another week or so, so there's no hurry and he'll have a mountain of stuff to get through when he gets back. I'll put on a covering note, pointing out that the implications of what you've unearthed are profound and asking for a personal meeting with him, to which you will come. If I get an off-putting reply, we'll know that someone is playing silly buggers and then we'll play a few other cards, like getting questions asked in the Lords."

One of the duties of Assistant to the Harbour Master, Angela Smart, at Poole, is to collect the harbour dues or mooring fees from those who sail into the harbour. If they forget, Angela would contrive to remind them in a not too demanding way. This morning she looked down her ledger and noted that the fees for the yacht Sea Raven were two weeks overdue. That would be the dark haired young man who had a blonde girl friend.   She looked for his name in the ledger, Raymond Farrell.   They made an attractive couple, him six feet, dark haired and bronzed and her five foot eight, blonde, slender and shapely. She came down to the Sea Raven most afternoons and they were obviously happy together, like Angela and Fred.

Angela looked out of the window and day dreamed. She'd been married for over two years and it still seemed only yesterday that Fred had climbed the steel stairway to her office to ask about the arrival of the charter cabin cruisers. Not to hire one but because they were suspected, it proved correctly, to be bringing in stolen antique French furniture. He had accompanied her to her usual lunch place, the Harbour Tavern, and had finished up in hospital from punches by one of the smugglers. After that she'd fallen in love with him.

The offices resembled a ship's bridge, those of the Master and his assistant were of the same size, end to end at first floor level and each accessed by a steel stairway and door at the ends. The front of the offices were of glass with a long chart table beneath and the windows at the back or town side, were high up behind the desk and filing cabinets.   The ship's bridge illusion was added too by referring to the storage spaces and toilets at ground level as the 'lower deck.'

It was no part of Angela's duties to note people's comings and goings but a girl couldn't help noticing and she realised that she hadn't seen either Raymond Farrell or the blonde girl for several days. On the other hand, earlier in the week, she had seen two men who didn't look as if they belonged there. But all sorts came and went in the charter boats.   The tide had just turned and she reasoned that anyone who planned to sail would have done so and those sailing in were more likely to come in with the tide –although lots did it the hard way – so she could go out in her dinghy.

This was what she enjoyed. Her father had been a sea captain, finishing up as skipper of a cross-channel ferry, and she had been messing about in boats ever since she could walk. She wheeled her boat out from beneath the offices and launched it from the slipway. She had a few calls to make and they took some time.   She finally pulled herself alongside the Sea Raven and said, "Ahoy, there," as she secured her boat.

There was no reply so she clambered over the gunwale into the cockpit and knocked on the door to the cabin. Still no reply. She then realised that the wood of the cabin door was damaged close to the lock as if a jemmy had been pushed in. She pushed the door and it opened. She called out again and went in. The cabin was as it should be, if a trifle untidy.

She turned to leave but something made her pause and turn back again and go through to the bunk space beyond. There was a wide bunk on either side of a narrow aisle and on one of the bunks lay the dark young man

"Oh I'm sorry," said Angela, turning to retreat, then she saw the small red stain on his shirt front and she knew that he was dead.

Angela didn't know whether she should dial 999 or 911 or the number of the local police station as the police ask citizens to do when it's not urgent. It wasn't urgent, the man was dead and his killers long gone. A few tens of minutes wouldn't make much difference. So she rang Clare Thornton, Clare would know what to do. She pressed out the number and after what seemed to be a long time Clare replied,

"Police here, Sergeant Thornton,"

"Clare, it's Angela, Angela Smart. I've just found a man's body in a yacht."

"Are you sure that he's dead?"

"Yes, he's got blood on his shirt."

"Where are you Angela?"

"I'm in the cockpit of his yacht. He hadn't paid his harbour dues so I rowed out to remind him."

"I'll come out and see. You stay there. No, I mean you row back to the slip and wait for me there, I'll probably be about twenty minutes."

Angela filled those twenty minutes by rowing to the shore, ringing Fred and telling the harbourmaster.

When Clare arrived, she rowed her out to the Sea Raven and waited in the open cockpit while Clare went inside. Clare came out and said,

"I'd guess that he's been dead for about two days. Did you touch anything Angela?"

"No." Then she thought for a bit and said, "I expect that I put my hands on the door frame, I always do in yachts and I also touched the outside of the cabin door, see, it's been forced by someone."

"Yes, I noticed that," said Clare. "The problem now, as I see it, is whether to do our police work out here at considerable difficulty or whether to move the yacht alongside the wall. Would it be difficult to do?"

"No," said Angela. "We could bring her alongside but what about looking for the murder weapon on the harbour bottom?"

"Well, presumably this mooring has a number?"

"Yes, it's painted on it, Number 23."

"OK then, I'll leave it to you to bring the yacht alongside the wall while I go and square things with my governor. How long will it take?"

"These things always take longer than you expect, let's say an hour and a half."

The scene of crime officers and an ambulance were there an hour later, just as Angela had secured the bow and stern mooring ropes to the harbour master's satisfaction, with sufficient slack to account for the rise and fall of the tide. Detective Inspector Wyatt and Clare arrived soon after and after a brief word of thanks to the harbourmaster and Angela, climbed down to the deck of the yacht.

Looking at it, Angela thought that it was a moot point whether it would have been better to do things on the level, as it were, and put up with the bother of rowing out and back to mooring buoy 23 or whether being alongside and free of the chore of rowing, but having to climb up near vertical ladders to gain the dockside would prove easier. One evident snag would be removing the body.

She got on with her work, the most immediate of which was to identify Raymond Farrell's next of kin and, as politely as possible, point out that the Sea Raven would have to be moved when the police had finished with it. Clare Thornton looked in and asked her to go over her story once more. She asked,

"What else can you tell me about Raymond Farrell?"

"Very little, I'm afraid. He was a fairly regular visitor, paid his bills and handled his craft well. He had a girl friend who spent most afternoons with him. I'm told that they both went off, separately, in the evenings."

"Do you know who the girl is? You said that you hadn't seen him for a few days. Did you see her?"

"No, but that doesn't mean that she didn't come, only that I didn't see her."

"Anything else?" asked Clare.

"No, except that I think that he worked nights."

"Why?"

"I don't know, I suppose because he was never about in the mornings and they went off separately in the evenings. If he'd been coming back she wouldn't have gone, would she?"

"Unless she worked as well. By her absence it's possible that she may have killed him, can you describe her?"

"Only in the most general terms," said Angela, "good looking, about five-seven or eight, slender, smartly dressed with long blonde hair and I'd say, a good few years less than thirty."

Clare thanked her and left.

When the time came for Angela to go home, the evidence of police activity had gone except for a single police constable looking lonely and bored, keeping guard at the top of the ladder.

Clare now had two bodies on her hands, Raymond Farrell and the unknown blonde girl who's description sounded very similar to Angela's description of the yacht girl. The forensic people had found four people's prints in the yacht. Two people's were on a number of things in everyday use, Angela's were on the bunk-space door-frame as she had said and stood out because they were recent and the fourth person's were on the saloon door frame and were fainter and incomplete.

She compared the prints taken from the boat with those taken as a matter of routine from the river girl. She'd leave it to the experts to confirm but she'd bet that the river girl was Raymond Farrell's girl friend. So in all probability she didn't have two separate murders but a double murder. She spared a thought for Inspector John Wyatt's square law, namely that if a murderer commits two murders, the chance of him being caught is four times greater than if he committed only one murder. She wondered if the law applied to simultaneous killings at the same place, which led her to wonder if the killings had taken place at the same place. If so, what was she doing in a river miles away, dressed for a cocktail party?

This made her think of transport. Did Farrell have a car and where was it now? Tomorrow she'd go back to the yacht and look through his personal effects and also ask Angela if she'd seen him in a car. If she found a driving license she would consult the DVLA people. She'd already asked them to check the ownership of the cars that her officers had found higher up the river following the discovery of the river girl's body. She was awaiting a reply but none of the cars had contained a girl's shoes and handbag.

Her phone rang, it was Simon.

"Hello darling, you're determined to keep me busy, aren't you? The latest one should certainly have died from the knife wound in the chest but I'll know more tomorrow. What I'm ringing about, apart from the pleasure of speaking with you, is to tell you that your river girl died from a blow to the head. It wouldn't necessarily have had to be an extra hard blow because she had a thin skull."

"Could it have been caused by a fall, Simon?"

"I don't think so. Of course, anything is possible, but deaths due to fractured skulls due to falls almost invariably are due to the victim falling on to the sharp corner of something. The river girl has a relatively long cranial depression, if she fell she must have fallen on to something cylindrical and hard, like a bath-rail."

"You're saying that she was struck by something cylindrical and hard like a club."

"Could be. There's one other thing and it might be important, she'd had intercourse in the hours before she died."

"Did you do a DNA test?"

"Yes, and that's why it might be important."

"How's that?"

"There were two different specimens."

"You mean that she'd had intercourse with two different men in the hours before she died?"

"Yes, dear, and I've got both DNA's. Now to something more pleasant, will I still see you tonight or does constabulary call?"

"I'll be there tonight my dear, thanks for your call."

She reflected on the change that Simon had wrought in her life. Before Simon she would have spent all the evening at the yacht or at her desk, going through the dead man's effects, now she'd do it tomorrow with the help of one of her detective constables. Which reminded her, where did Raymond Farrell live when he wasn't on board the Sea Raven? Was it possible that the Sea Raven was his permanent home? In the last resort his clothes might provide a clue, did he have an all the year wardrobe on board or just summer clothes?

She thought about living on a boat. It sounded rather romantic to live on a yacht and follow the sun. There must be a snag in it somewhere or everyone would be doing it. The objections started to line up in her mind. There would have to be mooring places within commuting distance of ones employment and those would soon fill up at big cities. The yacht would have to have a shower and a WC which said something about its size and the mooring places that would have to be connected to the public sewers and then there was schooling for the children. All in all, she could see why everybody wasn't in the living on their yacht business.

The following morning she let DC Tomlinson drive her to the harbour. She climbed the stairs and looked in on Angela who said,

"I've been ringing your number. It occurred to me last night that you'd be looking for his relatives, so I looked up what he wrote on his sailing manifest when he last sailed away from Poole. Here it is."

She held out a sheet of paper . Against the printed words, Next of Kin was written Mrs Barbara Nash, Holly Tree Farm, Alveston, South Glos.

"Thanks, that's a great help, something to work on at last."

Clare walked down the stairs debating her best course of action. This wouldn't be simply a case of informing a grieving relative, she needed to find out all she could from the grieving relative. Making a telephone call or asking the Gloucestershire force to do it for her wouldn't suffice; she had to do it herself. That decided, she went down into the yacht, told DC Tomlinson about Angela's find, told him to carry on searching and that she was off to this place called Alveston.

She was in Alveston half an hour after noon. Knowing how she herself hated people calling on her at meal times she had a coffee and a sandwich and found Holly Tree Farm at the end of a rutted track, an hour later.

Mrs Barbara Nash was a slightly older version of the murdered man with dark hair, skin bronzed from farm work and an upright bearing. Clare introduced herself and said that she was the bearer of bad news

"He's fallen off that yacht of his and drowned, hasn't he?" was the instant reaction.

"No," said Clare. "He's dead but not that way."

143

"Then he's crashed in that car."

"Not that either," said Clare, slightly taken aback. "He was stabbed."

It took Mrs Nash a moment to absorb this.

"Stabbed? Do you mean murdered?"

"Yes, he named you as his next of kin."

"He's my brother, you see, four years younger and a bit of a handful when he was small. Didn't like school, you see."

"I'd like you to tell me all about him if you will," said Clare.

"Like I said, he was a handful when he was young but everybody liked him, you see, could charm a monkey down from a tree, could our Ray."

Clare wasn't sure if that was the correct saying but she got the message.

"So he left school with few qualifications but lots of charm?"

"Yes, he could charm a bird down out of a tree, you see."

Clare let that pass.

"What did he do, how did he earn a living?"

"We had both been left a small legacy by our grandparents, on my mother's side, you see, and he worked his way through that. He stayed at home until he was over twenty, sponging on our parents while he wasted money on horses. Then he went and worked for a bookmaker in Cheltenham and seemed to be doing well until he was sacked at a minutes notice."

Barbara Nash tapped the side of her nose. "Working there, he'd figured out a way to put money on horses that he knew had just won a race."

"Sound a good way to pick a winner," said Clare.

"Like I said to him, he should have backed a few seconds and thirds as well."

"What did he do then?"

"He hung around sponging on our parents and spending half the night in Bristol and then he took off for London with a woman old enough to be his mother. He left her when her money ran out, you see and then we didn't hear from him for a while."

She paused and looked sad.

"My mother and father both died and I had no address to write to, to tell him, you see. Then he turned up looking all la-de-da in that smart blue car. He said that he had a good job working for a man who had a license to print money and that he was going to buy himself a yacht with some of it."

"Did he say who this man was?" asked Clare.

"No but he gave me a phone number to ring in an emergency. I said what emergency, they're both dead, you see."

"What did he say to that?"

"Told me that was water under the bridge, this number was for future emergencies."

"I'd like to have that number," said Clare.

Barbara Nash went to a dresser in the corner of the big farmhouse kitchen and pulled open the drawers in turn, muttering to herself while so doing. In the end she said,

"I remember now, I wrote it in that phone book."

She disappeared and came back with the telephone book. She studied the inside first page upon which a large number of numbers were written.

"You see, it's one of these," she explained, thrusting the directory at Clare.

If she had been asked what she considered to be the most useful modern invention, Clare would have put the mobile phone among her top five. But not at that moment. She searched in vain among entries that seemed to have been written with a very blunt pencil, for a good old fashioned number that told one where the phone was. There were no London numbers, Raymond or Ray.

"Oh, I remember now, he said that emergency numbers should go on the emergency pages."

She laboriously turned the pages looking for the list of emergency numbers. There were no pencilled additions.

"Oh, I remember now, this is a new one, I wrote it in the old one."

She disappeared again and reappeared with a pile of old directories that she could scarcely carry.

"It'll be in one of these."

To Clare, not yet 30 years old, it seemed that Barbara had enough material to write a history of the GPO Telephone service but she sorted through them and picked out the two that immediately preceded the one they had examined. She scanned their first page and Emergency Numbers page. There were some entries like the Doctor and the Vet on the emergency page of one of them.

Clare was about to close the older of the two volumes when a stubby finger shot out and pointed to one of the entries,

"There it is, I said it was somewhere there, didn't I?"

She was pointing to a number against which was pencilled, Boy.

"My parents always called him Boy."

Clare noted the number, explained that the sister would have to do something about the yacht and 'Boy's' other possessions when the police had done with them, thanked Mrs Nash for her help and thankfully departed to drive back to Bournemouth before she tried the number that Boy had given the sister who hadn't uttered a single word of sorrow or questioned the manner of his death or asked by whom.

That evening Simon gave her the portrait photographs of the river girl and Clare took them round to Jane's Boutique in the morning.

Jane recognised her as a customer but didn't know her name, she thought that she worked in one of the clubs and suggested asking the doormen, they'd know.

DC Tomlinson found himself deputed to visit all of the night clubs in the area and ask if anyone recognised the girl in the picture. He didn't relish the duty because most clubs didn't really get going until eight o'clock or later and it could mean a long night of trying to get answers from doormen and others whose continued employment depended on them behaving like the proverbial three brass monkeys.

Long experience told DC Tomlinson to try the Half Moon Club first, not because it was known to harbour girls who were likely to be struck on the head and fall into rivers but because Chalky White was the doorman. Chalky was an ex-soldier, a tank gunner who had been serving at the tank testing establishment at Bovington when he was demobilised. He liked the area and had taken the 'chucker-out' job until he could find something better. That was seven years ago.

Chalky was as straight as they come, he saw to the patrons and he saw that in the wee small hours of the morning, the hostesses and entertainers got taxi's driven by people that he knew and could trust. He had looked after Jane in her exotic dancing days.

He was also a friend of young Will who, in his days as a Commando, had been sent to Bovington to learn how to disable tanks, or as Will would put it, blow them up. Chalky had been the instructor and they had struck up a friendship.

DC Tomlinson had anticipated Chalky's reaction.

"Can't say as I recognise her, she's not one of ours but I think that she's been here, nice looking girl, what do you want her for?"

"Nothing, we only want to know who she is and where she lives, we fished her out of the river."

"Oh dear. I can't leave the foyer. You leave her picture with me and I'll ask the girls later and give you a bell tomorrow, OK mate?"

He had much the same but less friendly, reception at most of the other clubs. He didn't get to all of them and he'd run out of pictures, even so it took him to past 2 a.m.

Chapter Fifteen

THE following morning Clare picked up her phone to ring the emergency number that Barbara Nash had given her. Then she thought, why the secrecy, why had he been so insistent that his sister should only use it in an emergency? There had been a phone among his effects and it wasn't that number. Her first thought was that he had a wife. In which case it would be better to know before she broke the bad news.

She asked the police system to get her the address of the holder of the phone number. Within an hour she had the answer, Mr Raymond Farrell, Crimpers Court, Golders Green, London.

She rang the number and there was no reply. Clare concluded that there was no wife or she was out at work. She went through his things that had been brought from the yacht and took the bunch of keys. After a quick word with Inspector Wyatt, she caught a train to London. If there was anything in it there would be time enough, later, to bring in the Met. By one o'clock she was inside the flat at Crimpers Court. There was no one there and a quick look in the wardrobes showed only male clothing. Within five minutes there was a knock at the door. Clare opened it to find a rather fat, middle-aged lady standing there armed with a rolling pin.

"Wot you doing in Mr Farrell's flat?" demanded the woman.

"May I ask who you are?" said Clare.

"Mrs Bell, I live in the flat opposite and keeps an eye on Mr F's flat when he's away in that boat of his. Ever so nice is Mr F, we all miss him."

Clare fished out her identification and held it in front of the woman's face,

"Police," she said.

"'ow do I know that you're a proper copper, I thought that you people always went round in pairs?"

"I'm from Dorset," said Clare, "and I came alone to save the taxpayers money."

That seemed to satisfy Mrs Bell. She remarked,

"You're the third person wot 'as been askin' for him."

"Oh," said Clare. "Who were the others?"

"There was a chap who came all la-de-da an' asked for him. He'd been before when Mr Farrell was here and I heard them going at each other hammer and tongs. He laughed about it afterwards. 'E came again an' wasn't best pleased when I told 'im as Mr Farrell 'ad gone."

"Did you tell him where?" asked Clare.

"'E didn't ask."

"Who were the others?"

"Well they was more recent, if you know what I mean. After Mr Farrell had gone. There was this old chap who looked like a boxer. He banged on the door a lot and when I came out to see what all the fuss was about 'e asked me where 'e was an' I said on 'is boat an' 'e said where an' I showed 'im the postcard as Mr Farrell sent me from Bournemouth an' 'e went away."

Clare took a moment to digest this, checked that her recorder was working, then asked, "and what about the other one?"

"'E was the last. 'E was younger an' sort of Italian looking, if you know what I mean. 'E was creepy, 'e said as I'd better tell 'im all that I knew or else."

"Or else what?" Prompted Clare.

"I didn' ask 'im, the look of 'im was enough," said Mrs Bell.

"Did you show him the postcard that Mr Farrell sent you from Bournemouth?"

"Yes an' the bit out of the paper, too."

"What bit out of the paper was that?" asked Clare.

"It was just after Mr Farrell left, he hadn't been gone more than a month when 'e sent it wiv a little note saying as 'e was now an 'ero. The paper said as 'ow 'e'd averted a possible tragedy."

"How?" asked Clare thinking that getting information out of Mrs Bell was like getting blood out of a stone. "Did it say how?"

"I was just coming to that," said Mrs Bell. "It seems as if 'e was rowing back to his yacht late one night when 'e seen smoke coming out of someone else's yacht an' 'e rowed over an' woke them up. They might 'ave been burnt alive."

"That was fortunate, wasn't it?" said Clare. "Did it say what he was doing rowing late at night?"

Mrs Bell regarded Clare as if she was out of her mind, then cackled, "Wot do you think 'e would be doing in the middle of the night? Coming home from doing some girl, I expect."

"I see," said Clare.

"Anyway," said Mrs Bell, "wot's he supposed to have done?"

"Got himself killed," said Clare.

"Oh my God," said the woman, "he didn't deserve that."

"Why, particularly?"

"Well, he was always so cheerful and had a word for everybody and he brought home little things from the club."

"What sort of things," asked Clare hoping for a lead to the club. After all, it might be footballs or cricket balls.

"Oh, you know, book matches, fags and chocolates, that sort of thing and at Christmas the kids got balloons and streamers."

"Did he have a wife or girlfriend?"

"I don't know about a wife but he had lots of girlfriends." She grinned and added, "wouldn't have minded being one myself."

"Do you happen to know what club he worked for?"

"It was on the matches; toff's place in the West-End."

Clare reasoned that there was bound to be something in the flat. She thanked Mrs Bell and said that she'd let her know when she was through.

She resumed her interrupted search of the flat. There were several book matches, all with a picture of a group of four trees on them and the legend, Four Oaks Club, Mayfair.

Chalky phoned late the following morning and left a message on the machine.

"Chalky White here. That girl who was drowned, her name's Laura Wells and they think that she's a croupier at the Cavendish Club. She has a flat near the centre but they don't know the address."

Clare got the message and spared DC Tomlinson another late duty by saying that she'd make enquiries herself. Meanwhile she studied the report that another of her people had prepared on the documents found in the yacht.

It seemed that Raymond Farrell was up to his eyes in debt and that his creditors were very tired of waiting. He owed over £15,000 on the yacht and £2,000 on his car and smaller amounts to sundry others. He was overdrawn at the bank and was also behind with the rent for the London flat. The important fact was that there was no evidence of income. No wonder that he was two weeks behind with his harbour dues.

What did he live on, how did he buy the petrol and above all, what had he to offer a girl like Laura?

The other interesting thing was the very small notebook that he had in his hip-pocket, containing a series of numbers going back over the past month. Crosses seemed to be distributed randomly against the numbers, and on the first page was written x black.

She was at the Cavendish Club by seven that evening, identified herself to the doorman who evidently had just arrived and asked to see the manager.

"What for?" demanded the doorman.

"Surely that's his business," said Clare, nettled by his tone.

"We've got orders to keep undesirables out." He considered this funny.

"And the police are undesirables, are they? I'll tell my Super that and he'll remember it the next time the club's licence comes up for review."

"No need to be like that, Miss, I was just having a joke."

"Well, keep your jokes to yourself and tell the manager that I want to see him."

He disappeared and returned a minute or so later and escorted Clare to a door marked Manager, with the name Clyde Marks beneath, opened the door and said, "the police, boss."

A man in evening dress rose and said,

"How can we help the police, er Miss?"

"Detective Sergeant Thornton. I understand that a girl called Laura Wells works for you, Mr Marks."

"Yes," said the Manager, "but I don't think that you'll be able to speak to her."

"Why do you say that?" asked Clare.

"I think that she must be sick, she hasn't turned up for work on the past two nights, very inconvenient of her, I must say."

"She won't be turning up in future either, Mr Marks, she's dead."

"That's dreadful, how did it happen?"

"How did what happen, Mr Marks?"

"Well, how did she die?"

"We found her body in the water," said Clare.

"She fell off that boat," said the manager.

"What boat?" asked Clare.

The manager seemed a trifle surprised at the question and said,

"I don't know, I suppose that I assumed that she was on a boat because people fall off boats."

"You can do better than that Mr Marks, you knew that she visited a boat in the harbour, didn't you?"

"She told one of the other girls, I think that they share a flat."

"I'd like to speak to that girl, what's her name?"

"Sally Bechler, I think she's arrived, I'll get her for you."

Clare would much have preferred to meet Sally Bechler without the presence of the manager but that could come later, what she wanted was her address.

The manager reappeared accompanied by a most attractive brunette dressed in the sort of cocktail frock with a low neckline, that Laura had been wearing. It was plain that he had told her about Laura's death.

"This is Detective Sergeant Thornton, Sally, she'd like to ask you some questions."

"Yes," said Clare. "When did you last see Laura?"

"Three days ago. We slept until mid-day; people do, in our job, and then off she went to see her boy friend on his yacht. He was all that she talked about these days."

"How was she dressed?"

"As usual, undies, T shirt and shorts."

"She wasn't dressed for work then?"

Sally grinned. "She always took her dress with her. They're crease resistant and she dressed and did her make-up on the boat, she didn't come back to the flat."

"Was she serious about this boy-friend?"

"I got the impression that she was more serious than he was," said Sally.

"Did you ever meet him?"

"No. She was a bit secretive about him. Being the police you probably think that I could have sort of hung about the harbour and spied on her, but the thought never entered my head." She looked Clare in the eye and went on, "people like us don't pry into our friends lives, they might be going out with a married man or be getting a divorce or attending the hospital and didn't want the manager to know that they had a problem, we accept what they want to tell us and leave it at that."

"Very sensible," said the manager.

"Did she have any relatives?"

"Yes, a sister somewhere in the Midlands. She used to get Christmas and birthday cards from her."

"I'll have to have her address and I'll need to come and go through her things."

"Why?" said the manager.

"Quite obviously to get her relative's addresses but more importantly to see if there are any clues to who killed her?"

"Killed her?" Sally's voice went up an octave.

"Didn't I say?" said Clare artlessly. "We found her body in the water but she didn't die by drowning."

"Oh My God," said Sally, still in high gear. "Laura didn't have an enemy in the world, she was a nice care-free girl. The only places she went were this club, the boat and shopping."

"What exactly did she do at the club?" said Clare.

"She was a croupier, she worked the roulette wheel," said the manager.

"Successfully?" asked Clare whose knowledge of gambling could be written on the back of a postage stamp.

"Yes," said the manager.

Clare thought that it didn't sound like a 100% yes but decided not to pursue it at the present time.

She left after getting the address of the shared flat in East Cliff.

At noon the following day, she and DC June Sanoya were at the flat that the two girls had shared. A bright-eyed Sally in a short housecoat let them in and pointed to Laura's room. They were going methodically through each drawer and cupboard when Sally appeared in a shirt and belted skirt and asked if they'd like a coffee. They both said yes and Clare followed the girl into the tiny kitchen and perched on one of the two stools.

Sally took the coffee for June into the bedroom and returned and perched on the other stool warming her hands gently on her mug. Clare made certain that her pocket recorder was switched on and said,

"You like being a croupier, don't you Sally?"

"Yes, I like meeting people and I like the money."

"Is it one of the rules of the job that you don't date the customers?"

"Yes. At our club, if you're seen with a client you're fired."

"And Laura was breaking that rule, wasn't she?" said Clare to her mug of coffee.

Hesitantly, "Yes."

"Last night, in front of the manager, you said that you'd never seen Laura's boy-friend but you had, hadn't you?"

"Yes," again she said it hesitantly. "He comes to the club."

Clare produced a photo of Raymond Farrell that she had found in the Sea Raven and put it on the table in front of Sally, saying,

"Is this him?"

Sally picked up the picture, studied it and said,

"Yes, that's the man who comes to the club."

"He won't any more," said Clare, "he was killed as well."

"Oh My God," said Sally in her higher register, "both of them."

"Yes," said Clare, "and you must help us catch who did it."

"Oh yes I will," said Sally, "but you must promise that you won't tell Clyde Marks that I knew, will you? Otherwise I'll lose my job."

"I won't let you down, Sally, you must trust me. Let's start at the beginning, the reason that the club forbids its girls dating the clients is to avoid the possibility of cheating, isn't it?"

"Yes. Although the arrangements on each table are made to prevent the possibility of the rules being bent and there are assistant managers always on the prowl, they insist that there is no familiarity. They also tell us what to wear and you couldn't hide a chip under our dresses without it showing."

"You said that Laura's boy-friend came to the club."

"Yes, for the past two months he's been a regular. We girls remember their faces you know and we'd remember him because he was rather good looking, a welcome change from the fat young and old men and women we usually get."

"What did he do?"

"You mean Laura's friend?"

"Yes."

"He drifted round playing all the tables, not high stakes, you know, it's up to the punter how much he or she bets, and in the last six weeks or so he's played the wheel."

"Roulette," said Clare.

"Laura's table," said Sally.

"Now I'll let you into a secret, Sally, he owed money everywhere and had no job, so the reason that he came to the club was to get some money. How could he do that?"

"The club operates to make a profit for the owners and all the games of chance are weighted in the club's direction," said Sally. She smiled, "otherwise how could they afford to pay us our wages?" She went on, "to be sure of winning he would have to cheat."

"How could a client cheat?"

"People like Mr Marks have made it practically impossible for a client to cheat. Some try and are always escorted out of the club and told never to return."

"What you're avoiding saying, Sally, is that the croupier has to do the cheating for him, isn't it?"

"Yes although I find it difficult to believe that Laura would."

"Don't you believe it dear, we women do the daftest things for men," said Clare. Like going on the pill, she thought. Dear Simon.

"How could she have swung the odds in her man's favour?"

"You promise that you won't say anything to Mr Marks?"

"Yes," said Clare. "Cross my heart."

"Well," she said, "It's meant to trim the odds and I don't properly understand how it works but there are magnets under the wheel and the ball has a piece of iron in it. It sticks in my mind because the girl who told me about it said that it's soft iron and that's silly, isn't it? Because all iron's hard."

"Is it intended to make the ball always land in certain numbers?"

"I don't know but the croupier can switch the magnets on and off."

"They're electro-magnets then?" asked Clare.

Sally shrugged that off and said,

"There are switches under the table where the croupier stands and she can push them with her fingers or thumbs with her hands always in view. An experienced girl leans forward and all the men clients are so busy looking at her cleavage that she could be playing the piano with her hands without them noticing." Sally was evidently pleased with this evidence of male sensuality.

"What is the purpose?"

"If she can see that most money is on red, she switches on the magnets under the black numbers to persuade the ball to fall into a black hole. The owners also know which numbers are the usual favourites, like 13 and so on and there are two other switches that make the ball avoid these numbers. It's very complicated and remember it's meant to make sure that the casino makes a profit."

"What could Laura have done then?"

"Well, they must have had a code to tell him whether the red or black magnets were switched on," said Sally, "something quite natural and simple like leaning on the table with her left hand or right hand. He would know to keep off of the popular numbers. In that way he would probably finish up with a small profit at the end of the evening."

"Sounds a bit hit or miss to me," said Clare, "and in any case he could see for himself where the big money was being bet, couldn't he?"

"Yes, I suppose that he could. It's probably more complicated than I've described and he could make a small profit. That's the beauty of it, he never drew attention to himself by breaking the bank and the club still made a nightly profit on roulette."

"You heard no hint that the management was concerned that the profit from the wheel was less than they expected?" asked Clare.

"No, not a word."

"If management had suspected that she was bending things to favour a client, what do you think they would have done, called in the police, or the heavy mob or just shown her the door?"

"Shown her the door. The last thing they would want is the bad publicity that public mention of cheating would attract."

"They wouldn't think the offence was worth killing someone?"

"Good Lord no, they're quite nice people."

"Thanks Sally, that has given me a valuable insight into Laura's world. I'll just see how June's getting on and then we'll get out of your hair."

"You're the least of my worries, I've got to find someone to share this flat. I can't afford to live here on my own."

DC June Sanoya had collected all the documents that she could find in Laura's bedroom and they took them back to the station. There weren't many. A quick sort produced a recent letter from 'Your loving sister, Eileen' and an address in Warwick. A diary gave a phone number for Eileen.

Clare rang the number and conveyed the sad news. Eileen explained that – being a single mother with two children to bring up – she couldn't drop everything and come to Bournemouth but she'd like to be kept informed. No, she didn't know anything about the life that her sister led except that she worked at a club, wore nice clothes, met some nice people and didn't have two kids round her feet all the time. There were no other relatives and Clare suggested that she'd better get someone to act for her to clear up her sister's affairs and rang off.

Clare discussed the case with Inspector Wyatt.

"The girl was employed as a croupier at the Cavendish Club and she fell for a no-good who lived on a yacht who seems to have done nothing for at least the past two months except gamble there. She was breaking the club rules by seeing him and the suspicion is that she was helping him to win modestly at roulette."

"Is there any proof of that?"

"No, Gov and there would seem to be no rhyme or reason behind these killings. On the facts as we know them at present, no one had any reason to kill the girl, Laura, and there seems to be little reason for killing the man. The only thing that we've found at the moment is that he owed £15,000 on the yacht and £2,000 on his car and people don't destroy their chance of ever getting payment."

"What about their next of kin?" asked Wyatt.

"The girl has a sister in Warwick who doesn't want to know and the man has a sister near to Bristol who he kept at arms length. All she had was a telephone number to be used only in an emergency. That number took me to a flat in Golders Green and a woman who lived opposite said that he worked at a club and used to bring home book matches and chocolates. In his flat there were a number of book matches advertising the Four Oaks Club in Mayfair."

"If he had been living in a yacht in the harbour and frequenting the Cavendish Club he can't have been working at the club in Mayfair, can he?" said Wyatt.

"Then why did he keep the flat in London?" asked Clare.

"Did you speak to the Met?"

"No Gov, I thought that I should speak with you first."

"Have you got any of your hunches?" asked Wyatt with a smile. Their chief, Superintendent Harding placed great store on Clare's hunches.

"Not really, Gov except that whoever did it is utterly ruthless and they were killed before seven in the evening."

"How do you get that?" asked Wyatt.

"Laura always went to the yacht in a T shirt and shorts and changed into her cocktail frock in the evening to go to work. She was found dead in her frock, ergo, she had changed ready to go to the club."

"Or perhaps she changed early to go somewhere with somebody before going to the club," said Wyatt. "She might not have expected to come back to the yacht."

"There is that possibility, of course."

"Why do you say that they are utterly ruthless?"

"Because they killed her as well," said Clare.

"But the manner of death was different in both cases. Why didn't they stab the girl?"

"I don't know, Gov, it looks as if they didn't mean to kill her."

"How do you get that?" said Wyatt.

"From their dress," said Clare. "They always went separately to avoid the club becoming suspicious. On the face of it, she was dressed ready to go to the club and he was still in his casual shirt and trousers and would usually come along anything up to two hours later. But we know that she must have left the yacht in the afternoon. Perhaps a visitor arrived and clambered aboard, and she was the person they encountered. Perhaps they looked belligerent and she told them to push off and there was a struggle and she fell down and hit her head on one of those square corners that seem to abound on yachts."

"You always make things seem plausible but in that case how did she come to be dressed in her frock and in that river and why?"

"That beats me Gov."

"The body in the river could stand your theory on its head," said the Inspector. "How about this. Laura is in the cabin in her pants and bra perhaps repairing her make-up after making love. Some men come over the side, Raymond Farrell goes out into the cockpit to see who they are while Laura hastily pulls on her dress. Farrell is forced at knife point back into the cabin and then into the bunk space, protesting loudly. Shut up, they say, we've come for the girl. Farrell lunges forward and is stabbed and falls back on the bunk. Laura is appalled and terrified and the men force her to go with them. They drive out into the country and she either tells them or gives them what they want and they then hit her on the head. They didn't know that she had a thin skull. How's that?"

Clare smiled at him and said, "It's as plausible as mine, Gov. and I forgot to tell you a piece of evidence that supports a theory like yours"

"And what's that?"

"Two men had sex with her in the hours before her death. One of them was Raymond Farrell."

"And we don't know the other?"

"No, Guv but we've got his DNA."

"Where do we go from here, Clare?"

"I think that we've got to look at the Four Oaks Club in Mayfair."

"We'd better ask the Met, hadn't we? Otherwise there could be an official complaint, they're very possessive about their territory and, of course, they may already have an operation in hand that involves that club. You write it up and I'll get the Super to speak to someone at the Yard."

Chapter Sixteen

THE Prime Minister and his Chancellor were both back from their summer hols.

William couldn't speak for the PM but he, himself, felt like a new man, despite finding that poor girl's body in the river in the middle of the first week. It had done Peggy good as well, he thought that she was still as lovely as the day that he had married her and, if it was possible, he loved her even more than he had then.

He knew that she'd been pleased that he'd struck up a friendship with young Will. Over the bar one evening, Will had invited him to come round the estate with him the next day. They'd visited each of the six farms, putting a new hinge on here and a new tap washer on there, and several cottages in the village, with him fetching and carrying and holding things when young Will told him to. In one cottage Will had opened a washing machine door that had jammed, in another the washing machine filter was blocked and in a third a knob had come off the cooker. It was evident that the elderly residents welcomed Will's visits and chatted with him non-stop while he did the jobs. He'd said to William as they drove away,

"A problem with old people is that they're lonely and I'm one of the few people who they'll talk to in the week. Gloria pops along for a word and they might see the sisters who run the tea room and the man with the mobile grocers shop, but that's all."

William had said, "I'm surprised that they've got washing machines, I didn't think country cottages ran to that sort of thing,"

"That's thanks to Tim and Helene. They provide the money to run the Manor House estate. The General and his wife had used up all their money trying to keep the cottages in repair so Tim took over. He won't inherit it or the title, that will go to his brother David who followed the family tradition and went into the army. He's got an American wife and Tim's got a half-French wife, funny, isn't it?"

Young Will had gone on,

"Tim and Helene said that the cottages ought to have inside loos, bathrooms and washing machines. We said 'don't be silly, there isn't any room.' So they built them on the back."

"It doesn't show."

"No, they had me scour Dorset for old stone and planted shrubs when it was finished and most of the old people still live there practically rent free."

William had been impressed.

He wondered about the girl in the river, there hadn't been much in the papers. Same for the chap who was stabbed in his yacht, a person isn't safe anywhere these days.

He hoped that the Home Secretary didn't come up with proposals for more policemen, his budget was bursting at the seams already.

There were a whole lot of papers in his in-tray demanding an early answer. He didn't mind those sort of papers, in his first ministerial post an old civil servant had told him how to deal with them; 'say No, Minister, that always sorts out the men from the boys.' He'd never forgotten it and had found that it worked in four cases out of five.

Peggy phoned Jackie to say how much they had enjoyed their stay at the Tolbrite Arms, notwithstanding finding a girl's body in the river on the Thursday of the first week.

"I saw that in the paper," said Jackie, "do you know if they've arrested anyone for the crime?"

"Not as far as I'm aware," said Peggy, "and there was another murder in a yacht the same day, so your friend Clare was in the thick of things. Have you made any progress with the investigation into the death of Sir Stuart Harcourt?"

"Quite a lot," said Jackie. "It took me to Hungary. Before I went I was sure that I knew who had killed him and I went there to find out why."

"And did you?"

"Yes and my report is with the Prime Minister, I hope," said Jackie.

"Why the 'I hope' Jackie?"

"Well, he's so busy and there are those in the old-boy-network who try to shield him from unpleasant news."

"Oh, it's like that, is it?"

"Sort of Peggy but its history now."

"You must tell William and me all about it one day."

William arrived home at his usual time, picked her up and kissed her and told her that he loved her. That small ritual over, he asked her what sort of a day she had enjoyed in the heady world of public relations.

Peggy mentioned the clients with whom or for whom she had done something during the day and that, among other things, she had told Jackie Fraser how much they had enjoyed their holiday at the Tolbrite Arms, adding,

"There was one thing. I asked her about the murder of Stuart Harcourt and she said that she not only knew who had killed him but why."

"Good for her," said William, holding out his glass for a second pre-dinner sherry. Peggy carefully filled his glass and gave herself half a glass feeling a little self-righteous at so doing but a girl has to look after her figure, doesn't she?

"I thought that she'd tell me but she clammed up and said that her report is with the PM and she hopes that he gets to see it. That was a funny thing to say, wasn't it?"

"You know as well as I do, lover, that there simply aren't enough hours in the day for the PM to read every document that's sent to him. That's why he has six private secretaries."

"I know. That's what Jackie's afraid of, that the old-boy-network doesn't sweep whatever she found out in Hungary, under the carpet."

"Why on earth would they want to do that?" said William, then continued, "don't bother to tell me, I know already."

It was four days after the prime minister had returned to duty following his holiday that the DMS was summoned to see the PM at ten the following morning and invited to bring Captain Fraser with him. Major-General Lowe was beginning to fear that Jackie's report and his covering note had been side tracked.

He and Jackie were in Number 10 by five minutes to ten. Roger Stevens muttered to Jackie,

"You were right. We must all have been blind for all those years."

Roger showed them in. To their surprise they found the Chancellor there. He smiled and mouthed "Hello Jackie." There were two other people occupying chairs at the conference table. The prime minister said,

"Good of you to come across, General and you too Captain. You know Sir Lancelot Braceford, the Permanent Secretary of the FCO who is responsible for MI-6 and Anne Wallinton, the Head of MI-5, don't you? I invited them to be present due to the nature of Captain Fraser's report. I suggested that the Chancellor might stay because he and his wife were in on the ground floor, as it were."

He looked down at the file on the table.

"I must say that I find your report very disturbing, Captain, it's all predicated on the supposition that this Hungarian agent," he looked again at the file, "Sonia Berolinka, killed Sir Stuart Harcourt."

He looked at Jackie and she said "Yes, Prime Minister."

"And you have no doubt that she entered upon this elaborate charade for that purpose?"

"No doubt whatsoever, Sir, and Colonel Franz Matyev, the Head of the Hungarian Security Service, confirmed it."

"Ah yes, Colonel Matyev."

He suddenly smiled at Jackie and said, "I must say that was very ingenious, the way you got to see him." Then he became grave again.

"How do we know that this isn't a plot to discredit two distinguished Crown servants who are no longer able to defend themselves?"

"The evidence is in the Stasi documents and the copy of the secret communication that their London agent handed to Sir Roger Hollis in the middle eighties," said Jackie. "Your PPS was serving in our Budapest embassy at that time and he can confirm what I have written about Stuart Harcourt's behaviour. As to discrediting two distinguished Crown servants, what would be their reason?"

The prime minister reflected on that for a moment and said,

"To discredit the chiefs of the British security services."

"I thought that the Sunday papers had already done that," said Tubby Lowe.

"Touche," said the prime minister.

He studied the document before him and remarked conversationally,

"Now, what do I do?"

"I don't see that you need do anything, Prime Minister," said Sir Lancelot. "If the Captain is correct in what she alleges, and I don't necessarily agree that she is, it's all ancient history and best forgotten."

"And you don't think that there are any lessons to be learned?" asked the prime minister.

"Perhaps you should have somebody look at the security arrangements at Number 10 Downing Street," said Sir Lancelot, a trifle smugly.

"What about the Stasi report?" asked the Chancellor from the end of the table, "are you suggesting that they faked that as well?"

"The KGB have been known to do some funny things," said Sir Lancelot.

"Yes," snapped the Chancellor, "like recruiting two of your star diplomats called Burgess and MacLean."

The prime minister decided that he'd better step in.

"And what have you to say, Anne?"

"Well, Prime Minister, you only showed us Captain Fraser's report five minutes before this meeting and so I haven't fully digested the contents but it would appear that my organisation failed to detect yet another public school rotten apple in the Foreign Service."

Good on you girl, thought Jackie. She didn't know it but those were William's sentiments too.

"Oh come now," said the FCO man, "that's a bit steep, Hollis was yours."

"I agree," said the Head of MI-5, that's why I agree with DMS that someone should take a hard look at the methods of recruitment, and the through-life screening, of the officers in both of our organisations."

"Did you send copies of your documents to anyone else General?" put in the prime minister.

"No, Prime Minister, that's the only one unless..."he looked at Roger who quickly said,

"We didn't copy it to anyone, Prime Minister."

"I shall require a copy," said Sir Lancelot.

"Why?" asked the prime minister.

"This young woman has made serious charges against a member of the service and by implication, the service itself, and that will have to be investigated through the proper channels."

"A moment ago you were arguing that it was all ancient history and would best be forgotten," said William.

"That was before I knew that the Prime Minister was taking the General's proposals seriously," said Sir Lancelot.

"On recent experience if I give copies to the Home Office or the Foreign Office, extracts from the report or inspired rumours of a shake-up in the security services would appear in the press in a matter of days," said the prime minister. "None of us wants that and so there are to be only the two copies, mine and the General's."

Sir Lancelot looked down at the table and muttered something. The prime minister went on,

"It is in the country's best interests not to make this affair public. The two people who we have good reason to suspect committed treason of the foulest kind are already dead and dragging their names through the mud would only damage the security services which, God alone knows, have been criticised badly enough already in recent times. But we have a duty to ensure that this sort of thing can't happen again. For a start I agree the proposal that you made, General, that the base for recruitment be widened and the most senior appointments subjected to public review. The way the US Congress does it deserves serious consideration, but we have two problems."

"The Home Secretary and the Foreign Secretary," grinned the Chancellor.

The prime minister smiled and said,

"That's one way of putting it."

"If you set up a committee they'll waffle it into the ground," said William.

"What would you suggest that we do then?" asked the prime minister.

"I'd tell the General and Roger and whoever else they recommend, to make proposals and then you implement them, telling the other members of the cabinet to lump it," said William. "After all, you won't be sacking anyone, simply setting in place the arrangements for future recruitment and promotion."

"Our cabinet colleagues will argue that they are the best people to do that," said the prime minister.

"Then give them two weeks to agree and if they don't like it, they can resign," said his Chancellor.

"What do you think, Roger?" asked the prime minister.

"The DMS case is persuasive. On the evidence provided by the Stasi and the Hungarians, it can be argued that past Foreign and Home Secretaries failed in their duty to manage their departments. I know that it's far-fetched but it can be so argued. In these circumstances, Prime Minister, you should have no problem in convincing members of the House that you were acting in the best interests of the country and the party in taking a top-down approach to the system of future appointments in the security services."

Roger sat back and William smiled and said,

"He means Yes, Prime Minister."

They all smiled, except Sir Lancelot. The prime minister said,

"Then it's agreed then, Roger will prepare a note instructing the General and himself to make proposals for recruitment and appointments in the security services, co-opting others as they might wish. Including any recommendations for modifying the 1996 Security Service Act."

"I want it understood from the outset, Prime Minister, that I must have a representative on this ad-hoc committee," said Sir Lancelot.

"But you have," said the prime minister, "that's why I put Roger on it."

"I mean an MI-6 representative."

"Sorry, Sir Lancelot," said the prime minister, "that's precisely what I don't want."

"The Foreign Secretary won't like it."

"Nor will the Home Secretary, I'll be bound," said the prime minister, "but that's my decision."

He closed the file and slid it across the table towards Roger and stood up.

To the General's surprise, Jackie remained in her seat and said,

"There is one other thing, Prime Minister, what do we tell the Hungarians?"

"Why should we tell them anything?" asked the prime minister.

"For one thing to prevent them from publishing in the press what they found in the Stasi file. They clearly feel strongly on this," said Jackie. "I think that, at least, we should reply on Number 10 paper, thanking them for the information that they provided, pointing out that both of the people named are dead, that there would be little purpose in making their treachery public and that you, Sir, have taken steps to see that such a situation cannot happen again."

"Phew," said the prime minister, "and who do we send this to?"

"Colonel Franz Matyev," said Jackie.

The prime minister thought about this for a moment, then said,

"Very well, you draft something Captain and give it to Roger and he shall send it."

Jackie thought that the Colonel would know that Roger had been in Budapest in the mid-eighties when Stuart Harcourt had been there and would probably have a small question mark against his name in their records but what the hell, she'd write to the Colonel as well.

She and the General walked back to the MoD, dodging the traffic en route and discussing the outcome of the meeting and the Chancellor's presence. Jackie thought that her friend Peggy might have had something to do with that. Tubby professed himself well pleased with the outcome and particularly that that pompous ass Braceford had been sent away with a flee in his ear.

In the manager's office of the Four Oaks Club in Jermyn Street, Mayfair, Guiseppe Maranti was worried. He was usually worried about something, worrying was a way of life with Guiseppe. Would the train be on time? Would the supplier remember the olives? Was the wine at the correct temperature? And equally weighty items in a restaurateurs life. But this was different, he'd just had a visit from the police. He'd had visits from the police before, of course, but this one was different.

Even that shouldn't have worried him, he and his brother Francesco ran a good clean club frequented by what he regarded as the best people, no drunkenness, no drug taking and no rowdiness. Everything was discreet at the Four Oaks Club, from the cellars with their exquisite (and costly) wines to the discreet rooms for the use of clients and their lady friends on the upper floors.

But this was different. The police inspector had come to ask about Raymond Farrell. It seemed that he was dead. That was certainly something to worry about because that same Raymond Farrell had stolen £35,000 from the club and it's difficult to get your money back from a corpse. But the big worry came from the policeman saying that Farrell had been murdered. Guiseppe Maranti, worried because, he thought, he might have been indirectly responsible for that.

He hadn't said so to the policeman. A true Italian, born into a back street in Naples, wouldn't be that stupid, but he was worried. Should he tell Francesco or bear the burden of worry on his own broad shoulders? He decided not, then couldn't decide if he'd decided not to tell Francesco or not to bear the burden of worry himself.

Half an hour later his brother Francesco walked through the door.

He always arrived at this time, coming by train and taxi from his smart house in Virginia Water. The people of Virginia Water and the smart school to which he sent his children, knew him as Mr Francis Martin, a name that he had adopted in his early twenties to better realise his ambition to become an English gentleman.

Guiseppe, for his part, had realised that the English prefer the proprietors of the best restaurants and gaming clubs to be Italian, a preference that, he thought, probably dated back to when the siblings of the best families made the Grand Tour and were fawned upon and flattered by waiters. So Guiseppe worked at keeping his accent and fawning and flattering and laughed all the way to the bank.

"Good morning George," said Francis.

"Buon Giorno Francesco," said Guiseppe. "I've just had a visit by the police."

"Oh have you, what did they want this time?"

"They came about Raymond Farrell, he's been murdered."

It took a moment for this to sink in, then Francesco called Francis said,

"That's rotten luck, we can say goodbye to our money."

"That's what I thought."

"I trust that you didn't tell the inspector that our ex-employee had departed with £35,000 of our money?"

"I'm not stupido," said Guiseppe.

"How was he killed?"

"The inspector said that he was stabbed in a boat."

"I've heard of people being stabbed in the heart but never in a boat," said Francis. It was the sort of joke that an English gentleman might make. "Are you sure that he didn't say throat?"

"No, a boat in Poole. The inspector said that he regards the dagger as a southern European sort of weapon," said Guiseppe, "and he asked about our staff."

"Meaning, I suppose, that we employ southern Europeans and he wonders whether one of them bore him a grudge."

"I told him that everybody liked Raymond Farrell."

"One big happy family," smiled Francis.

"He asked me for a list of their names and addresses and how long they had worked for us and whether they had permits to work in Britain. It's very worrying."

"Why should it worry you, we can prove that we were here or at home when he was killed. By the way, when was he killed? "

"He didn't say exactly, just that it was about ten days to a fortnight ago," said Guiseppe. "It's very worrying."

"Stop going on about it," said his brother, "what's more worrying is that the money he stole was going towards the improvements to the club that we planned for the winter. Can we make it up in time, should we borrow some more or should we postpone the improvements?"

"We'll have to borrow more from the bank. I'd hoped to avoid doing that. That's why I did it."

"You lost me somewhere there among the that's," said Francis. "That's why you did what?"

"Asked Michael Bernoulli to find him and collect our money," said Guiseppe.

"You did what?" exploded his brother.

"I asked Michael Bernoulli to try and get our money back. I promised him ten percent of what he got out of him."

"I can't believe what I'm hearing, you asked Mick the Knife to collect our money?"

"Yes," said Guiseppe, "I didn't see why Farrell should get away with it."

"Have you seen him since?"

"No but he phoned up and said that he hadn't found Farrell. "

"Is that all that he said?" asked his brother.

"Well no, he said that he'd try again when he came back from the Bahamas. Now he needn't bother."

"The time that I tried to collect our money from him at his flat," said Francis, "Farrell said that if we wanted it we'd have to take him to court and he'd tell the world what went on upstairs at the Four Oaks Club. He said that if we were sensible we'd make it up on the tables in a week."

"It's a question of principle," said Guiseppe, relieved to have got it over with. But his brother wasn't finished.

"When exactly did you ask Mick the Knife to collect our debt?"

"About a month ago."

"And when did he phone and say that he couldn't find him?"

"A week ago, before he went away."

"And Farrell was stabbed about ten days ago?"

"You don't think that Michael stabbed him, do you?" asked Guiseppe, giving voice to what had been worrying him ever since the police inspector had called.

"How would I know?" said Francis. "He's mad enough to have done it. What you must do, little brother, is keep your head down and if anyone asks you if you told Michael Bernoulli the debt collector with dubious associates, to collect the money you say that you didn't. Understand, you tell them that you didn't?"

"Michael wouldn't like that. He might turn really nasty."

"Well then, admit that when speaking with Michael you did mention the outstanding debt that Farrell owed and that he must have misunderstood your meaning."

"Alright but it's worrying, isn't it?"

But Francis was already on his way, hoping to bump into that rather nice girl who helped wealthy business men relax in the rooms upstairs.

Chapter Seventeen

DETECTIVE Inspector Don Donovan of the Metropolitan Police had revised his opinion of the provincial police in the past few days. Well, not provincial police as a whole but Dorset police in particular. He'd rather liked that girl sergeant who had come to London to brief him. None of the 'it's our case really and you can whistle if you expect any co-operation from us' attitude that often accompanied requests for assistance from provincial forces.

What was her name? Clare Thornton. She wanted enquiries made in London concerning a Raymond Farrell, deceased, who had lived in a flat at Crimpers Court in Golders Green. Instead of the bald request, the Dorset Super had sent the girl and all her case material. He now knew that she thought that the Farrell killing was one of a pair, his girl-friend had also been killed on the same day but not at the same time or place. She'd been found in a river but she hadn't drowned.

Don Donovan knew that you can't solve crimes and get convictions without clues and the Bournemouth sergeant had brought two vital clues, a partial fingerprint and DNA. His mind dwelt on the nature of those clues. To him they spanned the forensic timeframe. It had been the realisation that fingerprints were unique to the person owning them that had sparked the explosion in criminology at the end of the nineteenth century and it had been the discovery of the uniqueness of a person's DNA that had done the same at the end of the twentieth century.

He expected an early result. The fingerprints that the sergeant said had been on a door frame in a yacht weren't of the best quality, they were partly obscured by later prints put there by the girl who had found the body. Inconsiderate of her but, the inspector presumed, there can't be too much spare space on a door frame in a yacht. Incomplete though they were, they had run the fingerprints through the files on the computer and had got a few partial matches. One of those partial matches suggested that the little finger of the left hand was that of a small time thug called Sailor Nesbit

Inspector Donovan suspected that a good defence counsel would be able to challenge the fingerprint evidence as open to reasonable doubt, but it gave him a starting point, especially when he brought up the man's record and saw that he was had a string of convictions for assault. He sent his boys out to bring him in. They returned and reported that he wasn't at his last known address, or the one after that, or the one after that. In fact no one seemed to know where he was.

A not unusual situation but annoying and time consuming, as and when his small staff weren't engaged on more pressing investigations, they would have to haunt his favourite watering holes and such like until he turned up. The law has a long memory. What a blessing it is that criminals, like all beings, are creatures of habit.

Inspector Donovan found time to study the copies of the more important documents that Clare had found in Farrell's flat and yacht. It appeared that he was up to his eyes in debt and to Donovan's certain knowledge, the sort of people to whom he owed money, weren't choosy as to the means that their agents used to persuade bad payers to pay. What fools some men were. That rang a bell, Sailor Nesbit had been an enforcer in his time, perhaps he was again. Donovan decided to call on the loan shark who held Raymond Farrell's promissory documents. He knew precisely where the office of Celestial Loans was, in a back street in Whitechapel.

He buzzed for his sergeant, Sidney Tyler

"Sid, about this murder on which the Dorset police have asked for our help, it occurs to me that the people he owed money to may have employed Sailor Nesbit to lean on Farrell. I thought that I'd call at their office in Trenter Street in Whitechapel, and see what they've got to say for themselves and I'd like you to come along."

"OK Gov, we still haven't been able to find him. Shall I get a car?"

"No, we'd spend most of the afternoon stuck in traffic jams, we'll go by tube, what's the nearest station?"

"Whitechapel I suppose, on the District Line from the Embankment, couldn't be more convenient," said Tyler.

"St James's Park would be better," muttered Donovan.

"True," said the sergeant, "I thought the walk would do us good."

"What do we know about Sailor Nesbit, Sid?"

"His proud parents christened him Albert Basil Nesbit. He put up with a lot of ragging at school where the kids called him Basil and said that it was a cissy name. Albert Basil fought the lot of them until one of his teachers, taking the attendance roll, called out AB Nesbit and remarked that he'd better join the navy when he left school. He was Sailor Nesbit from that time on but the fighting habit stuck and he was continually in trouble at school, then with the young offenders people and eventually prison."

"Employment?"

"Left school with no qualifications and drifted from one labouring job to another, then petty crime for which he was usually caught because he wasn't very clever. Then he joined a travelling boxing circus and, of course, he was billed as Sailor Nesbit, the Cruiser Weight. He got a bit punch-drunk and the doctors forced the owner of the boxing outfit to sack him. Since then he's been a hired bully-boy existing mainly on petty crime and what state benefits the government can be fooled into paying him."

"Does he have a wife and family?"

"No, not any longer," said the sergeant, "he married the girl who worked the box office at the boxing ring and she divorced him years ago."

"And we've no idea where he is at present?" asked Donovan.

"No and that, I suggest, is a question that we should ask Celestial Loans."

The registered office of Celestial Loans consisted of the front two rooms of the ground floor of one of the houses in Trenter Street. A small sign advertised that the proprietor was a Mr Vinji Singh and underneath that 'The sky's the limit.'

They went in and found a young woman in a sari seated behind a desk. A triangular prism announced that she was Miss Parveen Singh. Evidently a family business. She greeted them with a smile,

"Good afternoon, can I help you?"

"We're the police. We'd like to see Mr Singh," said the inspector showing his identity card.

"You haven't got an appointment," said Miss Singh.

"I don't think that you understood what the inspector said," said the sergeant. "We're the police and we want to see Mr Singh."

"I heard you the first time. My father is a very busy man and he can't simply drop everything because two policemen happen to call. What did you want to see him about?"

"Mr Raymond Farrell," said Donovan.

"Is he one of our customers?"

"Judged by the letters that you have written to him this summer, I would certainly think so," said Donovan.

The girl turned to the keyboard of her word-processor and tapped in a command. She studied the monitor and said,

"Yes, I see that a Mr Raymond Farrell has an account with us. How does he concern you?"

"We wish to discuss that with Mr Singh," said the Inspector.

"My father isn't available," said the girl and turned away from them.

This was a tactical error. The sergeant promptly walked past her and opened the door into the rear room. A grey haired man was sitting at a desk studying some papers. "Good afternoon Mr Singh," said the sergeant, "we're the police and we have some questions to ask you."

Miss Singh arrived at this moment, shouting in Hindi, and endeavoured to pull the door shut but Sergeant Tyler was not to be budged by a slip of a girl.

"Your daughter has refused to let us see you," said the Inspector who had followed, "so please understand this, you either answer our questions now or we will send some uniformed officers to take you to the police station for questioning."

"And what would that do your reputation, Mr Singh?" asked the sergeant who rather wished that would happen.

The man's daughter was still shouting and her father said something curt to her in Hindi. She shouted back and the man turned to the inspector, saying,

"I'm sure that won't be necessary, my daughter clearly didn't understand your request."

"Yes I did," said the girl in English, "you told me that you didn't want to see anyone this afternoon."

He said something else to her and she sulkily took a few paces back and stood in the doorway.

"Now gentlemen, of course we want to assist the forces of law and order, how can I help you?"

"They want to know about Raymond Farrell," said the girl.

"Ah yes, Raymond Farrell. Not one of our best customers I'm afraid," said her father. "You'll understand that I can't discuss the details of his account with you. If I did I might possibly be rendering myself open to a claim for damages."

"We don't want to discuss the details of his account with you, Mr Singh," said Donovan, "we want to discuss the methods that you use to collect the sums outstanding from people who are behind with their payments."

"Has someone complained?" said the man.

"Many people have complained," said Donovan, he was sure that it must be true. "How do you go about collecting bad debts?"

"We send them letters pointing out how far behind they are with their repayments."

"And if that doesn't produce the money," said Donovan, "do you take them to court?" He knew that such action would be the moneylender's last resort.

"We try the personal approach," said Mr Singh.

"You mean that you or your daughter go and see the debtor?"

"Well, no, we use an agent."

"I need to know the name of the agency or agent who you use," said the inspector.

"I don't see why I should tell you all my business," said Mr Singh. "Suffice it that we use an agent. If Mr Farrell has a complaint about my agent he should discuss it with me, not the police."

"He's in no position to discuss it with you, Mr Singh, he's dead..."

This was clearly news to father and daughter.

"... and he didn't die from natural causes. Your refusal to reveal the nature of the agency who you used to collect from Mr Farrell could lay you open to a charge of conspiracy or worse. Do you understand me?"

The daughter said, "We should claim against his estate, father," and he said abstractedly,

"Yes, I suppose that we should."

Donovan said,

"Now do you understand why we need to know who you used to lean-on Raymond Farrell?"

"Sailor Nesbit," said Mr Singh after some hesitation, "but I'm sure that he would have had nothing to do with the man's death. How did he die?"

"That will come out at the inquest," said Donovan. "What instructions did you give to Sailor Nesbit?"

"My father had nothing to do with it," said Miss Singh. "He came in looking for work and I told him that Mr Farrell was weeks behind with his repayments and we wanted our money."

175

"Is that all that was said?" asked Donovan.

"Of course not," said the girl, "he asked me where Mr Farrell lived and I looked up his address, the address to which we'd been writing."

"Crimpers Court?" asked Sergeant Tyler.

The girl went back into the front office, tapped some keys on her keyboard, looked at the monitor and came back to the doorway to say,

"Yes, that's right, Crimpers Court, Golders Green."

"Parveen told me about it when we were chatting at the end of the day," said Mr Singh.

"And that's all that you know?" asked Inspector Donovan.

"Yes," said the girl, "Sailor Nesbit walked out of the door and we haven't seen him since."

"I'd like his address, please, Mr Singh."

The father looked at his daughter and said, "Do you have it?"

"No, but I have a telephone number."

"I'd like that please."

"The garage might know where he lives," volunteered the girl.

"What garage would that be and how do they come into it?" said Sergeant Tyler.

"We got to know about Sailor Nesbit's debt collecting from the man who owns the Ace Garage in the Whitechapel Road. He gave us the telephone number."

"I see," said the inspector.

They thanked Mr Singh for his assistance, collected the telephone number from his daughter and left.

On the pavement, Sergeant Tyler said,

"Where to now, Gov?"

"You know already, Sid."

"OK then, it shouldn't be far."

It proved to be further than they had thought but eventually they came to what might have once been a bomb site but which was now covered with brightly polished second-hand cars, each proclaiming it to be a bargain in perfect working order and displaying a price ending in 995 or 495. To the rear was a workshop with a hydraulic platform upon which was a car with a man in oil-stained overalls crouched under it.

In front was a white painted cabin that announced in large black letters above the door that it was the office. Donovan and Tyler went in at the open door. There were two desks at right angles to each other, behind one of which a shapely blonde in a low-cut blouse was filing her nails. She looked up and said,

"He's out," and went on filing her nails.

"How do you know what we want?" asked Tyler.

She flashed him a smile that transformed her face and said,

"Well, when you walked across the forecourt you didn't look at any of the cars, so I figured that you don't want to buy a used car and you're both too old for me, see?"

Donovan looked in the direction she was looking and saw a CCTV screen on the wall behind him, displaying the forecourt scene. So she wasn't a dumb blonde, perhaps it came out of a bottle.

The younger Sergeant Tyler looked at her and thought 'that's what you think, darling.'

"When are you expecting Mr er ahem back?" asked Donovan.

"Archie? Oh you never know with him, he often doesn't get back until after I've gone home."

"Perhaps you can help us," ventured Donovan. "We're police officers…"

"I didn't think that you were holy gospellers," smiled the girl.

"…and we're making enquiries about Sailor Nesbit."

"What's the poor old sod been up to this time?"

"Nothing, as far as we know," said the inspector, " but he might have been in the vicinity of where a crime was committed and we'd like to ask him some questions. We've got his phone number but there's no reply."

"He lives in a council flat just round the corner," she took a sheet of paper out of a drawer of her desk, studied it, and said,

"Here he is, Mr A.B. Nesbit, Number 25 Peabody Building."

Her eyes flickered to the screen on the wall and she said, "Here's Archie now."

They heard the noise of a powerful engine which stopped abruptly and less than half a minute later a man bustled into the office. He was dressed in a somewhat shiny suit and suede shoes with thinning hair brushed straight back. Only one word came into Don Donovan's mind, Spiv.

"Hello, what's this Delores, I can't leave you for a minute without some customers chatting you up, can I? Have you shown them our motors?"

"No Archie, they're the police."

Archie's bonhomie disappeared instantly, he snapped,

"Why can't you people leave us alone, you won't find any hot auto's on my lot."

"They're not looking for stolen cars, Archie, they've come about Sailor Nesbit."

"What about old Sailor, wot's he done now?"

Donovan thought that it was about time he got into the act.

"We wanted his address and your secretary has given us that."

"What d'you want his address for?"

Donovan ignored that and asked,

"Do you employ Sailor to collect bad debts?"

"Sure, is that wrong now?" said Archie.

"Depends how he does it. The law's getting stricter on that sort of thing," said Donovan. "It appears that you recommended Sailor to Celestial Loans and the man they sent him to collect from, a few weeks ago, was found dead."

Delores caught her breath and said,

"I'm sure that old Sailor wouldn't kill anyone, but he can get very angry and that frightens people, look what he did to that chap who bought the yellow Porsche and then defaulted on the repayments."

"Sailor was going up to Golders Green again the other week," said Archie, " do you know how he got on darling?"

"He phoned and said that he wasn't there and that some old dear in the flat opposite had said that he was away on his yacht," said Delores.

"There's no justice, is there?" said Archie. "Here am I working my fingers to the bone to earn an honest copper." He paused as if to make some clever remark about the mutual incompatibility of honesty and policemen but decided not to push his luck; they might decide to look a bit more closely at the red BMW that he had on the forecourt, "and this guy owes me money for a car and now I hear that he's got a yacht. Did the old bint say where he had his yacht?"

"No," said Delores, "but she told Sailor that he'd sent her a postcard from Bournemouth and Sailor said that there's a big harbour right next door called Poole. I remember because I thought that it was funny. You can float boats in pools, can't you?"

"Did I understand you correctly? Did you sell a car to a man who has an address in Golders Green and a yacht in Poole?"

"If old Sailor is to be believed, yes."

"Would his name happen to be Farrell?"

"Yes," said Delores, "Raymond Farrell, he tried it on with me. Kept asking me to go to some club up West with him. I nearly did."

"You didn't tell me that," said Archie.

"I didn't want to upset you," said Delores, who had nearly given her all to Farrell. "He offered me a job as well."

"I don't believe what I'm hearing," said Archie. "When old Sailor turns up I'll send him down to Poole again to sort that bleeder out."

"Somebody already did," said Tyler. "That's why we want to question Sailor Nesbit."

Delores was quicker on the uptake than was Archie. She asked, "Sorted him out permanently?"

"Yes," said Donovan.

"Did he hit him too hard?"

"No, somebody stabbed him."

"I'm sure that Sailor wouldn't do that," said Delores. "People who have made their living with their fists wouldn't use a dagger."

Donovan privately agreed with her.

Archie was overwhelmed by the realisation that he would never get the two thousand two hundred and fifty pounds owing and that would put him even deeper in the red with that old skinflint money-lender Singh and his daughter.

"Is my auto down in Poole?"

"I suppose so," said Donovan.

"I'd better get dahn there and bring it back, hadn't I?"

"You'll have to talk to the Dorset police," said Tyler.

Inspector Donovan and the Sergeant asked a few more questions but nothing that would be useful in their enquiry emerged. After getting instructions from Delores on how to get to number 25 Peabody Building, they left.

"What now, Gov?" asked Sergeant Tyler.

"It's getting on a bit isn't it and I think that it would be better for us to interview Sailor at the station. I'll ask uniform to bring him in tomorrow morning, assuming that he's at home."

"What about if the garage tip him off?"

"I can't see Archie doing that," said Donovan, then added, "Dolores might."

"You think that she's one of the girls with a heart of gold?"

"Haven't you noticed, most girls with big boobs are kind hearted," grinned the inspector.

"So it's back to St James's?"

"Yes."

Chapter Eighteen

SAILOR NESBIT wasn't overjoyed to find two policemen at his door the following morning. It had happened before and, he supposed, it would happen again. He wasn't surprised when they invited him to come with them to assist in their enquiries, or, that when he asked them politely (for Sailor) what precisely those enquiries were concerned with, that they merely said that it was a serious matter. He was, however surprised to find that he wasn't taken to the local nick but to Scotland Yard. It must be serious.

He was taken to an interview room where Donovan and Tyler were waiting, having been alerted while Sailor was being processed.

Sailor got his protest in first.

"Wot you brought me 'ere for, I ain't done nufink."

"We just want to ask you some questions, Sailor, and we thought that it would be quieter here than in your flat."

"Wot about me time? I might 'ave 'ad somefink important to do this mornin' like going to the doctor or collecting me uncmployment pay."

"I thought that they paid that into your bank account these days," said Tyler, idly.

"I don't 'old wiv banks," said Sailor.

Inspector Donovan brought the talk back to the matter in hand.

"We'll see that you're taken back, if you help us with our enquiries."

"Wot about?"

"Raymond Farrell," said Donovan.

"Who's Raymond Farrell when 'es at 'ome?"

"He's the man who you went to Poole to collect money from."

A sly look came over Sailor's face.

"Oh, 'im, what you want to know about 'im? Wot's in it for me?"

"Only going home tonight instead of down to the cells," said Tyler who thought that his inspector was too kind to crooks.

"If you're goin' to say things like that I ought to 'ave a lawyer. I know my rights."

"Look Sailor, you can have a lawyer present if you wish but it will take time, all I want to do is to ask you a few questions."

"Wot you want to know then?"

"Why did you go to Poole?"

"I went there because Archie arst me to collect his money."

Again that sly look.

"Is that all?" prompted Donovan.

"Well, when Archie arst me I remembered that the geyser owed old Shylock money as well, so I went and saw that daughter o' 'is – she's as mean as 'e is – an' she arst me to get theirs as well." He thought about that and added, "that's not exakerly true, she said that if I wanted any more work from them I 'ad to get their ten grand first."

"How did you know where he was?"

"The old bint as lives opposite showed me a postcard 'as 'ed sent 'er from Bournemouth, so I went there and looked in all the places where there were boats."

"But how did you expect to know which one he was in?" asked Tyler. "There must be thousands of boats."

"Easy, I looked in the car parks for that blue car wot Archie sold 'im. The one he owed the money on."

"And you spotted the car?"

"Me an' a few seagulls," laughed Sailor.

"You found the car?" persisted Donovan.

Sailor was disappointed that his joke hadn't had the detectives rolling in the aisles but it confirmed his view that they weren't like other people, otherwise they wouldn't be policemen, would they? Stands to reason.

"You found the car?" repeated Donovan.

"Yus, in the 'arbour at Poole. Big place Poole with a big 'arbour wiv 'undreds of boats in it an' I didn't know which one was 'is but I fort it must be one near to where 'is car was parked, close to the 'arbour master's offices."

"What did you do?" asked the inspector.

"I decided to wait until he came for his car but after a while I decided that I'd borrow a rowing boat and row round the bigger boats and see if I could spot 'im. There was a boat under the 'arbour master's place but it didn't 'ave any oars. Then I spotted a boat coming towards me wiv a chap an' a girl. The girl was doin' the rowing, dressed in a dress which I remember because it was a nice day and everybody else down there was dressed in shorts, an' the man wasn't sittin' at the back but at the front, close up behind the girl. When they got to the slip, he jumped out and pulled the boat up a bit for the girl to get out. He hurried 'er away, leaving the oars behind."

"Did you get a good look at the man?" asked Tyler.

"No I was looking at the bint, she was a good-looker and she 'ad no shoes on. I fort it was to get out of the boat but she didn't 'ave any to put on. I fort that she looked frightened. Perhaps she didn't like the sea, some people don't you know."

"What did you do then?"

"I borrowed their boat and rowed past some of the yachts. When I came to the boat where the geyser and the girl 'ad come from, I noticed it's name, Sea Raven, and then I remembered that Farrell had put something about being a sea raven in the writing on the back of the postcard that he'd sent to the old girl in Golders Green. "

"That was very clever of you," said Donovan. "Did you go aboard?"

"Yus an' I wish I never 'ad. I tied up my boat and climbed over the side but there was no one there. So I went through the cabin and looked in the next room. I found a man wiv blood on his shirt, lying dead on one of the bunks. I fort either this is Farrell or the geyser wiv the girl was Farrell and I didn't want to get mixed up in it, so I rowed back to the slip an' scarpered."

"What did you tell Archie and Mr Singh?"

Again that sly look.

"There wasn't any point in telling them that I'd found him either dead or alive so I said that I couldn't find 'im. Arter all, they might 'ave arst me to make another search, mightn't they?"

Sergeant Tyler placed a picture of Laura Wells in front of Sailor, asking,

"Is this the girl who you saw in the dinghy?"

Sailor picked up the photo and looked at it closely, finally saying,

"It could be, except that she looks more peaceful in the photo."

Amen, thought Inspector Donovan.

"That's been a great help to us, Sailor. The man who you found dead on the bunk was Raymond Farrell and the girl was his girl-friend, Laura Wells who was murdered that same day somewhere out in the country. Our conclusion is that the man who you saw with the girl in the boat murdered them both, so we'd like you to tell us all that you can remember about him."

Coffee and biscuits were brought in and Sailor realised that he was a valuable witness. It might be worth a few quid.

"Well, Gov, I didn't really get a good look at him, I was looking at the girl."

"Yes Sailor, we understand, that was entirely natural because she was a strikingly beautiful girl but try to remember, what colour was his hair, what colour were his clothes, did he speak to the girl, was he white, did he have a weapon? Try hard to remember anything, imagine that you're standing near to the slipway watching them coming towards you, she's doing the rowing and he's close behind her partly obscuring your view of her."

"He had a light blue shirt without a tie, dark blue trousers and a jacket of the same colour in his left hand when he got out of the boat." Sailor looked down and moved his arms, miming the movements the man had made. "He had dark hair, much darker than either of you two and he was sun tanned."

Sailor thought about this and added,

"That might 'ave been 'is colour, 'e might 'ave been an arab or from Spain dressed in our sort of clothes."

"Mediterranean?" prompted the sergeant.

"Yes, that too," said Sailor.

"Did he say anything?"

"Yes, he said, 'Come on' sharp like. Come to think of it, he didn't sound like us."

Don Donovan shrugged aside the implication that he and his sergeant had also been born within the sound of the bells of Bow Church. He said,

"He had an accent?"

"Yus, like some of them waiters you gets in pubs these days. Give me a good old-fashioned barmaid any time."

A possible interpretation of this remark occurred to Sailor and a smile spread across his face. He added,

"Not 'arf."

"I know that this might sound like a silly question, Sailor but bear with us. Did you see any indication that the man who you saw was carrying a weapon?"

"You mean a shooter?"

"Yes, a gun or a knife," said the inspector.

"No, but he might have had one, that could have been why he was sitting close to the girl and why he had his coat over his arm and why she looked so scared."

A question that he realised he should have asked earlier occurred to Inspector Donovan,

"How tall was the man and was he fat or thin?"

"Oh, Gov, I don't know, he was bent over most of the time, in the boat and pulling it up the slip."

"Think back to when he said, 'Come on' and they walked up the slip, was he taller than the girl, the same size or shorter?"

Sailor creased his brow and screwed up his eyes as he thought about this and said,

"She came up to his ear level and he wasn't fat, but square looking."

"By that do you mean that he didn't have a narrow waist?"

"Yus, that's it, he didn't go in."

They went over the ground a second time but Sailor had nothing to add and he was thanked for his valuable assistance and taken back to Peabody Building.

Later in the day Inspector Donovan summarised what they knew about the man who had left the Sea Raven with Laura. About six feet tall, not fat but starting to lose his waistline, black hair, a Mediterranean complexion and speaking with a slight accent. He also probably took care of his clothes that included a dark blue lightweight suit and a light blue shirt. It wasn't much but was better than nothing.

Sergeant Tyler thought that he'd read something about a dark suit and a light blue shirt in that Dorset sergeant's account. He'd look it up when he had the time. Dark suits and light blue shirts were fairly common.

What could have been the motive for the murders? Killing the girl may have been unplanned or at least unintentional and had occurred because she could identify the man who had killed Farrell. So Farrell was the key, why had he been killed? The most common reasons for murder were bound up with money or women, I want your money, I want your woman or you've had my woman. Jealousy is wrapped up in those as well.

Donovan recited this to his sergeant and was disappointed that Tyler seemed to be unimpressed, saying,

"So?"

"So what, Sid?"

"So where does that get us?"

"Well, for one thing, I don't think that he was killed because he had been having an affair with somebody else's woman because he had been going with Laura Wells for at least six weeks."

"A rejected female lover might have taken that long to accept that he had rejected her and then to find a hit-man," said Tyler.

"There would have been letters at his flat or in the yacht and there weren't any."

"OK then, Gov, where does that get us?"

"Money," said Donovan.

"But Farrell didn't have any."

"That I admit is a problem," said the inspector.

"Apart from his clothes, he appears to have had only two possessions," said Sergeant Tyler, "his car and the yacht and he hadn't paid for either of those. We know that he owed the Ace Garage most of the money for the car, and he still owed the yacht company £15,000. What about the yacht, it must have cost more than the £15,000?"

"He had borrowed from Mr Singh," said the inspector.

"The ten grand that he owed Celestial Loans and the money that he still owed wouldn't cover the purchase price of that yacht," said Tyler with great authority.

"How much would it take to get a yacht like that, then?"

"I don't know but even second hand it would be more than that."

"So we could be looking for another lender?" said the inspector.

"Or someone who he swindled," said the sergeant.

"There was no trace of another creditor in the papers that were in his flat or boat."

"Then where do we go from here, Gov?"

"Two places, we ask the people who sold him the yacht for details of the transaction and we go and have another chat with his employers."

Sergeant Tyler went through the dead man's papers and found that he had purchased the yacht Mermaid 2 from a yacht brokers in Lymington. He wondered if you have to tell anyone if you change the name of a yacht?

They drove to Lymington the next day and called on the Fairbrother Yacht Company (1975) They were received in a sumptuously furnished office by a Mr Fairbrother who was dressed in white trousers, white shirt and blue blazer with a blue tie with little yachts on it. His bonhomie faded when he found that they were policemen and he returned to sit behind a large desk and asked, condescendingly, to what he owed the visit.

"We've come about the yacht Mermaid 2 that you sold to a Mr Raymond Farrell," said Inspector Donovan.

"Let me see, Mermaid 2?" He took a ledger from one of the desk drawers and turned over the pages. He stopped at a page and said,

"What about Mermaid 2, there was nothing wrong with her when we sold it?"

"As far as we know there is nothing wrong with the yacht, it's the man who bought her who interests us, " said Donovan.

Mr Fairbrother looked down at the ledger and said,

"Yes, I can well understand that. Between you and I, he still owes a substantial sum on the vessel. We contemplated taking legal action and he seemed such an affluent gentleman, too."

"Most confidence tricksters do," said the sergeant.

"How did that happen?" asked Donovan.

"He paid £40,000 and sent us a cheque for the balance after we'd let him take delivery of the yacht. The cheque bounced and he still owed us £15,000. Our legal advisers are in process of getting the vessel back. He renamed it Sea Raven."

"Do you have a record of how he paid the £40,000?"

He consulted the ledger once more.

"Yes, he paid by two personal cheques, one for £30,000 and the second, a week later for £10,000. He said that he'd had to sell some shares and would wait until their price went up before he paid the balance of £15,000. We should have realised at the time that this was a ruse."

"I'm sure that it all seemed to be reasonable and above board at the time," said Donovan, helpfully.

"Oh yes it was," said Mr Fairbrother. "My wife, who's the other director, was quite taken with him. Such a well mannered young man, she invited him home to meet our daughter."

Inspector Donovan could sense that his sergeant was about to comment and said, hastily,

"Thank you very much, Mr Fairbrother for sparing us your valuable time, it has been most useful."

With which he stood up, shook Fairbrother's hand and led the sergeant out and back to their car.

Sergeant Tyler could scarcely contain himself.

"Took him home to meet their daughter, eh, it's a wonder that Farrell doesn't own the firm by now. What mugs some people are."

The topic kept him amused for most of the way back through the New Forest.

After a while the sergeant said,

"I wonder where the thirty grand came from?"

"I was just thinking about that," said Donovan. "If you recall, the bank statements that we found in his flat, he paid in £35,000 about three months ago. The bank immediately took something over £3,000 to pay off his overdraft and within a week he paid £30,000 to the Lymington yacht people. Which still leaves us with the question, where did the £35,000 come fro?"

"The usual sources, could be a legacy, a win at the races or on the Premium Bonds or a bonus from work."

"He had a sister somewhere near to Bristol, she might be able to help," said the inspector, "although the sergeant from Dorset got the impression that the sister didn't think much of him."

"She must be a good judge of character," smiled the sergeant.

They were silent and occupied with their own thoughts for a few miles and then Donovan said,

"It couldn't have been winnings."

"How's that?"

"The timing, Sid. He got the £35,000 and paid £30,000 almost immediately for the yacht. That must mean that he'd already decided to buy the yacht and must have known where to lay his hands on the money."

"So it's a legacy or a bonus," said the sergeant.

"The bonus might be severance pay."

"If it was, why did he keep the flat at Golders Green?"

"Resigning or getting the sack doesn't mean that you have to move, Sid."

"No, I suppose not," said the sergeant somewhat doubtfully.

They drove for a further few miles and the sergeant said,

"It probably wasn't a legacy. Remember in the lady sergeant's note of her meeting with his sister, she said that the rotter took all of their parent's savings."

"True," said the inspector, "but it might have been from a maiden aunt who liked boys."

"I favour the bonus from work idea," said Sergeant Tyler, "partly because it was a nice round number."

"That might be significant, Sid. Tomorrow, I want you to ring his sister and ask her if she knows anything about a legacy. Then we'll go and see his employers again.

Chapter Nineteen

THE next morning Sergeant Tyler phoned the sister who lived at a farm near to Bristol. After saying Hello a number of times he heard a female voice complaining that the dratted phone had gone wrong again. He put his phone down and called again ten minutes later.

"Hello?"

"Hello," thundered a voice in his ear, "What are you playing at?"

"This is the police," said the sergeant quickly, "Is that Mrs Barbara Nash?"

"Yes, Who wants her?"

"This is the police, Mrs Nash. I'd like to ask you a question about your brother Raymond Farrell."

"He's dead. It's no good asking me."

"Do you know if he received a legacy within the past six months?"

"What's that, you mean somebody left him something in their will?"

"Yes."

"If they did I never heard of it."

This clearly wasn't going in a helpful direction. Tyler tried again.

"Have any of your relatives died in the past six months, Mrs Nash?"

"Yes."

"And did they leave any money to your brother?"

"No, silly, he's the relative as died."

"Not any aunts or uncles?"

"No only Boy, that's what my parents called Ray. He's the only one who's died and it seems that he's left me a peck of trouble."

Sergeant Tyler decided to call it a day. It seemed conclusive that no one had left Raymond Farrell a legacy.

He prepared a file note and on re-reading Clare Thornton's account of her visit to Holly Tree Farm, realised that there was another possibility. Say that the older woman with whom he'd had an affair and who's money he had squandered, had died and left him something? Surely there would have been a piece of paper somewhere in his flat? He decided not to raise this red herring with his inspector.

He reported to his boss that the deceased's sister had no knowledge of any legacy and doubted that there had been one.

"OK," said Donovan. "After lunch we'll visit the Four Oaks Club in Jermyn Street, there's probably no sense in going earlier."

The receptionist at the club asked them to wait while she checked to see if one of the brothers was available. The inspector thought about what he'd say to the club owners while the sergeant studied the receptionist's vital statistics and thought that she probably wouldn't be as kind hearted as Delores but well worth the try.

The girl knew that Guiseppe was the only brother in. Not ten minutes before the arrival of the police, brother Francis had leant over her desk and told her that he was stepping out for a minute. That meant for at least an hour. She told the secretary who did for the brothers that two policemen wanted to see one or other of the brothers..

The girl buzzed Guiseppe and told him that two policemen wanted to see him.

"What do they want?" said Guiseppe.

"They want to see you. Mr Francis is out."

"He's always out when he's wanted. Ask them what they want."

His secretary spoke into the phone. The receptionist said to Inspector Donovan,

"I'm afraid that Mr Francis is out and Mr Guiseppe is in conference and wants to know what you want to see him about?"

"Mr Raymond Farrell, deceased," said Donovan.

The receptionist passed the message.

From the time that whoever was at the other end of the telephone was taking, it was evident to the inspector that someone was making up their mind whether to see them or not. That suggested to Donovan that someone knew that there was something illegal going on at the club or at the very least, that there was something to hide concerning Farrell. The receptionist sat with the phone clamped to her ear. Finally she said,

"I'm afraid that Mr Guiseppe is terribly busy and it will be at least an hour and perhaps two, before he can see you. He'd prefer it if you could make a proper appointment to come tomorrow."

Donovan was torn between being awkward and demanding that he see him now, sitting it out for perhaps two hours and coming back tomorrow. Common sense and the demand of his wife that he gets home at a reasonable time that day, prevailed and he said,

"Very well, ask whoever is at the end of that telephone what time would be convenient tomorrow."

The girl spoke down the phone, then turned to them and asked.

"Would 11 a.m. be convenient?"

"Quite," said Donovan, "and tell whoever you're talking to that if they stall us tomorrow like they have this afternoon, I'll have them brought in to the police station and question them there."

The following morning the receptionist phoned through that they had arrived and the brothers' secretary came out and escorted them into Francis' room.

"Good Morning gentlemen," said Francis, "please sit down, would you care for some coffee."

That settled and served, he went on,

"I understand that you wish to ask us about Raymond Farrell. Very sad."

"Yes, Sir, we're making enquiries into the circumstances of his death."

"I thought that he was stabbed in a boat," said Francis, smiling.

"We're trying to put together his finances," said Donovan, "and we wondered if you might be able to help us."

"We're always ready to assist the forces of law and order."

"Good," said Inspector Donovan, "then perhaps you would start by telling us the nature of Farrell's employment at the Four Oaks Club."

"When he was employed by us he wasn't a permanent member of our staff, he was employed on a casual basis as and when the need arose."

"So he wasn't a salaried employee?"

"No, more like self-employed. He wanted it that way." This was said with a knowing grin.

"So you didn't deduct income-tax and didn't have to provide for sickness, holidays and pension."

"Exactly," said Francesco called Francis, "there are advantages to both sides."

"What did he do at the club?"

"He was an assistant manager in the casino, which meant that he circulated among the clients, saw that they had gaming chips and that nothing untoward occurred."

"He was there to prevent or detect cheating," said Donovan.

"That too," said Francis righteously.

"You said that he was employed on a casual basis. Over what period was he so employed?"

Francis looked down at the file on his desk.

"I have his details here. He came to us last October when things started getting busier on the run-up to Christmas and the New Year, it seems to get earlier each year, and he left at the end of May."

"On mutually acceptable terms?" prompted Donovan, hoping for a mention of a bonus.

"If you mean that we weren't at loggerheads, yes."

"You didn't give him a bonus?"

There was a slight noise from a door on the side of the room. The Inspector and Sergeant exchanged glances and Tyler got up quietly, moved across the carpet and opened the door to reveal Guiseppe in a crouching position on the other side.

"You'd hear better if you came this side of the door," said the sergeant.

"You imbecile," screamed Francis, "I told you to leave it to me."

"I was worried," said Guiseppe.

"You're always worried," said his brother, "go back in your room."

"Oh no," said Donovan, "since you're not busy you must join us and tell us why you sacked Raymond Farrell."

"We didn't sack him, he took our money and didn't come back."

"Be quiet you fool," said Francis.

"Well, it's true," said Guiseppe, "we took him on because you said that he was an English gentleman and what did he do? He stole our money."

"£35,000 to be exact," said Donovan.

Both brothers looked at him, aghast.

"You knew?" said Guiseppe.

"You just told us," said Donovan. "Did you report your loss to the police?"

"Oh no," said Francis, "that would look bad for the club. We prefer to deal with these matters privately."

"Like hiring someone to kill him, mafia style?" said the sergeant.

"We had nothing to do with that," said Guiseppe. "I told him that he could have ten percent of what he collected."

"Told who?" asked the inspector.

"Be quiet you fool," shouted Francis, "can't you see that he knows nothing and is just leading you on?"

"He knew about the £35,000."

"Lucky guess. They've got his bankbook. Now don't say another word. I forbid it."

Guiseppe looked as if he would burst but sidled towards the door where he had been caught listening at the keyhole.

"We shall have to ask you some more questions Mr Maranti," said Donovan.

"Only with his lawyer present," said Francis.

"That's his privilege," said the inspector, "but you should realise that it heightens our belief that you both might have had something to do with Raymond Farrell's murder. I must caution you both not to leave the country."

"I said that for his own good, he's a born worrier and doesn't think about what he's saying."

"Many innocent people do that when we question them," said Donovan. "It's the crooks that remain tight-lipped."

Like you, thought the sergeant, eyeing Francis.

"There is little point in continuing this discussion," said Donovan. "If either of you wishes to provide a statement, here is my card. Next time I will arrange for you to be brought to a police station to continue the interview. In handcuffs if necessary."

The secretary, who served both brothers, gave them an old-fashioned look as they passed. She couldn't have failed to hear most of what had transpired.

That afternoon Don Donovan phoned Clare Thornton and brought her up to date with their enquiries. He described the interview with Sailor Nesbit and remarked,

"You really uncovered a mass of worms. Farrell owed money to all sorts of people, any one of whom might have invited a heavy-handed debt collector to recover their money. There's the garage owner, the money lender, the Four Oaks Club, the yacht-broker and I suppose that club in Bournemouth. And that's only the ones we know about."

"You can probably exclude the two down here, there's no indication that the Cavendish Club knew that he and the girl were cheating. If they had known she would have been instantly sacked and he wouldn't have been allowed in and as for the yacht man, he's a JP."

"They're sometimes the worst," laughed Donovan, "but I agree with you."

"That leaves the garage owner, the money lender and the club in Mayfair."

"The first two employed, if that's the right word, Sailor Nesbit," said Donovan, "and I don't think that old Sailor would use a dagger, he might rough someone up but he wouldn't stab them."

"And there's the girl as well," put in Clare.

"True, Sailor wouldn't have killed a girl and he's our prime witness at the moment which brings me to another of the reasons why I phoned you; would you make enquiries to see if anyone else had seen a man in a dark suit and light blue shirt with a girl leaving the slipway, presumably to get into a parked car."

Clare said that she'd see if any of the harbour CCTV tapes for the fateful day were still available, they were usually wiped after a week. She asked if they would send her a transcription of the interview with Sailor, she thought that there was something that rang a bell but she couldn't put her finger on it at the moment. Inspector Donovan said that he'd e-mail it right away.

Early the following morning Clare phoned Donovan.

"I'm sorry to say that all the CCTV tapes for that day have been wiped. The good news is that the people who found the body had earlier seen a man hurrying away from the river. This is what the Chancellor said,

The only person we saw was a chap walking back to a car which he then proceeded to back along the farm track.

And his wife said,

We weren't closer to him than the length of a football pitch but he didn't look country, he had a dark blue suit and a lighter blue shirt.

And her husband added,

His car was light green. Looked like a Mondeo saloon or estate from the distance.

An hour or more later they found the girl's body in the river. It's all in the file that I gave you."

"Thanks love," said Donovan. "Did I hear you say Chancellor?"

"Yes," said Clare. "It's hush-hush but he and his wife were staying at the local pub as Mr and Mrs Smith to get away from it all and bingo, they go for a country walk and find a girl who's just been murdered. And before you make any cracks about blood-suckers, they are very nice, down-to-earth, people."

"It looks as if they may have seen the killer, doesn't it?" said Donovan.

"Yes, he was supposed to have his detective with him but he'd told him to take the day off and sent him home to his wife and kids," said Clare.

"OK love, thanks for your help, I'll keep you posted."

Much later that morning, Inspector Donovan took a phone call from the Maranti's solicitor stating that he was preparing a statement for Mr Guiseppe Maranti and asking when it would be convenient for him to bring it to the station.

"You mean for Guiseppe Maranti to bring it to the station?" asked Donovan.

"No, I'm afraid not, Inspector," said the solicitor. "I know that it sounds irregular but wait until you see the statement."

The solicitor came at eleven and presented Donovan and Tyler with a typewritten statement which was signed by Guiseppe. It read,

Raymond Farrell was employed as an assistant manager at the Four Oaks Club, Jermyn Street, Mayfair from October 2004 until May 2005. He left voluntarily. When he left it was found that a sum of £35,000 was missing.

We visited his residence and he rudely refused to return the money, making untrue allegations and threatening to damage the club's reputation.

Subsequently I invited an agent to endeavour to collect the money by promising him 10% of whatever sum he recovered.

I have not seen or heard from the agent since that day.
Signed Guiseppe Maranti

Donovan said, "You know that this isn't good enough, don't you? When we say that we want to question someone who might be able to help us with our enquiries, we mean just that."

"I understand that but my client won't have it. He says that he knows nothing about any murders and he won't be budged."

"We don't think that he had anything directly to do with the murders," said Donovan, "but its possible that he might have triggered the chain of events that led to them."

"That, too, I appreciate," said the solicitor. "I pointed out to my client that if he persisted in withholding information he could render himself liable to charges, but he is adamant. He admitted to me privately when his brother was out of the room, that it's not the police that he's afraid of; they can only put him in prison."

"That's a most interesting observation," said Donovan.

"Yes, I thought that you'd be interested. What will you do now Inspector?"

"We shall have to bring him in and go through the motions, in your presence of course, and see if the mention of vendetta's and the mafia elicits any response. When would be convenient for you?"

The solicitor consulted his pocket diary and said, "I could manage after eleven the day after next."

"OK," said Donovan. "I'll have uniform at the club at ten-thirty to bring him in, in handcuffs if necessary."

Two days later uniformed police went to the Four Oaks Club in mid-morning, walked past the receptionist and told Guiseppe that they had come to take him to the police station for questioning. He protested, he shouted, he wept and he tried to lock himself in the washroom. The officers patiently explained that it was to discuss the statement that he had already provided but to no avail. Eventually they practically had to carry him to the car. They had the same bother at the station until he was delivered to the interview room where Donovan and the solicitor were waiting.

Sergeant Tyler was at the Four Oaks Club. His duty was to interview the receptionist and the brothers' secretary. He started with the receptionist who, according to what he now called the inspector's Delores rule, he judged was likely to be kinder than the secretary.

She said that all sorts of people came to see the brothers. Many had Italian sounding names. Well, they would, wouldn't they, the brothers being Italian? She lowered her voice,

"Mr Francis likes to pass himself off as an English gentleman and it confuses some of our clients, one brother being so obviously Italian, you see."

"Yes, that must puzzle them," said the sergeant. "Do you ask them their business?"

"Of course, then I pass them straight on to Dorothy, the brothers' secretary."

"We're interested in the man who brother Guiseppe asked to collect a debt. Being a licensed club, I suppose that some of the clients do sometimes owe the club money?" tried the sergeant.

"We don't see any of that, thank the Lord. It's done very discreetly by Mr Francis, he handles that side of the business, that's why he was so angry with Mr Guiseppe when he found out."

"Found out what?"

"Dorothy told me. It seems that one of the assistant managers has stolen a large sum of money and Mr Guiseppe had asked one of the Italians to try and collect it, not the usual people."

"Do you happen to know who the Italian was?" asked the sergeant.

"No, like I said, we don't see that side of the business but when I'm here at night I see some clients who look a bit like gangsters going in."

"I suppose that it would be difficult to keep them away if they behave themselves."

"Mr Francis says that their presence helps to prevent other people making trouble," said the receptionist.

"And you wouldn't have made a note of the name of anyone coming in?"

"No, I ask visitors their name and what they want, contact the club person concerned and pass them in or tell them to go away and write or phone for an appointment, and that's all. It's up to the person I pass them to, to get the details."

"So I should go and see your friend Dorothy?" said Tyler.

"Yes but don't tell her what I said about Mr Francis, she's very protective."

Sergeant Tyler walked through to the secretary's room from which separate doors opened into the brothers' rooms.

"Good morning Dorothy," said Tyler. "You know who I am don't you? Detective Sergeant Tyler and you know why I'm here?" said the sergeant.

"Yes, how can I help you, Sergeant?"

"Mr Guiseppe Maranti commissioned someone to collect a sum of money from a man called Raymond Farrell. We think that whoever that person was may be able to help us in our enquiries into two murders."

"Mr Guiseppe wouldn't hurt a fly."

"We don't think that he murdered anybody," said the sergeant, "but he may have spoken with the person who did."

"When was this?"

"We think, four to six weeks ago."

"They were very upset about Mr Farrell stealing that money so I suppose that it would be after he left and that would be a lot longer than that."

"They would have tried to get the money back themselves before employing an agent," said the sergeant.

"I suppose so and it would be before the brothers had their big row about it."

"What row was that?"

"I couldn't help overhearing bits of it, it seems that Mr Guiseppe had asked someone called Mick to collect the debt from Mr Farrell without consulting Mr Francis and Mr Francis didn't like it."

"Did this Mick come here?" asked the sergeant.

"He may have done while I was on annual leave. So was Mr Francis."

"Didn't one of the others provide secretarial duties for Mr Guiseppe while you were away?"

"No, Mr Francis insists that we get a temp. I can't understand why."

I bet that I can, thought Sergeant Tyler. He said,

"Can we look at Mr Guiseppe's engagement diary for that time."

Dorothy turned back the pages of the A4 sized book on her desk while the sergeant walked round to look over her shoulder. It was quite evident when she had been on leave, the meticulous entries in her hand suddenly changed to scrawled entries, often across several of the ruled lines, blots and areas of intricate doodles. Dorothy said,

"The temp was very untidy and doodled in the appointments book when she spoke on the phone."

She turned over the pages. The only entry that might refer to someone with the name Mick was one for 9th July that read 11.45 MB. That was all.

Sergeant Tyler thanked her for her help, assured her that Mr Guiseppe would come to no harm provided that he told the police the truth, thanked the receptionist and emerged into Jermyn Street where he stopped to phone Inspector Donovan. After what seemed to be a long time the inspector came on the line.

"Gov, it's Sid. The brothers had a big row because when the other one was on holiday, the one who's with you asked someone called Mick to collect the Farrell debt. All that I have is that someone with the initials MB called on Guiseppe at 11.45 on 9th July."

"Thanks Sid, I'll spring it on him."

Chapter Twenty

INSPECTOR DONOVAN had taken Guiseppe through his statement for the fourth time. Even the patient solicitor was becoming restless. Then Donovan had left the room to take the phone call. He returned and said,

"Now Mr Maranti, let's go through your statement one last time."

"I say, Inspector," said the solicitor, "you've been through it four times already."

"I know but I want to know what your client said to Mick when he gave him his instructions on 9th July."

The solicitor looked surprised and Guiseppe said,

"What I already told you, I said that he could have ten percent of what he collected."

"And you haven't heard from or seen Mick B. since?"

"No," said Guiseppe, " not a word…"

Then he stopped, realising what he had said,

"I don't know anyone called Mick B."

"But you just admitted it. He called on you at the club at a quarter to twelve on the morning of the 9th of July."

"I don't know anyone called Mick B."

"So that there's no confusion," said Donovan, "Mick is a Christian name and B the initial letter of a surname. Now, who is Mick B?"

"How many times do I have to tell you that I don't know anyone with those names?" cried Guiseppe.

"You may rest assured, Mr Maranti that we will find this man and when we have established that he is the murderer of Laura Wells, we will arrest you as an accessory to her murder."

"I thought that you said the murder of Raymond Farrell?" said Guiseppe.

"Yes, I'm a trifle confused myself," said the solicitor. "Who is Laura Wells?"

"Oh, didn't I say?" feigned Donovan, "she was Farrell's girl friend who was murdered the same day, after being raped."

"Do you have DNA evidence?" asked the solicitor.

"Yes," said Donovan, "ironic, isn't it? He might have got away with killing Farrell but he has to go and rape the girl before killing her and so he left his calling card behind."

"I didn't tell him to murder a girl, I mean, I didn't tell him to murder anyone," said Guiseppe.

"That will be for the courts to decide," said the inspector who was becoming sick of Guiseppe's obtuseness. "If you hadn't asked this Mick B to collect your debt, two people would still be alive and enjoying life on a yacht."

"I can't tell you his name, they'll kill me."

"Who will kill you, Mr Maranti?"

"They will. You English don't begin to understand the power of the mafia to exact vengeance years afterwards."

To the solicitor's surprise, Donovan said, "This interview was concluded at 11.30." He switched off the recording machine and pushed his note-book across the table, saying,

"This is off the record. You don't need to tell me a name, just write it on this page of my notebook and I'll guarantee to produce a cover story that shows that the police got the name from somewhere else."

"Before my client does anything, Inspector," said the solicitor "how sure are you that you can do any such thing?"

"We have a witness who saw him bring the girl off the yacht and another two witnesses who saw him hurrying away from the place where the girl's body was found. If I could show them a photo of this Mick B they will be the ones who have put the finger on him, not your client."

"You're sure of that?"

"Oh yes," said Donovan with his fingers crossed underneath the table. "I'm sure that he'll have form and we will say that they picked him out from the police mug-shots."

"What shall I do?" wailed Guiseppe, looking at his solicitor.

"I suggest that you do as the inspector asks."

Guiseppe laboriously wrote Michael Bernoulli on a blank page of Donovan's note-book and said,

"I don't think that he'd do anything like that, he phoned me about a week after he started looking and said that he hadn't been able to find Farrell and would look for him again when he got back from the Bahamas."

"And you haven't heard from him since?" said Donovan.

"No."

Donovan digested this piece of information and said "Remember both of you, this discussion never took place and you don't mention it to anyone."

"Not even to my brother Francesco?"

"Especially not to your brother Francis," said Donovan. "Don't tell anyone, if you tell your wife, she and your children will be in danger as well as you. Simply forget it, we won't come near to you again but you'll probably be required to give evidence at the trial about asking this Mick to try and recover your debt, there's nothing wrong in that, people are doing it all the time."

"Will you be producing a written record of the recorded discussion, Inspector?" asked the solicitor.

"In the circumstances I thought not," said Donovan, "unless you want one?"

"We're quite happy not to have a written record, Good-day Inspector."

With which he led a slightly bemused Guiseppe from the room.

The solicitor dropped Guiseppe off at the club. Guiseppe stopped worrying for long enough to be pleased that the solicitor would have to pay the cabbie, then realised that it would go on his bill anyway. He should have been a solicitor.

The solicitor went on his way deep in thought. He arrived at his destination, paid the cabbie and instead of entering his office building, walked back to the nearest underground station and entered a telephone booth. He took out his pocket diary and phoned a number that he found therein. The distant phone rang and was answered on the second ring.

"Hello, who is this?" said a cultured female voice.

"Silvestro Bessani, I wish to speak with Mr Luigi."

"What about, Mr Bessani?"

"A private matter, Signorina, I'm a solicitor."

There was a long pause, the solicitor couldn't decide whether the girl was consulting someone, thinking, or had forgotten him. In the end he said "Hello."

"Hello Signor Bessani," said a deep resonant voice, "it's a long time since we talked."

"Yes Signor Luigi, I guess that we're both too busy, we should let the young people do all the work."

"My secretary tells me that you want to talk with me on a private matter."

"Yes Signor," said the solicitor switching to Italian. "I don't know if it is of any interest or concern to you but the police are looking for someone called Michael Bernoulli in connection with two murders."

There was a long pause. Eventually the voice at the other end of the line said, in Italian,

"How do you know this?"

"I'm told that the police have witnesses who saw him forcing a girl to go with him after a man was stabbed in a boat. The girl was killed later, they think by him."

"Where is all this supposed to have happened?"

"In Dorset where he'd gone to collect a debt for Guiseppe Maranti."

"From the Four Oaks Club?"

"Yes."

"What did Guiseppe tell the police?" asked Signor Luigi.

"Nothing, he has insisted that he didn't know the debt collector's name."

"Good, that is wise of him. Tell me Signor Bessani, you're a solicitor and you know how witnesses evidence of identification can go wrong under expert cross-examination, how strong would you say the police case is?"

"They have DNA evidence taken from the girl."

Another long pause.

"What do the police make of that, Signor Bessani?"

"You must understand that I am not in their confidence. The police took Guiseppe Maranti to the police station. They almost had to carry him to their car because he's scared at even the mention of the word police and he insisted that I should be present when they questioned him."

"Yes, I understand all that but what do you think that they think?"

"They seem to think that the man who they are seeking, stabbed the man on the boat, took the girl ashore in full view of witnesses, drove her into the country in a light green car, raped her, killed her and threw her body in the river. Two more witnesses saw him by the river afterwards."

"It sounds as if they could have a pretty strong case."

"Yes, Signor Luigi, when they find this Michael Bernoulli and compare his DNA with the samples taken from the girl, they should have enough evidence to secure a conviction, I thought that you might wish to know."

"I thank you for your consideration and I would be grateful if you didn't share your thoughts on this matter with anyone else, not even your law partners."

"That I understand, Signor," said the solicitor and he heard the phone at the other end disconnect.

He'd covered his own back and, he hoped, Guiseppe's.

Luigi Coroneli was deep in thought. Despair would be a more accurate description of his mood. On a professional level what an absolute idiot Bernoulli had been. It sounded as if instead of waiting until his target was alone, he had gone straight in and found him with a girl. Then instead of backing-off, something had happened to make him stab the target. Then to cap it all, instead of killing the unfortunate girl, he'd drawn attention to himself by taking her off the boat so that he could have sex with her before killing her and in so doing had left behind something to tie him to the girl for ever more. So although there might be insufficient evidence to convict him of the murder of the man in the boat, the murder of the girl would ensure that he got a life sentence.

What fools men were. Of course if they weren't, a good slice of his 'family's' income would disappear but at the moment his thoughts were more personal.

What had made his only daughter marry the rotter? What was more to the point was, why had he allowed it?

He knew the answer to that, too. She was the apple of his eye, the jewel in his crown and ever since she had been able to talk she could wrap him round her little finger. It was his own fault, really. His wife, God rest her soul, had asked him why the men who were his constant escorts – his soldiers – were always ugly. Couldn't he have a few good looking ones? So he had introduced a few smoother looking guards. Eventually Michael Bernoulli had become one of them. How was he to know that his precious daughter would fall head-over-heels in love with the fellow?

They had married a year ago. He'd given her a house in a very quiet part of Highgate for a wedding present and provided her husband with a legitimate job collecting rents. Ever since then the fellow had been asking for more. He should have known that he would cause trouble. Thank goodness that the house was in Sophia's name.

Maria, his secretary, came in and placed some papers on his desk. He barely noticed her. She lingered a moment, thinking that he might want to mention something about the phone call and then withdrew. Her boss didn't know that she was teaching herself Italian and had listened to the whole thing and she wasn't surprised, Michael had propositioned her, too.

Luigi, the boss, pondered on, assessing possible courses of action open to him under omerta, the strict moral code that controlled their operations, the obligation never to assist the authorities in any way in the detection of crimes or to apply for assistance or justice to those authorities. In the circumstances he wouldn't confide in Salvatore his underboss or Leonardo, his consigliere and hence nor to his caporegime or lieutenants who acted as a buffer, distancing him from the soldiers who ran the mob's legal or illegal operations in London and the Home Counties.

He thought on. What if he did nothing? The police weren't stupid and would get Michael Bernoulli in the end. There would be a trial and Michael would go-down for 20 years. His daughter, who was a devout Catholic, would become what he called a prison-widow, the best years of her life would be wasted and if she had any children everyone would know that their father was a murderer. Furthermore, he wouldn't put it past Bernoulli to 'do a Valachi' and tell the authorities all about Luigi's mafia family in an attempt at plea bargaining.

The next thought was get him out of the country and settled in southern Italy. There were two obvious objections, one, his daughter would go as well and, two, the English police would apply for his extradition with all the attendant publicity.

In each case it would reflect badly on his position as boss in the 'family'. How much better if his daughter had never met the fellow.

It was but a small step to how much better it would be if the fellow no longer existed. This thought reinforced his decision not to tell his underlings. This was something he must deal with himself and quickly, the police would find out where his daughter lived soon enough.

Could he rely totally on his secretary's silence? He thought, Yes, she didn't speak Italian. He fell to plotting.

Inspector Donovan and Sergeant Tyler spent an instructive afternoon looking through the police records. There were three Michael Bernoulli's on record but only one was a resident of the UK, the other two were visitors who's form had been provided by the Italian police. The UK resident had convictions for three separate cases of assault and the nickname Mick the Knife.

Armed police were sent to his last known address in North London to arrest him on a charge of murder. They returned empty handed, the present occupant of the flat said that she'd been there for a year. Mail had arrived for someone with an Italian name and she'd popped it back in the pillar-box, having no forwarding address.

Donovan remembered what Guiseppe had said that Michael Bernoulli had said about 'when he got back from the Bahamas.' It was a long shot but it was all they had, so he set his team checking the passenger lists of aircraft flying from and to, the Bahamas while being aware that many people who visit the islands travel via Miami. He wondered if you need a US visa to transit through Miami these days but he had the Heathrow – Miami flights checked as well, just in case.

Sergeant Tyler went to the East End with a picture of Michael Bernoulli to ask Sailor Nesbit if that was the man in the dark blue suit and open neck light blue shirt that he had seen bringing a girl ashore in Poole harbour.

Like so many witnesses before him, Sailor said that he thought so but couldn't be absolutely sure. Sergeant Tyler could see a good barrister for the defence tying Sailor up in knots in the witness box.

The search of the airline passenger lists produced nothing. Donovan told them to keep looking but he knew, in his heart of hearts, that it would be a waste of time.

When it was dark, Luigi the Capo set the video beneath his TV to record the programmes between 8.30 p.m. and midnight, then left his house by the back door and walked by a circuitous route to a lock-up garage more than a mile from his house that only he knew about and backed out the car that was within. The garage and the car and the substantial sum of money hidden in it, were part of his escape arrangements if ever things went horribly wrong. He stopped at a public call box and phoned Michael Bernoulli's mobile phone number.

"Michael, it's the Capo, don't say a word to Sophia but I'd like you to meet me at the corner of your road in half an hours time. I've got a little job that I want you to do. If it goes right you could soon be a caporegime. Remember, not a word to our girl, if she asks say that you have to see Leonardo."

"OK," said Michael in a familiar condescending voice that Luigi had come to dislike, "see you in half an hour."

Luigi was standing beside the car in the tree-lined street when his son-in-law approached.

"What's this then?" said Michael in an amused voice. "I haven't seen these wheels before and driving yourself, it must be something very special that you want me to do."

"It is, get in and I'll tell you all about it," said Luigi, starting to move round to the off side of the car, then stopping. "No, just a moment, first let's get the packet that I put in the boot."

Curiosity made Michael the first to reach the boot and open it. It was the last thing that he was to do on this earth, for Luigi struck him a terrible blow on the back of his head with a small crowbar that he had concealed until that moment. He then calmly pulled the body into the kerb in a position that made it appear that Michael had been struck by a passing vehicle. Luigi had thought for some time that some of the side mirrors on coaches and lorries were dangerous. He looked around, there was no one in sight. He closed the boot, resumed the driver's seat and drove back to his secret lock-up garage. He was in his room watching the recordings of the earlier TV programmes, when his daughter phoned to ask him if Michael was with him. He switched the video off,

"No, pet, he isn't here. What made you think that he might be?"

"Nothing Papa, it's just that about three hours ago he had a phone call and said that he had to go out. I asked him what for and he wouldn't tell me except to say that it was something to do with Leonardo." She added, "he's been going out alone a lot these days."

"That's not good, baby, do you want me to talk to him?"

"Oh no, Papa, we have to work these things out for ourselves."

"Why don't you both come to dinner tomorrow and we can have a little family get together."

"Alright Papa, I'll call you in the morning."

He resumed his catching-up with the TV and then went to bed. Tomorrow he'd send his suit to the cleaners and one night next week he'd take the car to a car wash. The small crowbar had been washed-up with his dinner dishes in the dishwasher and was now back where it belonged.

It was gone 8 a.m when she phoned.

"Papa oh Papa, Michael's been killed. The police came here and said that he's been killed in the road."

"Oh baby, that's terrible. I'll come right over."

He leisurely finished his breakfast and phoned for a taxi. He was there before the police came to ask the widow what her husband had been doing wandering on, or close to, the road the previous evening?

Sophia recited what she had already told her father, that her husband had received a phone call and had gone out after muttering something about Leonardo.

Luigi asked the nature of the injuries and suggested that his son-in-law might have been hit by a lorry's wing mirrors. The constable thought this to be unlikely and asked if the victim had any enemies.

Luigi told the officer that his son-in-law ran a debt collecting agency and, he supposed, although it was most unlikely, he could, conceivably, be the victim of one of the debtors and that the only Leonardo that they knew, worked for him and was at present on holiday in Italy.

The policeman wrote it all down and departed.

Luigi took Sophia back home with him and set about arranging Michael's funeral to take place when the authorities released the body. His wish was to have it cremated as soon as possible.

Another road-death wasn't front-page material for the local paper and barely made Page 9

Sergeant Tyler lived at home in Hampstead with his parents and sister and a springer spaniel called Prince. His father fervently hoped that he'd meet a nice girl, marry her and move out. His mother thought that, what with the peculiar hours that he worked, he'd be lucky if he ever met a nice girl. His sister didn't think about it, she was in her first year at university reading physics. Prince slept in the kitchen and dreamed doggy dreams. A newspaper was put down in case he couldn't wait until morning.

It was when she was taking up the dog's paper that his sister noticed it and even then she wouldn't have done so had she not been doing 'hydraulics' in her physics course at the time. The word Bernoulli caught her eye. What on earth could the local rag be writing about Bernoulli's law? But it wasn't, someone called Bernoulli had been killed in the road in Highgate. She thought that it was a hoot and mentioned it at breakfast and was surprised at her brother's instant reaction.

"Bernoulli? Where is it Cis?"

"In the recycling bag, of course."

He got up and went outside and rummaged about until he found some sheets from the previous night's paper, then brought them in and spread them one-by-one on the worktop.

"It was down the bottom on the right hand side," said his sister, helpfully, "on a page that had a holiday advert."

Eventually he found it and read,

Late last night the body of a local resident, Mr Michael Bernoulli, 29, of Lime Gardens, Highgate, was found lying beside the road. It is believed that he had been struck by a passing vehicle. His distraught wife, Sophia, 22, stated that he'd gone out sometime before 9.p.m.to attend a meeting.

Sergeant Tyler cut the piece out of the paper and said,

"That may be the chap we've been looking for. If it is, he murdered two people in Dorset a few weeks ago."

He took it to the station and showed it to the Inspector who agreed that it was worth a try, it was time that they had a bit of good fortune. They phoned the local police station and arranged to visit the mortuary to which the body had been taken prior to an inquest.

Notwithstanding the damage inflicted by the blow that had caused his death, the corpse did resemble the Michael Bernoulli who had once resided at the address in North London. Inspector Donovan asked that the body be fingerprinted and its DNA taken.

The next day he had the answers, the fingerprints identified the corpse as the North London offender and the DNA identified him as the second man who had been intimate with Laura Wells on the day that she was murdered. The local station later confirmed that the dead man owned a light green Ford Mondeo.

The next day Scotland Yard issued the following statement,

It is confirmed that the Michael Bernoulli who was killed by a hit and run driver in Lime Gardens Highgate two nights ago, is the man who the police were seeking in connection with the murder of Raymond Farrell, who's body was found in his yacht in Poole harbour and Laura Wells, his fiancée, who's body was found in the River at Tolbrite in Dorset on the same day. The enquiry into those deaths is now closed.

When the Chancellor of the Exchequer got home that evening and was settled with his second sherry, Peggy plopped herself down beside him on the settee with one of her legs tucked under her and showed him the brief announcement in the Times.

"So they got him in the end," said William.

"With a little help from God," said his wife.

Had he heard it, Luigi would have thought that fitting. Family affairs must be settled within the family and he felt like an avenging angel.

God and the Mafia move in mysterious ways.

Printed in the United Kingdom
by Lightning Source UK Ltd.
118383UK00002B/190-198

9 781846 853289